ANAX | KEREN OULIEL

Keren Ouliel
ANAX

Cover Design by: Alice Blake
Page Design by: Liron Maliah
Graphics by: Niv-Books

Printed in Israel 2021

Niv Books Publishing

www.nivbook.co.il

ANAX

Book One of The Order Series

Keren Ouliel

May this book inspire you to follow your dreams
like so many other books had inspired me.

CHAPTER ONE

"Ladies and gentlemen, we're being held up at a red signal. We should be on the move shortly."

The train conductor's announcement is a blessing in disguise, as this must be the fifth time Naya has heard the words since the moment she boarded the train more than half an hour ago. She knows that it might not help her, but she can at least huff out her frustration along with everyone else in the carriage.

It takes another minute before she decides to turn her attention back to the book she was reading and just in time too as the train pushes forward. Her focus on the words lapses and, though not uncommon, it still bothers her. Unbidden, her mind wanders off, and she tries to wrestle back once more into the written word. She would have succeeded, if not for the odd tingling sensation that can only mean someone's eyes are upon her.

Naya likes to think that there are a few unwritten rules when it comes to riding in public transport — one of which is not staring. She can handle it most of the time, giving people that do it the benefit of the doubt that they are not aware, or are simply tourists, but the intensity of this particular stare makes her slightly on edge.

At half past five on a Friday afternoon, the carriage is pretty full, but Naya can still pick up on the person who is staring at her with no trouble whatsoever. She supposes anyone could, what with how conspicuous he is; he is standing next to the middle set of doors and doesn't look familiar at all. It strikes her as odd, as usually people turn their gaze elsewhere when they realise they are caught, but he holds her gaze as she examines him.

He is probably taller than her, not that it's a challenge, with dark hair and a firm posture. While there's nothing about him that seems special enough to remember, she still thinks she would have recognised him if she knew him. He seems to be more engrossed with her than with his companion who is talking, and it's evident the attention from her is upsetting him too.

The train slows down again and just before stopping completely, it hauls forward in order to regain momentum to rush past again. Naya would admit to be petty enough to gloat silently as the staring man almost loses his balance but, at the very least, it causes him to avert his glance.

Happily, Naya thinks that at least karma still works as she tries to go back to her book.

It proves futile as the robotic voice of London's underground trains announces loudly, "The next stop is Finchley Road," so Naya tucks the book into her bag.

Something is bugging her, and she looks to her right, catching the stranger's attention again, as she stands and moves to the doors. To try and relax her anxious mind, she counts the seconds until she will see the blissful sign of the station at which she needs to alight, which would hopefully mean good riddance to the weird passengers on the train.

Naya can't help wondering what made him stare at her as she catches a glimpse of her reflection in the door windows. The image is distorted in a way that only a moving train's window can, but it confirms that nothing is out of place. Her brown hair remains in the loose French braid in which it has been all day; her makeup still looks somewhat presentable — which she gives herself some slack for, as she is, after all, after a long and tedious shift at a restaurant — with her black parka coat still covering her work clothes. There's not even a hint of dirt on her tanned face, nor any remnant of food that was thrown her way from the last table at work.

Even her colleagues had assured her that she looked just fine.

There must be something, she thinks anxiously, but she brushes the thought away just as the train advances to the station.

A sense of alarm hits her again when she notices the two strangers getting ready to leave the train as well. Once the doors have opened, Naya steps out, hearing the soundtrack of the same robotic voice, asking everyone repeatedly to mind the gap.

The platform is busy, as it always is during rush hour, and she squeezes past the passengers to the other side, where she will wait for the next train to take her to West Hampstead station. The men flit in and out of her focus, and she tries not to appear visibly shaken when they board the same train that she does.

There are only a few passengers on the short five minute ride. This doesn't help her nerves, but she has the experience of knowing the layout of the station, so when they arrive, she is ready to negotiate the station in order to avoid them and hopefully shake off these remaining ominous feelings.

There's a queue on the way out the station, but at least she can't see them anymore, which relaxes her just a tiny bit.

The early October breeze helps to keep her sober-minded to the point where she can scold herself for thinking anyone is after her and she scoffs, sliding her card by the station's barriers and then taking a sharp right. By the time she does make it outside, she forces her mind to focus on more important things.

She is almost an hour late. She would need to have a fairly good excuse, other than being caught up at work, to use on her friends. That statement is far overused and she is such a bad liar that it has never done the trick anyway, but she would do what she can to minimise the damage. The brisk walk keeps her warm, which is the only perk of being late, so not before long she is standing in front of the pub right across her flat building, hurrying to get indoors.

The pub is busy, but it's their usual hangout and she loves it. It is quite dark, with only a few lamps scattered along the dark wood-panelled walls; the only part lit up enough is the bar, but it's too crowded for her to try and get a drink at the moment.

It doesn't take her long to spot her friends sitting at a table. She'll never admit out loud, but perhaps this is the other upside of being late — it takes the weight off her shoulders of needing to find a place for them to sit. It is a task really, and usually involves them hovering over a table until the current occupants leave.

She's glad to see that they are sitting at one of their preferred tables, the one by the wall-length windows that overlook the back garden, which is temporarily closed due to renovations combined with the upcoming winter.

Naya takes in her friends as she makes her way to them. She gets a dirty look from one of the twins, as she suspected she would. With their sandy hair, dark eyes and pale complexion, they are similar enough to be confused by others, yet Naya had the unfair advantage of growing up with them and thus, unlike most people, she knows to relate to them as two different people. The other twin, as usual, is more sympathetic, and was smiling at her as he waved her way. He shares a playful look with the blonde woman sitting next to him, and they both wait to see his brother's reaction when she arrives at the table.

"Ah, her Royal Highness Naya," he says, and Naya chuckles, throwing her braid behind her shoulder as an act of defiance and sits down, but not before winking at the pair next to him.

"I think Lucas might be afraid someone will steal his throne," Naya tells them and nudges the twin in question, earning yet another angry glance in her direction which doesn't cause her to back down. "I figured by now you would have been able to make sure he was onto his next drink, so at least he would be more tolerable."

Lucas scoffs, his eyes rolling condescendingly. "At least my go-to reaction in problem-solving isn't drinking alcohol."

As if to emphasise his jab, the woman pushes a glass filled with what is undoubtedly Pinot Grigio, in front of

Naya, making Naya smile, and she turns her attention to participate in the banter.

"No, you just sleep around," the words roll off her tongue, and it's oddly comforting how he just laughs.

The blond woman takes a sip of her gin and tonic, before saying, "Either way doesn't sound too healthy, you know?" Her question is innocent, yet with a hint of curiosity there.

"Julie, just because you've had your chance—"

Julie laughs loudly, successfully shutting Lucas up. "Oh, my God! Don't finish the sentence, please!"

Naya briefly looks over at how Lucas's twin, Logan, falls silent, his smile disappearing. She offers him a small glance, one she hopes is supportive and helpful before trying to avert the subject. "Well, with all due respect to who you're letting in your bed and who you're not, I think we're here for a special occasion."

Logan grins gratefully at her and nods. He raises his beer, prompting the others to do the same, and when they do, he toasts, "To Julie!"

As they all repeat the toast, Julie sits there, completely content, watching Logan pull a decorated plastic bag that screams *happy birthday!* before Julie tries to take it from him. Naya stops her, elbowing Lucas, who springs into action.

"Wait!" He exclaims, "The cake!"

Without waiting, he makes his way to the bar, whispering a few words to the bartender and returns with a victorious smile on his face as if he hadn't just missed his cue to have Julie's birthday cake presented at the same time as their toast.

"Unbelievable," Naya shakes her head, though it doesn't surprise any of them. "Please tell me you asked them to light the candles."

"Hey, give me some credit."

He doesn't bother turning to Naya to see her raised eyebrows, but simply waits patiently for the cake to be delivered to their table. They all know this is one of the few pubs in London in which they can actually get away with lighting birthday candles indoors, and so they all wait in anticipation. The cake is presented by one of the bartenders, who is Lucas's friend, and he leaves shortly after making sure they all have what they need.

Lucas begins the toast he meant to open with before. "I just want to say—"

Naya and Logan groan in annoyance, but Julie just smiles, urging Lucas to go on.

He does, blatantly ignoring the other two. "Julie, thank God you met Naya, I don't think we would have tolerated her ranting as well as you do. So, here's to you, for basically saving me from a heap of trouble!"

Naya rolls her eyes; both Julie and Logan laugh with

Lucas soon joining them as he half hugs Naya, assuring her it was a joke. Without admitting he is right, she goes on to wish her best friend all the best.

Almost everyone in the pub joins in when Lucas starts singing *Happy Birthday*, and Naya takes out her phone, quick to snap a few pictures and videos of an extremely cheerful Julie and then takes some of them together. She's enjoying how normal it all feels, and despite the cliché, she really hopes it can stay like this forever.

The street is mostly silent by the time they leave the pub, save for Lucas's incessant declarations of love for his flatmates — Logan and Naya — and the birthday girl herself. He had almost persuaded them into getting another round until he fell as he was getting up to go and buy the next round, which sealed the deal. They had to get home.

"Good luck with him," Julie says standing next to Naya. They had been walking around West End Lane, hoping to sober Lucas up a little, and both girls were more than happy to leave Logan in charge of this.

Naya smiles, watching as the boys negotiate over the pizza place right next to them. "Logan was off today. He can take care of this mess," she says in between Logan's firm *no* to buying pizza and Lucas's very good argument that it might clear his head a bit.

She must admit that he is pretty convincing, and she hadn't eaten anything other than a slice of cake and her lunch at work.

Julie interrupts her musing. "How was work? You seem stressed."

"When am I not?" Naya answers truthfully, adjusting her coat.

Julie chuckles. "Good point. Still, overworking yourself might not be the solution."

Naya nods because there's not much else she could offer in reply. They have the same discussion at least once a week, and that has yet to make a difference. In Naya's defence, Julie is not very good at following her own advice and, more often than not, they find themselves helping each other in projects when they get overwhelmed with deadlines and ideas.

Naya is fairly sure that she still has the draft to one of Julie's very first law cases in her flat.

Julie hums to get her attention and asks, "Is it work, though?"

She asks it loudly enough that it piques Logan's curiosity as well, and he shoots them a glance before attending to his brother again. Naya thinks of mentioning the people on the train, but the words get caught in her throat; she's not sure she has enough energy for a conspiracy conversation right now.

She's silent for a few more moments, before relenting to give Julie what she wants to hear: "I have a deadline tomorrow."

She doesn't do that often. It's usually quite easy for Julie and her to just be with each other without the need to try and squeeze unnecessary words out. Julie doesn't comment, and Naya is thankful enough not to look a gift horse in the mouth.

It is at times like these that she really dislikes living far from the city centre. It makes her long for the consistent hum of sound from the world around them. Here it's quieter, despite being less than twenty minutes by tube to Central London, but it makes the silence of the night even more prominent.

Her friends adore being here though, and she knows she can't really complain. Especially not when Julie is more than happy to help ease her mind.

They separate from the twins, quickly falling into a brainstorming discussion, without even meaning to.

Sometime around eleven, Naya bids Julie goodnight and starts walking to the direction of her own flat. It's not much, just a small three-bedroom flat on the main road of West Hampstead, located in Queens Court, but she's living with her best friends and she couldn't ask for anything more.

Lucas had used his connections and charisma as a realtor agent and managed to find the flat at a fair price and with a decent landlord, and ever since they moved four years ago, it had become the home Naya was hoping for.

The foyer lights up when she opens the door, and she gives one wishful look at the broken lift that had yet to be fixed and sighs. She is not looking forward to climbing three flights of stairs in her state of exhaustion.

When she leaves the green carpet and white wooden walls of the hallway behind the flat's closed door, she finds Logan already sitting in her favourite seat of the corner sofa of the living room, which is really just the small space between the flat's rooms and kitchen. She smiles and quietly closes the door after her.

As she takes off her coat and shoes, Logan updates her on the pizza Lucas made sure to leave for her and gestures at the mug in his hand. "There's one for you in the kitchen," Logan says, and it's this thoughtfulness that warms her heart.

Leaving the pizza for later, she greedily snatches her own mug from the kitchen counter and joins him at the other side of the sofa. She supposes she can still get comfortable enough in its dark grey surface, and she's sure she's being coy enough as she reaches to her laptop, sitting innocently at the edge of the sofa.

"The website can wait, stop pouting."

Her face twists into a scowl, one she knows all too well. Mostly, because she does not pout and secondly because she swears to Logan, "I have a deadline!"

It usually doesn't work, and she's not expecting it to either, but this time Logan must see reason, or so she tells herself, assuming he was just as tired from dealing with his brother to try and stop her. So he only nods, leaning back in his place and says, "At least change your clothes because you know you're going to fall asleep on the sofa again."

She's almost tempted to defy him, but past experience had taught her that he has a point. Only after he has promised to wait up for her does she get up, doing as he suggests.

Her bedroom is the smallest of all of the rooms, but she has fitted wardrobes and an ensuite bathroom, so all in all, she feels — even after a few years of living in tight quarters — she has the best room in the flat.

The double bed does take up most of the space, but she has pushed it up against the wall with the window, and she has enough space to take four full steps if she doesn't have to open the door.

But again, she shouldn't complain. Julie lives in a studio half the size of the shared space of her flat.

She's quick to go back to the living room, dressed in her coziest pyjamas and her hair in a high ponytail, which could only mean she was about to start working.

Logan sits with her for a while, and they talk briefly, but it doesn't take more than half an hour before he leaves to retire for the night.

Long after her tea is finished and her slices of pizza are eaten, she's alone again which means she can get back to business and continue working on her next article for the environmental website that one of Julie's contacts managed to secure for her.

She's so absorbed in it, that she doesn't even notice her eyelids close as she falls asleep.

CHAPTER TWO

Naya is jerked awake by a series of constant knocks on her flat's front door. Judging by the sunlight streaming through her living room window, even in her half-asleep state, it is not hard to gather two things. The first is that Logan was right once again, and the other — this she confirms by looking at the clock hands that show quarter past eight — is that it is far too early on a Saturday morning to be up and about.

She's got half a mind to just ignore whoever that is at the door and go back to sleep.

Naya never considered herself to be lucky, and this was not going to change today apparently. If it was not the incessant knocking shaking any remainder of sleep off her, it is the horrible pain in her neck, which is her own punishment for not listening to Logan and dozing off on the sofa.

It had been a rough week and she was really looking forward to sleeping in.

In the few moments it takes for her to get up, move around the laptop's charging cable and order her legs to function properly, she lists off at least ten words she can use to bite this person's head off.

However, before she has a chance to spit out the words, they disappear when she opens the door and takes in the man. He's two heads higher than her but shares her tan skin tone and, while his hair is a lot lighter than hers, it is unmistakable that they are related. He smiles fondly at Naya, revealing one dimple in his right cheek — an attribute she wishes she had inherited.

"Papa!" All resentment towards the hour melts away as she welcomes him in with a hug. Quickly, she adds in Hebrew, "Good morning, how are you?"

She always slips back to Hebrew when it's just her and Dom. He had taught her his spoken languages when she was growing up, and while she could probably hold a decent conversation in his dialect of Moroccan Arabic, they rarely spoke it as a whole. French is a whole other matter, though, and she can't grasp it for the life of her.

Usually, when they were alone, it was a mix of Hebrew with some sentences and phrases in Arabic.

Saturdays are reserved for family, and it was the first rule she set out to her boss when she started working at his restaurant. She had however played the whole dead mother card, but eventually, she got her wish in the shape of almost all Saturdays off.

She wouldn't lie by saying she would have preferred his visits to occur at a more convenient hour but considering it saved her the time to travel almost an hour by tube, she was not going to protest.

It doesn't make it less suspicious that he chose to drop by unannounced, considering Dom was quite a planner and preferred scheduling something concrete or at the very least giving a proper heads up.

However, much to her disdain, lately their meetings had tended to shift between pleasant and nerve-wracking. It reminds her of when she was a teenager, and she knew that there was no middle ground, so she is waiting patiently to see what he might say. She had gotten pretty good at predicting the mood just by his first word.

Whenever he visits, Dom always starts by examining her home. He always starts from the twins side of the flat, with the two closed white-textured doors. Then he moves on to the doors on the opposite side of the flat, which are the ones to Naya's bedroom and the bathroom that the twins share. His eyes always linger on the corner grey sofa and the television, but this time he stops at the small kitchen.

She understands this gesture without words, and he follows her.

It puts her on edge. She only has their past experience to guide her, but nothing gives her an indication of how this will go, despite her usual confidence. While they have a good and stable relationship, Dom randomly stopping by without a warning is a rare occurence. Mostly it's up to her to go and visit him in his shop in Chiswick, always to find him engaged with the management.

She knows better than to prompt him into a discussion, though. If there is one thing she has learned from him, it is taking time with conversations.

He lets her go about the task of making them tea, moving around the kitchen with his hawk like stare on her back.

The kettle has finished boiling by the time he speaks. "You fell asleep on the sofa?"

Well, not what she expected, but she can work with it.

"I have a deadline." She uses the same argument she gave Julie and Logan last night. She knows it won't work; Dom had never been extremely supportive with what she thinks is her true calling. Trying to distract him, she hands him a mug with mint tea in it.

He sighs and takes it from her. "If this is about those natural disasters again—"

Naya sighs, it's way too early to have this argument again.

"I'm really onto something, Papa," she insists.

He pauses, probably to think of a better way to make her give up on her passion to be an environmental journalist, but does not continue to elaborate on the matter. Either way, she's taking it and guides them to go and sit in the living room.

What he does say, though, leaves a few questions in its wake.

"I want to keep a promise I made a long time ago," Dom starts, careful in keeping his tone as impassive as ever. It has always made her jealous how well he keeps his emotions on a tight leash, while hers are always up on display.

She crosses her legs, gesturing to him to continue.

"I was going through some of your mum's belongings the other day, and... well, I just thought you would want this."

From the pocket of his trousers, he takes out a long golden necklace with a key-shaped pendant. Naya examines it from where she sits; it looks ancient and quite expensive, yet she could not remember him owning anything like it.

Dom's life before Naya was born is taboo, or something akin to it. They don't talk about these things, and while it's always a subject that looms over them, Dom is never the one to initiate it. Especially when her mother's life is questioned as well.

Naya doesn't like the turn in the atmosphere. It makes her queasy and nervous.

"You're giving me a necklace?" She teases, trying to lighten up the mood. "Gee, Papa, thanks. You always know exactly what I want."

If he does not approve of her sarcastic comment or

her disregard for the object, he does not let it show, and instead thrusts the jewellery at her, like it's cursed. They are sitting far enough apart for her to know she needs to lean in to take it if she wants to, but she's not sure she does; not with how it dangles from Dom's outstretched hand like a menacing charm.

"This isn't a gift, Naya," his tone is quick like he might regret it. "If it were up to me, this thing would have been at the bottom of the Thames… But it was your mum's dying wish for me to give you this when I believed you were old enough to receive it."

The strong sense of immediate connection to the necklace throws her off since she had never bothered to actively seek out new information about her mother. Especially when she saw how much it pained Dom to talk about her.

She tries to sever the connection as far as she's able, but the anxiety it causes her does not leave her much choice. By now she knows the signs, and the tight handle she has on it won't remain for very long.

For now, she can't help but take advantage of her father's new revelation to dig further.

While she wouldn't breach the subject herself, more out of respect to Dom and slight resentment towards her mother, there are still many things she needs to know; so many unanswered questions and wonderings, so many loose ends she is unable to tie up without her mother's presence and so many ideas of who her mother might have been before she died.

Naya also thinks that today, being five months before her twenty-six birthday, it is not such a special occasion, so she doesn't quite understand what being *old enough* means.

If she were a superstitious woman, she would have blamed the necklace for making the atmosphere in the room take a turn for the worse, but she's too rational to think that. It's just an object, and even if Dom still had not lowered his hand, it can't be more than that. She tries to push anything else away, even if the feeling suffocates her.

At this point, she would say and do anything to loosen the pressure in her chest.

"Why?" She's giving Dom a free hand to choose the nature of her question.

But the man doesn't succumb to her logic. "It's your inheritance, Naya," he simply says, though something hopeful glints in his eyes. It baffles her, but he continues. "But you can choose not to accept it."

"Don't tell me this opens up a secret door somewhere in the world," she jokes in another futile attempt to address the subject.

Nevertheless, as Dom's hand starts shaking from being constantly help up in the air, she closes the small gap and clutches the necklace. He is not the only one with a sharp gaze. She notices that the moment the object is in her hand, any and all hope diminishes from his eyes. Clearly, he has misjudged how much she is guided by curiosity.

They sit in silence, and Naya turns the pendant around in her hand, feeling the coarse metal it is made of. It's nothing special — a skeleton key probably used for something some ancient time ago, but she doubts she'll get anything more out of Dom.

It's a mystery if she ever saw one, and it both intrigues her and frightens her at the same time.

"I don't know much about it," Dom confesses after a while, and Naya knows he is only saying it to clear the air and distract her from her own feelings.

This is one of the few things she had picked up from him.

"I only know she wanted you to have it."

Naya chooses only to nod and see where it leads her.

Dom's eyes land briefly on the necklace, and when he turns to look at her again, his expression is unreadable just as it had been when she first told him about befriending the twins or moving in with them to the other side of London. It makes her heart ache because she knows how much this had hurt him.

She wonders if he's disappointed or upset, and she hopes he knows he didn't really leave her much of a choice.

Then she figures it out. He is waiting for her to do or say something, and she wonders how much of her own emotions are written on her face at the moment. She wonders if the anxiety is evident, or if maybe her face is revealing how much she is beginning to struggle breathing...

"Naya?"

She's raises her head, meeting his eyes. Her heart's beating so fast she's sure he can hear it, as it drums a painful melody in her mind. She hates the vulnerability of it — how her lungs tighten and her throat turns dry.

The dam she works so hard to contain is just about to burst.

"I'm fine," she manages to push out the words.

He's not convinced, yet by the time he opens his mouth to respond, he is stopped by Logan calling out his name. Her flatmate hovers by his bedroom door, rubbing his eyes. Their conversation probably woke him up, and he crosses the room to sit by them, blissfully unaware of the exchange.

She's hoping her sigh of relief isn't too noticeable.

Dom goes back to speak in English for the sake of her roommate, and she knows whatever discussion they were having, was now over and done.

"Hey, Logan, how're you?" He asks.

Naya listens to them quickly catching up, slowly

detaching herself from them. She excuses herself, going to the shared bathroom, and closes the door, letting out a deep breath. The jewellery in her fist feels strange, its weight mostly emotional and yet still all too solid. She tries not to give it too much significance, even if Dom seems to be doing so.

As the same feeling from before returns, she stares at herself in the mirror, trying to anchor herself back to the present. Usually it doesn't help, but she can't show her father how much a simple gesture has affected her.

One — she counts down, trying to distract her mind with an easy task.

Two — she uses the sink as a surface to secure her back to reality.

Three — she opens the tap, listening to the soothing sound of the water.

Repeat — *one, two, three* — until she can breathe properly.

She does not know how much energy it takes until even the slightest trace of the anxiety is gone, but she feels exhausted. The necklace is still in her hand, so she throws it on the counter, hoping to forget it for now.

The chatting continues in the living room and, when she hears the men talking about football, her ears pick up the sound of Lucas, and she thanks him for waking up, because now with them both being there, they can distract her father for long enough.

She meets Dom's stare when she rejoins them, but just smiles, dismissing him. "I'm fine," she assures him once more.

"You're staying for breakfast, Dom?" Logan diverts Dom's attention once again, throwing Naya his *we are going to talk about this later* look. "We were planning on cooking."

They had not, but it's a good plan, Naya thinks.

"Oh, I don't think so, thanks though," Dom says and gets up. "I should get going, the store won't run itself."

The twins say their goodbyes as Naya accompanies her father across the room, where he hesitates. Naya hopes he doesn't think of saying something about their earlier conversation. But then he turns back to the door, mutters a simple "take care" and leaves the flat.

"So?" Lucas is the first to break the silence when Naya sits back down on the sofa. She rolls her eyes thinking about how well she knows him.

"What the hell did I interrupt?" Logan asks.

Naya scoffs at Logan's observation. "He gave me my inheritance — some stupid piece of jewellery my mum left behind or whatever."

They know her just as well as she knows them, so by the disbelieving looks they give her, she knows that they are not fooled.

"Let me get this right, the man wakes us up at this ungodly hour to give you your inheritance and it's not a big deal?" Lucas tilts his head in general consideration, even though they all know it's a courtesy more than anything else. "I don't buy it," he adds.

"My dad's a strange man, we know that."

That doesn't work either, by the smile on Logan's face. She hates that grin, it's like she's playing right into their hands.

"You were never a good liar, you know?"

"Fine," she relents. "So maybe it is a big deal, but I don't know much about it. He was very... ominous about it, so..." she trails off, not entirely sure how to explain what's going on.

They sit in silence for a while, but it's a much easier silence than the one she and Dom shared. It gives Naya a moment to think for herself and try to make up her mind about the situation. Now that her mind's not fogged up by anxiety, it's clear the necklace means something, and judging by how hopeful Dom was that she would refuse to take it, it must lead to some secret he either wants to spare her or which can embarass him greatly.

It piques her curiosity, and she shares that with the twins.

"Whatever it is, I don't suppose we can do much thinking on an empty stomach." Lucas is the first to comment, and it makes them laugh. "I remember something being said about breakfast."

"You mean, us cooking and you watching us?" Naya says, happy for the change of subject.

"Well, someone has to stand and look pretty."

"Thank God you excel at that," Logan adds.

"And only at that," Naya smiles.

They do talk about it again, this time over scrambled eggs and pancakes, provided kindly by Naya and Logan, but after not arriving at any conclusion, they give it up for a while and settle on watching some television instead.

Naya can't let it go though, and as she goes back to retrieve the necklace from the bathroom, something in it beckons her. She puts it on, thinking perhaps this would be the answer. When nothing happens, she scoffs in annoyance and thinks she's way too influenced by Hollywood movies.

CHAPTER THREE

Naya spends the entire weekend trying to decipher the necklace. When she's in the comfort of her room, she traces the edges of the jewellery, begging for the mystery it holds to unravel so she can relax. It puts her on edge, like she's waiting for something to happen, and when nothing does for two whole days, it just doesn't make sense.

She doesn't seek out the twins again, since after a few sporadic conversations with them she knows it's not something they can help her with. Lucas even goes further to express how disappointing the necklace is, and how he would never give something like that to anyone; which Naya knows is a joke meant to ease her mind, but it doesn't help.

Whatever happens, she knows she has exhausted her attempts with her father, even if something tells her it doesn't end there.

On Tuesday, while she is waiting for the Metropolitan line with Julie, she tries to tackle the subject again in the hope that her best friend will have an answer ready just like she always does.

Julie, however, cannot seem to figure out what the problem is. She chuckles and examines the necklace closely. The golden chain is long enough for her to do so even with it still tucked beneath Naya's heavy scarf.

"So you're upset he gave you jewellery?" she asks in genuine wonder.

"First of all, I'm not upset—"

Julie gives her an incredulous look, which causes Naya to rephrase. "Fine, okay, maybe I'm a bit upset. It's just so bizarre!"

The train approaches, and the screeching of wheels makes them halt the conversation. Once they were boarded and seated — the carriage is near-empty save for a few passengers, so they have the guise of privacy — Julie turns to her and, over the train's announcement, says, "I think I'm missing the point, Nay."

"The point being, that in twenty-five years of me being on this earth, he never gave me jewellery. Most of the gifts I received for my birthdays were self defence lessons or gift cards for stores… Or money, you know, nothing that requires too much thought."

Naya knows Julie doesn't really get her's and Dom's father-daughter relationship, since Julie's relationship with her own parents never involved intense learning of anything — not for any school curriculum, nor training to protect herself.

Julie doesn't say anything for a few long moments, and Naya takes advantage of the silence to tilt her head sideways. Julie gets the message and starts working her fingers through Naya's hair, pulling it into a complex braid which only she manages to do.

It's one of the reasons Naya leaves the house twenty minutes before she really has to.

"Have you considered that your dad is not getting any younger and he thinks he should spoil you a bit?"

Naya wishes it was as simple as that. "You're kidding, right?"

Julie might not know Dom as well as the twins, but she had heard enough from her friends and occasionally the twins' mother, Lara, to know how ridiculous this sounds.

"What do you think it is, then?"

Naya shrugs, careful enough not to interrupt Julie's braiding, and huffs. "God knows, Jules. All I know is that I've been waiting for something to happen the entire weekend, because it clearly meant something to him."

"Maybe it's a tracking device," Julie says, and Naya hopes she's joking, though she wouldn't put it past her father to want to know where she is at all times. "I'm joking, relax."

"It just freaks me out, is all."

They both know it's not all, and it doesn't begin to scratch the surface at all, but she lets Naya have it.

"Well, considering there's not much you can do about it, maybe just let it be for now and we'll figure it out as it goes. For all we know, it's nothing and in a year from now you won't even remember being bothered about it."

Julie's argument does sound reasonable, but the nerves under Naya's skin have been tingling like small needles for the past few days and it doesn't feel like it will just pass by itself. It's ironic how usually she would always be the first one to stick to normalcy and now she's practically praying for something to happen, just so she can stop thinking she might be going insane.

"Yeah," Naya says instead. Expressing her thoughts can be at times complex, even if it's to Julie she needs to explain. "I guess you're right."

Julie hums in agreement and ties down the braid, squeezing Naya's shoulders to try and reassure her. "It'll be all right, you'll see."

When Naya gets to work, she finds her boss, Charlie, already hanging Halloween decorations outside the restaurant. She smiles, settles her bag by the door in close proximity and moves to take the part of the pumpkin garland he's trying to hang all by himself.

"Finally! One of my employees thinks to show some initiative," he jokes and hands her a creepy looking skull drawing. "Johnny's inside, I had to threaten him with morning shifts for the rest of the month for him to hang up fake cobwebs."

Naya laughs. "Imagine what chaos will erupt when Anna arrives," she says, knowing her co-worker's not too fond of the holiday.

"I already told her she's not taking the month off," Charlie says, scratching his red curls. "It looks fine there, we have a few more and then you'll be able to enjoy hot chocolate, on me."

Naya doesn't mention the fact she had been planning on it either way, and helps him for a few more minutes before he sends her inside to get warm.

Charlie's restaurant has been like a second home to her since she finished her years at Oxford University and the familiarity of the place will probably never stop being a comfort. She knows how lucky she is to work for a generous boss that allows her to take time off to invest in blog posts and slack off whenever it's acceptable, so she will never take it for granted.

The interior is already decorated, and she wonders how early Charlie had arrived in order to do it. John, one of the waiters working with her, waves her a good morning from one of the back booths, too entangled with cobwebs to come and say a proper hello.

Charlie's a business genius. When he bought the place upon relocating from Texas, it had been completely run down. The man had no previous experience in running a restaurant, but he was savant with fixing broken down places and with social media too, apparently, as he managed to do the impossible and turn a profit within the first five years.

Entering the restaraunt feels like stepping into someone's home, and while Naya had never seen where Charlie lives, if she needed to imagine it, she would see it as a replica of this restaurant. The restaraunt is open plan all through to the kitchen, which stands behind a wooden bar, with warm toned tiles and panelled walls. The maroon leather upholstery for the booths and chairs, and the dark wooden tables matched splendidly with the scattered art on the walls, all of which Charlie swears were painted by his family.

It's close to the end of her shift when she's met with a table of three children and two clueless adults who must be their parents. She stops in her tracks and seeks out Anna, who always seems to be immersed with children. Before she gets the chance to ask her anything, Anna stops her and asks if they can switch.

She's not about to look for a catch, so she nods and only hopes that she does not look as eager as she feels. The dark skinned waitress beams and thanks her, but it's only when Naya approaches the table that Anna was supposed to serve that she understands she was played.

The man sitting there can't be older than her father, though unlike him, he is wearing a sophisticated three piece grey suit and his hair is styled like it belongs in a different time. She can't explain why, but it makes her apprehensive just looking at him.

"Afternoon, sir," she swallows up her insecurities. "Are you ready to order?"

The customer looks up at her and after ordering a pot of English Breakfast tea and a croissant, sends Naya on her way.

Her boss looks up when she is at the bar to send her customer's order to the kitchen, and gives her a sideways glance from the cash register; she doesn't dare to talk to him though, and instead places the order down and waits patiently.

Charlie is tense; Naya can feel the emotion pouring out of him when she looks his way, but he stays silent for a few seconds, busying himself with preparing the tea.

"I can kick him out, if you want," the redhead suggests once he thinks it's been long enough.

She knows that there is no solid reason for that, but she doesn't say it.

"I wouldn't worry about it, Charlie," she replies instead, still unsure of what she thinks, but she wouldn't keep a man from having a quiet dine-in just because he seems strange.

London is filled with strange men and women and everything in between, and prejudice doesn't suit the city.

Charlie doesn't say anything in response, which makes Naya appreciate him even more, and just sets the order on one of the trays. She can feel his eyes watching her on her way back to the customer and has to remind herself that neither of them has a real reason to be alarmed.

Once Naya reaches the table, it seems as if the man wants to say something. Naya knows from past experience that it can lead to unwanted conversations, mostly with the elderly wanting to share their world views or discuss politics and life changing situations, so she pretends that she does not pick up on the change in the air as she puts down the teapot and mug.

Halfway from setting down the pastry plate, he decides to speak. "You're an environmental journalist, aren't you?"

Naya freezes, places the dish down with a loud noise and takes a step back to look at him. Hugging the now empty tray to her chest, she nods, not trusting herself to speak. It's the first time someone outside of her close circle has known what she does, and so she starts thinking back about what she could have said before to let him know.

He seems puzzled, probably by her lack of cooperation on the subject. He smiles fondly, perhaps noticing how it might seem. "I have read one of your articles," he clarifies.

It doesn't explain much, considering she posts under an alias.

"Yeah?" She prompts.

"Yes, it was about the connection between natural disasters and humanity's greed."

All thoughts of how he knows who she is are dismissed, and instead she gears up for a heated discussion in which she will be considered either a conspirator or delusional. She opens her mouth to correct him and say it was more about how humanity provokes natural disasters by working against nature, but he beats her to it. She manages to stay silent for the entire minute it takes him to talk again.

Logan would be proud.

"I am involved in solid research on a similar subject, and was interested to read your views on it," he continues, and Naya once again feels eyes on her, though she's not sure they belong to Charlie anymore.

She gives him a moment to stir the sugar and pour milk into his tea before saying anything.

"What's your research about?"

He smiles again, and this time Naya feels like she caught the bait he set out for her. "My name is Joshua Adams, and I have been waiting to collaborate with someone like you for a long time."

It doesn't go unnoticed by her how he avoids the question.

Raising her eyebrows, she says, "Fantastic". If he notices the sarcasm, he doesn't call her out on it. She shifts slightly in her spot — a subconscious move to try and stop anyone from overhearing their conversation. She is sure she looks like a complete fool, but he doesn't say anything about it, and just continues talking instead.

He smiles again, seemingly taking as much joy from the conversation as Naya takes nervousness. "I reckon you'd find our views correspond," he says.

"Is that so?" She asks just for the sake of it.

"I believe there is something more behind those reoccurrences, and that there is nothing natural about them. If I'm correct, and I think I am, they are a result of something that went entirely wrong, something that is definitely human."

She's not buying the possibility of stumbling upon perhaps the only other person in the world with the exact same theory as hers on Liverpool Street of all places. Despite the fact that they both knew she agrees with him, she had to test him.

Glancing around the restaurant she finds it almost empty. She sets the tray on the table and folds her arms in the hope that it makes her look skeptical enough to challenge him. "Don't you think that if something like that was true, everyone would have known it by now?"

When Joshua's smile turns a lot more pleasant, Naya can't help but be reminded of her high school teacher's expression whenever she gave a right answer in class. Joshua taps his fingers against the mug, seemingly somewhat impatient yet curious.

"Well, your world leaders do not care about anything that does not involve money."

Naya scoffs. "My world leaders? Need I remind you that we live on the same planet?"

She does not mean to sound disrespectful, though it probably is the case, but there is something extremely off about the man, and she switches her weight from one foot to the other, anxiously waiting to be scolded.

Instead, the man straightens himself, takes a twenty pound note out of his blazer pocket and stands up, handing it to her rather than putting it on the table. Naya doesn't miss the fact that he hadn't touched his food nor drank his tea.

"We may live on the same planet, but that does not mean we live in the same world. My world, Miss Tellus, has its own rules."

He's dangerously close to her, so much that she can see his pulse and the few grey hairs by his temple. She can tell the air is different, that he is peculiar, but not in the way she thought so far. There is nothing subtle about his next words, and there is no second guessing at how ominous it sounds.

"I can show you what that means, if you know how to look."

He doesn't wait for her to reply or to gain her composure. He places the money in her hand and closes it for her. He takes a step back and leaves the restaraunt. Naya feels momentarily paralysed, as if in a haze.

Now that he is gone, she's able to break free of her daze and open her hand, finding more than enough money and a card with only an address on it.

The invitation to investigate is undeniably there, and she can't tell if she likes it.

CHAPTER FOUR

As per her request, Lucas and Logan stay up and wait for her until she comes back home that same evening.

It's later than she would have liked, but it was stock day and Charlie had asked them all to stay a bit longer, and she can't find it in her to decline, despite the fact that the conversation with Joshua Adams had managed to spoil the rest of her day. Neither Charlie nor her coworkers had said anything regarding her sour mood, and maybe they had witnessed the exchange, but perhaps they were just giving her space. Either way, she was grateful.

She can't put her finger on what doesn't quite add up, or why Joshua had made her so nervous. It could be the opportunity he had presented, if she can even refer to it as one, that frightens her. Up until now, no one, other than a few low-ranking bloggers, whose real names she doesn't even know, cared enough to regard her theories in any way, with most of her work scattered in a few websites, and therefore not making much of a living.

It's not an income, as her father likes to remind her.

When she tells the twins about Joshua they are silent for a change. She can see them visibly thinking about how to react, and she gives them time. She may have left out how Joshua made her feel, but she trusts they know her well enough to pick up on it.

"Is this a job offer?" Logan asks, eventually.

Naya shrugs. "He didn't say. But he gave me his business card, so what else could he want?" She stops, looks at Lucas and adds, "Don't answer that, Lu."

He doesn't, in fact, and crosses his arms instead. "I don't know about it, Nay. How did he even find you? Aren't you at least slightly concerned about the probability of something like that?"

The simple answer would be the truth, but her mouth feels dry as she thinks of an answer that would satisfy them both. Especially since she knows, deep down, she wants to go and meet him to hear him out. She leans back on the sofa, thinking.

"I thought you posted under an alias," Logan adds to his brother's argument after a while.

"It seemed purely accidental," Naya says as an afterthought. It's vague enough to show she's not that bothered by the fact that Joshua had found her, and also lets off some of the suspicion she was still feeling.

It's a lie she tells herself, because if the opportunity is real, she can't risk losing it.

Logan must sense her resignation, since he tries to calm things down immediately. "Well, it does sound like a good chance at a proper job, if that's what he's aiming at."

"What's the bloke's name again, Joshua…?" Lucas interjects, his phone already out and Google at the ready. Naya gives his full name. His finger breezes over the phone's keyboard, and then randomly onto the screen, probably scrolling through unimportant information.

"Are you planning on meeting him?" Logan asks.

"I don't know," Naya replies honestly. "It's an opportunity I don't think I should miss, though."

"Thank God for Google," Lucas says, eyes still glued to the screen as he reads off what's written, "So apparently he's an expert in Seismology, having worked with some Japanese and American folk about the cause of natural disasters… didn't seem to do well in it, he got sacked halfway… then moved on to start his own small company here in London, which is near Bond Street, but we know that already."

He pauses, seemingly observing the information before repeating. Logan moves to sit closer, browsing through the same information. Naya keeps to herself, trying to form an opinion about the man.

"He says he can conduct a way to prevent natural disasters, and is recruiting young and open minded people with the same aspirations. Looks like he inherited quite a lot of money, otherwise there is no way he could be able to pay wages and research of that scale—"

"He could have gotten a sponsor," Naya adds, and is relieved how everything makes sense.

Even if he did use unconventional means to find her, or to make sure she would be at the restaurant when he came in, or even though he gives off an odd vibe — it doesn't sound like it is something that she can miss.

"This sounds like what you've been waiting for," Logan says, as if reading her thoughts. "A proper research to be a part of, maybe even change the world a bit."

Naya chuckles, "Yeah, yeah it does."

"Keep your head about you though," Lucas advises. "I know it's easy to get carried away but something doesn't sit right, and I'm not sure what exactly."

"Well, there is only one way to find out, right?"

Lucas doesn't look so thrilled by her words, but she chooses to brush it aside and focus on the prospect of her life turning out just the way she wants it to.

Whether it's curiosity or stupidity that leads her to schedule an appointment with Joshua will be determined by the outcome of such a meeting, and while she tries to reassure herself that she shouldn't worry about it, the feeling still gnaws at her stomach.

Even so, the journalist in her will be insulted if she didn't take up the challenge.

The GPS application on her phone takes her to the front of a white brick building in Brook Street, and she checks the address again before making her way inside. In all honesty, she had thought she would find the address to be a fake, a trick on her or somewhat of a trap. She's hoping the astonishment doesn't show on her face when she approaches the receptionist, asking for Joshua Adams.

The receptionist takes his time as he asks her to fill out a form with her name, time and date of visit and sign it before turning away from her, speaking in a hushed voice on the phone.

It gives Naya time to examine the lobby. It looks expensive with white marble floors and matching walls. There's an array of comfortable looking chairs in the right corner, scattered over a huge carpet and the sign behind the reception desk states *Enterprise House.*

When she feels a pair of eyes on her, she turns to look at a black haired woman leaning over the reception counter not far from her. She is probably a decade older than Naya, and is wearing a suit that looks so unfitting, with a ridiculous amount of makeup. Naya does not have enough time to inspect her properly before the man at reception calls for her attention and then accompanies her to the fifth floor.

He doesn't talk while on the way there, and Naya doesn't try to pry him into talking either.

Eventually when he opens up a door for her, she enters a moderate size office and sees Joshua rise from behind his desk.

"Miss Tellus."

Joshua looks surprised to see her, either because he was not informed that she was coming, or he thought that Naya would not show up. She thinks it is probably the latter, since she had thought about skipping the meeting altogether.

She stands by the door, not moving an inch, waiting for him to talk again, all the while taking in his office.

Somehow it doesn't shake the ground to know that his taste is old fashioned. The great dark oak desk in the middle of the room and the Moroccan carpet below it are as impressive as they come, but what really catches her eye are two tall bookcases, each one is on opposite sides of the window behind his workplace and are filled to the brim with leather-bound books, that she swears look like they each equal more than her monthly rent.

He gets over his shock easily, and invites her to sit on one of the reddish armchairs by the door. He sits on the other armchair and faces her.

"I was not sure you would come," he says, probably deciding to take the candid road.

There is no reason for her not to show him the same courtesy. "I wasn't sure myself," she mutters. "I'm not used to strangers showing up where I work, asking me to collaborate with them."

She doesn't get called out on the fact that he still hadn't asked, officially.

Joshua chuckles. "Yes, I can see why it would appear suspicious. Fate works in mysterious ways, and I had not planned on meeting you when I did. Rest assured that I mean you no harm."

"But you do understand why I'm not sure about this."

"Well, in all honesty I had not asked you to do anything but to hear me out." He shrugs, seemingly forced for some reason. He leans forward, and points to the teapot on the side table in between them. Naya silently refuses, and looks at him again.

"I'm here, aren't I?" Her question comes off a bit blunt, but she makes no move to correct it.

It seems to be the stimulation he was looking for to start pleading his case, since he nods and pours himself a cup of tea, and ignoring her decline, pours one for her as well. There's something methodical in the way he moves, like he's putting on a show.

"Historically speaking," he says, "this year has had the most natural disasters to have ever occured in the span of twelve months. However, I do not doubt that you know this. You also have your theory regarding this matter."

It feels like a question, even if it's not posed as one. "I just think that it's not a coincidence," she responds.

"But your editors do not approve."

She's not sure she would categorize the few blog writers that agreed to feature her articles as editors, but she's not picky about the term.

"They think I take it one step too far. They think that I'm too extreme," she says, hoping to convey that she doesn't really cares if she does. Criticism is important, but not when it makes her feel like a conspirator.

"Yes, and people do not approve of extremists." He stops as though the thought pains him, to which she almost relates. "Well, as you can see — I have the means and the time to do research, but I came across one of your articles and it got me thinking that, perhaps, what I require is a... fresh view on the matter."

"How did you manage to find me, Mr. Adams? I post under an alias."

He smiles and nods once again. "There's no reason for formalities."

It's a deflection, which causes her mind to signal a red flag. She's pushing it aside, knowing that she will get her answer one way or another. Instead, she raises her eyebrows and pretending she is not bothered, asks, "Is this a job interview?"

"I'm looking for a young, ambitious and open-minded person to take part in my research. You're one of the few I trust to have these attributes." He pauses to take a sip of his tea and gives her a pointed look.

Despite how sincere he looks and that it all fits in with what she has read online, she is still finding it hard to believe. "And you've picked me? There are bound to be others, a few successful researchers who would give you the publicity for it or the funds. Me — I don't..."

"Would seeking you out be so strange? Surely the job you currently have is not enough. I can give you the resources you would need — should it be your own office, books, income... Being a waitress isn't your destiny, Naya."

It is a motivational speech if any, yet while she had not planned on being a waitress for the rest of her life, she had worked for enough time to feel attached to it and therefore protective over it.

Instead of giving him a piece of her mind, she asks "And what would be the job requirements?"

"Well, for starters, I would need your full attention. Six days a week, so you wouldn't be able to keep your current job." It sounds logical enough, considering everything. "All I ask is how much further you intend on taking your theory?"

Naya's only response is to lean back and cross her legs. He takes it as a hint to elaborate, and resumes talking.

"When we think of a solution, we must consider how far we are willing to reach to achieve it. If I am right, and I most certainly am right, there are things to take into account when we look at the problem analytically."

"And what is the problem, exactly?"

Joshua takes another sip, narrowing his eyes at Naya, as if he is not sure if she's playing dumb or being serious. Nevertheless, he answers with great certainty. "Nature has a tendency to correct itself; it rids itself of waste, of species no longer useful to the ecosystem and creates diseases to control populations. Most importantly, and what is the basis of my thesis for my research, is that nature has no wrong or right, all it does is in the name of self preservation."

She lets him pause, using the time to consider his words.

When he continues, his tone changes to an admiring one. "If mankind did something to destroy that, surely nature must find a way to correct it, no?"

"So you think that natural disasters are nature's way of telling us to stop?"

Joshua shakes his head. "I am not saying anything yet, simply suggesting an alternative to what you think. You must clear your mind if you intend to work with me, Naya. As I said before, I will not ask for much, only that you keep an open mind."

Though she fears the answer, she has to ask. "What am I opening up my mind to?"

He smiles again, but his expression reminds her of the one he had back at the restaurant, and it sends a treacherous shiver down her spine. It's as if they're not supposed to be having this conversation at all.

She feels her chest tighten and wonders if it's a byproduct of delving into a subject that is considered taboo.

"If you had the opportunity to re-shape this world, would you take it?"

"I don't claim to have god-like power, Mr Adams," she replies. "I'm just a journalist."

She tries to ignore the ominous feeling overcoming her and sinks deeper into her seat, as if the armchair is supposed to grant her comfort.

"You underestimate yourself, my dear. You must, by now, understand that there are some things we can't explain. Some events that are so unnatural they appear to be made up, and some words that simply cannot be the truth."

The way he looks at her is too much. It's as if he is hanging all his hopes and dreams on her, as if she's the only one that can give him what he wishes, and suddenly it does not feel right.

The red flag is there again, this time blaring with horns — anything to get her attention, and she stands up abruptly. If this catches him by surprise, he doesn't let it show.

"I can understand why it must seem odd," he says instead, looking up at her. She must make an effort to hear him over her heartbeats. "Why I must seem odd," he simplifies his words. "You wanted the answers to the questions you dare not ask, and need I remind you that you took the opportunity to seek me out, not more than three days after we had met."

She knows he's right. She had come there all on her own, but she wonders how much of it was because he knew she would not be able to resist the temptation of digging out the truth, piece by piece.

She remains silent, not trusting herself to speak. The rational part of her brain screams at her to run with her tail between her legs, as far away as possible, but she stays, just for a moment.

"Soon you will have a big decision to make." This is all he offers before he stands to open the door for her. "All I can hope is that you make the correct decision and not the easy one."

Naya doesn't stay to ask, and she's not sure if she wants the answer either. She does exactly what her intuition tells her to do, and flees his office as soon as she gets the opportunity. It is all too much, and she cannot even pinpoint what has caused her such distress, but she knows it's because of him.

What he says may or may not be true, but the words spoken so earnestly feel like a death sentence. His presence in her life feels like a heavy weight on her shoulders, and she's sure if she chooses to stay it will come with a price, and she's not sure she even wants the truth anymore.

Not if it means risking her life.

Halfway to Bond Street's underground station, she stops, catches her breath and takes a look around, forcing her heart to slow down to a normal pace.

When she feels eyes on her again, she forces herself to move to the street again; the comfort of the busy street anchors her before the feeling disappears once she is safely behind the closing doors of the underground train.

CHAPTER FIVE

Saturdays are supposed to be Naya's fixed days off, but Charlie needed her in the early noon shift, and that is why she found herself in front of her childhood home in Acton Lane a lot earlier than she had intended.

One of the terms her father had set out for her when she left home was to schedule a meeting at least once a week, so that they could catch up and be involved in each other's lives.

They usually meet up at a coffee shop on Chiswick's main road or even in his small grocery shop — anywhere but home. Thinking back, Naya realises that she hasn't been at the flat she grew up in for over a year. It's not that the place has bad memories, it's more Dom's preference.

Her father greets her with a hug and a smile when she steps into the flat, using her key. The sound of the kettle heating up and the smell of breakfast fills the small space. Nothing about the two bedroom flat spells out family and, even if Naya knows that's where he and her mother used to live, it still feels like it belongs to a single dad and his only daughter, but it could just be her memory.

The flat is as she remembers it, with nothing out of place, and when she steps into the living room, her father makes sure to make her as comfortable as possible.

"I've made breakfast," Dom says, and his voice is gruffly, as if this is the first time he has spoken since waking up. "Pancakes and scrambled eggs, for old times sake."

Naya giggles, as she remembers a solid version of her younger self being spoiled on weekends and school holidays with a huge breakfast — the best meal of the day in her opinion. More often than not, Dom had included the twins, as well as Julie sometimes, when Naya was in university.

They sit down to eat, and Naya postpones telling him about Joshua Adams as long as she can, knowing fully well the argument it will surely bring on.

She does, however, end up telling him. She is extremely cautious about what she says and how she says it, to keeping a neutral expression all the time and not revealing to Dom that Joshua was a little odder than most people.

Dom doesn't say anything in response at first, which appeases Naya somewhat, and she thinks perhaps she has overreacted. However, his face hardens and he folds his arms.

"Why would you go and meet him?"

In hindsight, Naya should have seen the question coming a mile away and have mentally prepared a response before blurting out the first thing that comes to mind, which is usually something stupid.

"It's a job interview, Papa. Was I supposed to say no?"

She's happy she can occupy herself with eating and looking at her plate, so she doesn't have to suffer his scrutiny — she knows it's there, but it's not the same as experiencing it.

"You said he is an eccentric person," Dom offers as an excuse.

In fact, she hadn't said that and she would never have used that word, causing her to tilt her head slightly in question. It's an assumption even the twins had not made, and she had told them a lot more than she was telling her father. Even though Dom is usually in sync with her, Naya knows better than to confront him, she decides to try a different angle.

"You always complain how I don't make money from journalism—"

"That doesn't mean you should take a job offer from some random stalker!"

And once again, it's another piece of information he couldn't have known, at least not from her, since she had never told him she posts under an alias. As far as she knew, he has never read anything she's written, deeming it far too extreme but still supplying helpful advice whenever she came to talk to him.

Something doesn't feel right. While he has never tried to deliberately cut her wings, he has never showed such disapproval.

"Do you know Joshua Adams, Papa?" She asks instead.

The expression of being caught red-handed is quick and fleeting on his face, but it's still there and Naya has enough time to perceive it. She feels on top of her game, but maybe it's just Dom who's having an off day. Nevertheless, the fact that this has cracked his usual mask is enough for Naya.

"Why would I know him? As far as I'm aware, we work in different fields."

He's trying to divert the subject, but it doesn't work. Naya's not sixteen years old anymore, but she also knows it's not for her benefit to call him out on it.

He has taught her well enough to recognise when people are trying to hide things from her, though she's not sure if it's good or bad that he is showing it without hesitation.

"Right," she agrees nonchalantly to dissolve any suspicions he has. "Either way, his offer is a generous one, and I may accept it."

She's not really, however, about to accept anything Joshua has to offer, but she wants to test this new theory to the end and see how Dom reacts.

This time, Dom's face remains unfazed, and it almost disappoints her.

"I'm sure you can ask Charlie to give you a raise if it's about the money. I'd rather you stay where you are and work by yourself to succees and not use someone else's money to prove a theory that doesn't even make sense."

If she wasn't forcing herself to pay attention, she might have dismissed it as an attempt to show support and dissatisfaction at the same time. It's clear she must break down what he says, though, and find the true meaning there. She hates when it's like this; it reminds her too much of her childhood, working around the edges to avoid the knives in his words.

She doesn't have time, though, since he's looking for an answer.

"I'll prove my theory either way," she offers, and it's a half-truth that must irritate him.

He's silent for a few moments and lets her finish her breakfast before he gets up again and gestures towards the door. "I forgot I have a meeting," he says slowly, like he doesn't believe he has to spell it out, as if Naya should have read between the lines and known there was a time limit on their meeting when he suggested they catch up.

It's a dismissal she knows that has everything to do with their conversation, but there's nothing she can do about it.

"Sure," she swallows up her chagrin and gets up.

He walks her to the door, and she stops at the narrow hallway. Something pulls her to her old bedroom at the end of the hallway, and she mutters about forgetting something before walking towards the small room.

Dom lets her do as she pleases, and waits by the flat's entrance.

The room is how she remembers leaving it when she was eighteen; still pale pink wallpaper and white curtains that match the furniture. Even the bed — though unmade now — and dresser are all still in place… and yet something feels foreign.

Then she sees it on top of her dresser. She doesn't even know why it catches her eye. It is a simple wooden box, and looks like an antique. It has the letters K.T engraved in gold on its cover. It should have been insignificant, especially since Dom hasn't tried too hard to hide it, but those are her mother's initials and she cannot help wanting to stop and examine it.

She cannot, however — not without raising Dom's suspicion over her delay. So she leaves, setting out into the cold to make her way to Liverpool Street to her workplace.

Perhaps it is due to the long hours or the constant customers, or maybe it was due to the darkening skies that make her look twice before she starts walking to the underground station. Either way, she's grateful for noticing Joshua across the street.

She's even more thankful for the fact that he hasn't seen her yet, and so she can decide for herself whether to approach him or not.

The decision falls and she moves forward without even meaning to.

When she's about to catch up to Joshua — and do what her mind enquires in a voice that sounds too much like Lucas — she sees another man on Joshua's trail, clearly not even trying to hide the fact that he is practically stalking him. She can't help but bristle at this suspicious behaviour, that only adds to the number of oddities that seem to orbit around Joshua Adams.

She wonders about a lot of the things. For starters, who the hell is the dark skinned man spying on Joshua, and what his business with him. He doesn't strike her as friendly, since she knows there's no reason to stalk someone you're on good terms with. Then she thinks that's exactly what she's doing, but that thought doesn't linger for long. She suddenly becomes aware of the fact that London is such a big city, and the chances of these two showing up completely at random on the route she has chosen to cross the city are extremely unlikely.

And once again, she has zero ability to think of the matter.

They go to the other side of the train station, but the worst that can happen is that she might be a little later in getting home. In hindsight, she should have focused more on the stalker than on Joshua, because then she would have noticed him disappearing from the street.

But she doesn't, and immediately feels the consequences.

In the blink of an eye, before Naya can do anything about it, she is forcefully pushed into a nearby alley. The blow causes her to cough, but it's the forearm pressing just below her neck that makes her struggle for breath for a moment; she's trapped in between the solid brick wall and Joshua's stalker.

"It's hardly polite creeping up on people, you know," the man says with a clear edge of warning in his voice. His accent sounds American mixed with something else she can't pinpoint, but it is not a priority for her just now.

He seems to be scrutinizing her just as she is of him. Up close his skin looks lighter than what she originally thought, despite it being darker than her own. He is only about a head taller than her, but it's his wide shoulders and arms that make her feel like a small creature next to him, even though she's not of average size or as thin as she would like to be.

It's not easy, what with him only using a single hand on her. His intention is — not to harm her physically, she gathers, only to defer her, yet she at least attempts at giving him her best intimidating look.

He's not impressed, and she knows that fighting back is futile, but it's not in her nature to surrender, so she can't help but try.

"Let go of me!" She demands and wriggles her shoulders, trying to shake off his arm. His movements are quicker than hers, almost like he predicts exactly how she would try to escape; for a split second, he backs off, but not long enough to give her a sense of victory.

He pins her arms tightly to her sides by her elbows, not hard enough to hurt her but still in with a clear intention of restraint. It's funny how he obviously has the advantage of size and strength but still seems to be making an effort to be as gentle as he can. When it is obvious that she won't win this, she forces herself to relax. With her hands occupying his attention, she thinks she can still scream loud enough should the situation call for it.

He seems content with her submission, and his angular face softens slightly, yet in a way that makes it clear some of the anger is still there. When he speaks, she's surprised to find his voice modulated.

"Now, I'm usually not one to hurt women, especially someone as good looking as yourself, but don't think I won't make an exception for Mavro."

This ticks her off. What is she missing here that a stranger could hate her so much? This isn't an attempt to mug her or worse, she concludes, as he would have done so already, and there's also that word he used...

"Mavro?" She gives the foreign word a try. "What are you on about?"

He's silent for a moment, seeming to concentrate on something, and Naya finds the lack of movement menacing, much like the calm before a storm. Then, out of the blue just like how this whole encounter started, he loosens his grip on her. She doesn't waste time with her newfound freedom and thrusts her leg upwards in a well aimed blow to his groin — a blow that is intercepted by his palm on her kneecap, much to her displeasure.

He doesn't say anything, and his face is passive even as he stares at her chest. She's about to call him out on it, when he flat out gives her a reason — one that is far from what she was thinking of.

"Nice necklace," he forces out the words, and she's sure he's not talking about her Star of David.

She doesn't know what she wants more — to try her luck with hitting him again or to scream and run the other way. Thankfully, he doesn't let her linger on either thought, and tugs her away from the wall, causing her to feel unbelievably better.

It seems like he's looking to get to an even ground, in a way. He seems surprisingly unthreatening at the moment, like he's using the space between them to apologise and show her he's not there to harm her. If they would have crossed paths in the street, she would never think he has the ability to snap her neck if he wanted to.

He wears a black hoodie and over it a well-fitted motorcycle jacket, paired with dark jeans and sneakers. Normal and good looking without even trying, probably. When her gaze reaches his face, he holds it with arched eyebrows, looking extremely satisfied to have her check him out. He even goes the extra mile and crosses his arms, flexing them.

"I wasn't following you," she says quickly to keep him distracted.

His smugness turns doubtful. "So it's a hobby of yours to creep up on people?"

When she understands that she has no way of answering, she just huffs and mimics his posture.

He lets out a laugh that makes her feel considerably better. "Sorry about — well, the wall and all," he offers.

Naya turns to glance toward the street, and cannot see Joshua anywhere. She knows this man is to blame and groans when she feels small drops of rain on her. Before she can question her sanity by not listening when the twins told her to take an umbrella, she hears the man next to her shuffle and then opens up his own umbrella to shield the both of them.

She has no idea where he managed to hide it, but she makes no comment.

Apparently she looks as if the object is offending her, which only makes him laugh again. "What, no thank you for saving you from the big bad rain?"

"I'm not made of sugar, you arse, so you can shove that knight in shiny armour nonsense up your—"

"Well, aren't you sweet," he says, very close to her. She takes half a step back, still on edge from before. He doesn't say anything, but she doubts he didn't notice. "You're doing Britain such a bad service, we thought you were all really polite."

Americans, she rolls her eyes. "Why were you following that man?"

"Now, that's really none of your goddamn business, is it."

The sudden defensiveness in his tone doesn't go unnoticed, and she can't help but feeling intrigued now. "What is Mavro?" She asks instead of pressing on about Joshua.

He tilts his head as if to say, *seriously*, before once again arching his eyebrows and refusing to answer her second question. With that Naya gathers that whatever Mavro is, it is not good and she should be glad she's not one.

Naya sucks in a breath and before she is ready to put this weird encounter behind her and never think of it again, she decides to return his unexpected kindness and gestures at the umbrella. "Thanks for... whatever it is you were doing."

"I believe the term was saving you, but I don't suppose you'll ever admit it."

She won't add to his overly self-confidence by telling him he's right, and turns to exit the alley, more than willing to just call a cab and leave. But that would mean standing in the rain for however long it might take, so instead, she takes a left turn towards the underground station, choosing to walk in the rain.

When no rain hits her, she catches on to the fact that the man is still there, providing shelter from the weather with his white umbrella. Given the fact that not too long ago she was sure he was looking to kill her, walking alongside him doesn't have the same result he had probably looked for.

"You're still here," she mutters.

"And you're very observant, I like that."

She stops in her tracks, which causes him to do the same, and then narrows her eyes. She's silently demanding an answer.

"What's the problem?" he asks, and Naya ponders on his ability to keep up.

"You tried to kill me—"

"Hey, I apologised for that."

Naya inhales sharply, again, and tries to explain once more. "People don't really appreciate when strangers push them into walls to do — God, what were you trying to do?"

When he starts walking again, her shelter from the rain disappears as well. She takes the hint and falls into step beside him, completely baffled by how she doesn't feel entirely uneasy.

"I thought you wanted to attack me," he replies, and that's the most honest he has been with her. "So it really was self defence, and mostly your fault. You can't just sneak up on people, okay?"

She gives him a sideways look, clearly evident that she's not buying his crap, and he grins. They walk in silence all the way to the station, and it's nice not having to pick up on any insecurities she might have. Instead she rather enjoys the brisk air and the hum of the city, especially when she can shove her frozen fingers into the pockets of her coat.

"My name's Aidan Hall." He only speaks again when they're right by the entrance to the underground station. "Now that we are not strangers anymore, you should feel better about me almost tearing your head off."

She hopes he's kidding.

"Usually that's the cue to introduce yourself in return," he continues. It's a peace offering of sorts, and she looks at the hand he has extended. "I'll help you: what normal people say is 'my name is…' fill in the blank."

"Naya," is all she says, not really meaning to, but the word blurts out as an instinct more than anything else. He smiles softly, and she summons all her courage to turn her back on him and disappear into the ticket hall.

CHAPTER SIX

If there is one place Naya can call her haven, it's Tower Bridge.

It's the one place she always goes to when she needs to clear her thoughts or make an important decision. It is where the idea of moving out of her father's flat, or the pursuit of journalism surfaced. She goes there when she needs to cool off after an argument or a failed interview.

There's no reason for her not to be here, but as the wind sweeps past her and ruffles her hair out of its braid, she thinks back to what brought her here this time. She can't even remember leaving the flat, let alone waking up in the morning.

She glances at the people on the bridge next to her, which distracts her from the water below. None of the people are familiar. They all seem like silhouettes instead of the living breathing human beings she knows they are. As they pass her and catch her staring, they say something to her, though she fails to hear the words properly.

It takes some time for her attention to focus on trying to make out the syllables, without actually hearing them, but she eventually understands what they are meaning to say. It's not clear at first, and she has to empty all other thoughts in order to perceive this, but eventually she gets it.

It's your decision.

Their voices flow through her mind in a jumbled array of different tones and words. The words are coming all at once and she can't make much sense of them; it's deafening, and she covers her ears to try and block out the voices. It's futile, and she knows she's screaming at them to stop, to give her a moment to breathe and to find relief — but nothing helps.

They're not even using words, anymore — they're screaming, then they're shrieking, and the sound sends her body into a panic. All she wants is for them to stop, and when they do, it's only for a moment before everything comes crashing down.

The earth itself shake.

Nobody even tries to get to safety, despite the bridge starting to collapse. Blue and white stones fall from above, and she tries not to concentrate on their destination. It's chaos, and she must attempt to get them out of there, but when she touches the woman next to her, everything becomes still again.

It takes her a whole minute to make sense of what has happened.

Naya realises she had never left her flat, nor made it to the bridge, but what shocks her the most is that she can see the thin lines separating the two realities. She now sees the disharmony; from there it's easy to conclude she's having a nightmare.

The people on the bridge turn to her in sync, looking anything but human, and their voices are clear as day, as they point at her. *It's your fault*, they seem to be saying.

Hearing her name yelled out in the dream causes the first crack to appear in this fabricated existence and she sees it as well. As a result, it generates into a ripple until it all changes rapidly and she can hear someone calling for her, but it's only her heart beating that drums in her ears, blocking out any other sound.

She feels the hands on her before she comes to, and the silent urge to breath properly kicks in as she jumps back into reality again.

It must be few minutes before she shakes off the disorientation and the comforting smell of Logan invades her senses. She makes out his figure in the darkness of her room and his lean frame covers her.

Logan doesn't have to spell it out for her — her throat aches and she knows she had been screaming.

It explains why he's in her room in the middle of the night. She's almost sure she can see someone moving in the living room and then a door closes. She hopes she's not imagining Lucas trying to be as discreet as possible.

It's always difficult coming to — forcing her mind from its own abyss always leaves her disheveled and unsure, but the sense of touch keeps her anchored to reality even after an extreme panic attack.

Her legs are tangled up in the sheets, and she feels sweat coating her forehead. Her hands are clutched so tightly into fists that she is sure when she opens them she'll find blood; her breaths are unsteady, and she feels the weight of the dream heaving down on her chest, making it harder to breathe normally.

"Naya," Logan whispers, his eyes wild, searching for a response.

It must be a reflection of her own stare.

She doesn't reply, but forces her hands to lessen their grip and places them in her lap, so she can twist her body and sit up, crossed legged. She doesn't dare to look at Logan, as the embarrassment soaks into her slowly when she sees his worried expression.

"Naya," he tries again. "You've had a panic attack."

She grimaces, because she knows. She's been living with it for as long as she can remember to recognise the signs. It has been years since it has been this bad, though, but she doubts that he doesn't know that.

"I'm fine," she says, sounding hoarse.

He doesn't say anything, and she's relieved because they both know there's nothing he can say. When she sees he is about to say something, she takes the cue to collapse on the bed. Thankfully, he takes the hint as she covers herself with the blankets once again and turns away from him.

He sighs, but as always, he understands.

It takes her a while to get back to sleep, and when she does, it's the same nightmare again. Maybe it's her mind choosing to not delve too much into it, but at least she's not waking up screaming.

It's still relatively dark outside when she wakes up again, but by the blueish shade of sky she gathers it is around seven in the morning.

As she looks for her phone, hoping it will distract her, she can feel the nightmare still embedded into her awareness. She hears the twins in the living room. She can't face them now so she stays in her room in silent gratitude to herself for taking the day off.

She finds her phone after a few seconds of searching blindly and looks at the screen.

Being an environmental journalist should have reassured her that the chances of an earthquake with that magnitude of destruction in London are slim, but it did not hurt to refresh her knowledge on seismology.

Her mind nags about the connection to Joshua, but she dismisses it quickly, unwilling to go down that road.

She finds an article about the last earthquake in London, and about the fault lines in the city, but nothing that has caused anything more than tremors. It should set her mind at ease, but it has the opposite effect. By the time she hears the twins leaving the flat, she knows she needs a distraction and focuses her attention on making the best of her day.

Out of a necessity to settle everything and get a better view of things, Naya asks Julie to meet her in the afternoon, under the pretence of spending proper quality time together.

Julie, ever observant, calls her off on it but leaves it up to Naya to work out the details.

For the sake of her sanity and her own comfort, Naya picks a place randomly in Marylebone, which should be pretty convenient for the both of them, especially considering that Julie will arrive straight from work.

Naya gets there with plenty of time ahead to ensure a semi-private booth that should be secluded enough to have a proper conversation, and she waits.

It takes Julie thirteen minutes from the time she texts Naya that she is on her way till Naya sees her squeezing her way through the busy pub. Naya had been counting the minutes, and that alone tells her she's more on edge than normal.

Julie notices as well, if her stare is anything to go by.

"Oh no," is the first thing she says when she sees Naya. Naya would have been insulted, but she figures her appearance isn't as neat as usual, so she doesn't take it personally that Julie has decided to comment on it.

However, Julie's stare fixes on the opened bottle of wine on the table and, with a sigh, slides into the booth across from Naya, turning to look at her. "I suppose it's a six on a scale of one to ten, right?"

Naya chuckles, moves one of the glasses towards her friend and waits for her to take the first sip. "It's actually more of a nine out of ten."

"Nine?" Julie repeats. "That bottle's too full for a nine, and—"

"I think someone tried to kill me."

Naya hadn't meant to blurt it out, but her mind to mouth filter has never been good and really, she can't see how else she could have led up to it. She gauges Julie's reaction, watching as a few expressions replace the usually calm one on her face and waits.

"Excuse me, what? And why are we here instead of at the police station? I have a friend at Stockwell's police station, we can go—"

And for the second time, Naya cuts her off, this time intentionally. "We are not going to the police," she says, and begins relaying the events of the past twenty-four hours to Julie's shocked face.

She starts with her actual meeting with Joshua, juggles between her work shifts and her weekly meeting with her father, stressing how out of the ordinary it was and finishes with Aidan.

Julie is silent for the entirety of her tale, only nodding and humming whenever Naya takes a breath, as well as once she is done. It causes Naya to shift in her seat, anxious for her response.

Usually, Julie is the type to fire off a comment or a word of advice, and should she not have one at the ready, she'll provide a word of encouragement or a smile — anything that would guarantee Naya everything will be alright.

Now, though, Julie sits in front of her with her hand clutching the thin part of the wine glass and she's so quiet it's unnerving.

"Jules?" Naya tries to prompt her into talking, but it fails, and all Julie does is look at the bottle, with a contemplative look on her face.

"What the hell is going on, Naya?"

"Do you think I know?"

Julie sighs, once again. "I don't know what to tell you, honestly."

"Yeah," Naya says, a bit disappointed. "I had a feeling you'd say that."

"Logan told me you had an anxiety attack this morning," Julie offers instead.

Naya knows what she is doing. It is the oldest trick in the book, but she doesn't know why it makes her angry. It takes almost all of her energy to suppress her anger, reminding herself that Julie is only doing it to distract her and buy some time to form a proper answer.

Nevertheless, she would have preferred to tell Julie on her own, if she had thought that she needed to know.

"My anxiety has gotten worse lately," Naya says instead, not really able to hide anything from Julie. "I don't know why. I've had some bad times with it, but in the past few weeks — it's been almost unbearable."

Julie nods and takes a sip from her drink. "Do you think it has anything to do with what you're going through?"

"I suppose," Naya pauses just enough to steal a glance at the door, all of a sudden feeling self-conscious of the fact that they were out in public. "Would it be weird if I feel like everything's connected?"

"What do you mean?"

"Joshua, my dad and Aidan… my nightmares and my anxiety."

Julie seem to consider it before replying. "Maybe your anxiety is acting out because you're worried about Joshua's job offer? Because it feels real or—"

"Thanks, but if I needed a physiologist, I would have gone to Dr. Howard," Naya snaps at Julie, but by Julie's grin, Naya can see that she is not fazed. "Julie, I need you to use your proper lawyer intuition to tell me if I'm overthinking this."

"Well, I don't think you can figure out if anything suspicious is going on unless you actually start to dig into it." Julie stops for a second, and Naya knows she's only doing it to give Naya a chance to cut her off again. "If it means working for Joshua, or talking to your dad about it, then you need to do it."

"And this Aidan?"

Julie shrugs. "If he shows up again, you will know it's not a coincidence, and you'll confront him about it."

"And if it doesn't work," Julie chuckles, and Naya rolls her eyes at how well she knows her, "then we'll go together to the police. But, just in case you don't want to involve the authorities, I have someone you can talk to."

Naya raises her eyebrows in an attempt to make Julie elaborate, but Julie is too busy with her cellphone to pay attention. A couple of seconds later, Naya's own cellphone pings with a text from Julie. It's a contact number, and she looks up to meet her friend's stare.

"His name is Andre, and he can find out things for you. A colleague of mine is a good friend of his and he has helped me out with a lot of cases. I'm sure he can help you too, if you need."

"Please don't tell me he's a detective—"

"The term is private investigator, and he can help. Trust me."

With that, Julie settles the subject, forcing Naya to change it. They continue talking for a while before leaving the pub together, making their way back home.

CHAPTER SEVEN

"Joshua Adams, right?" Patrick says, and it comes off so casually someone would think Naya was sharing her inner most thoughts with him.

She was not however, which causes her to stop and glare at Lucas. He has the audacity to look innocent enough, which only serves her anger. Patrick is Lucas's coworker, and since Lucas considers him a pretty good friend, Naya feels obligated enough to be as nice as possible. This however, does not correlate with how Patrick seems to think he has any say in Naya's personal life.

Logan, quick to pick up on it as usual, tries to divert the subject.

"So this bloke, the stalker…?"

Lucas doesn't hesitate commenting on it, and as much as Naya wants to revert to the other topic, she can't at the moment. "You have a stalker now, too?"

"He's not my stalker, calm down, would you. Also, how do you know?" The question is directed at Logan of course, since she came home from work to catch them both with the sole intention of talking about Aidan.

"Uh, Julie?"

Naya scoffs — a response way too natural to be considered healthy. "Is that how it works? I can't tell you anything by myself anymore? Do you also have a group chat you use to spy on me?"

"Don't be ridiculous," Logan says. Unfortunately for him his brother adds just as quickly, "Also, don't be paranoid."

"We're all trying to help," Logan offers in a beat. "Patrick included, I suppose."

Whatever deflection he had tried before flies out the window, causing Naya to refocus her anger towards the black-haired man in her living room, whom she specifically had not invited to take part in their discussion.

"I can't believe you told him!"

Lucas folds his arms. "He asked what had happened. Was I supposed to lie?"

She sincerely tries to remain calm, mustering all her available composure and inhaling before replying. Deep down she knows Lucas is just trying to help, but however close Patrick and him are, it's still her life and she would rather Patrick stay out of it.

"Look—"

"No," Naya holds her hand up, knowing that whatever

Lucas thinks of saying is only going to make it worse. "Don't bother."

"Are you thinking of working with him?" Patrick asks anyhow, making Naya realise it is a lost cause.

"No," she's quick to reply.

He nods, and gives her a look before saying, "I think you should, if you ask me."

As Naya contemplates her next words in the line of *no one asked you*, Logan, who knows her better, is quick to come out and ask, "What makes you say that?"

"Well, it's sounds like it is a once in a lifetime opportunity, you know?"

Patrick's answer clearly doesn't add up to how Lucas thought he would contribute to the conversation, and Naya wonders briefly if Lucas had brought Patrick only as a voice in his favour. If Logan's stare is anything to go by, Naya barely manages to wipe the smug smirk off her face when she sees how Lucas's plan is backfiring.

"It does sound like a great opportunity! How refreshing," she says in delight. Patrick doesn't need to know she is only saying it to spite Lucas.

It works, and Lucas looks at her, outraged. "You said he looks strange and that you don't want to work for someone with secrets!"

"To be honest, everyone has secrets," Patrick says. "And really, you're not the most normal person, Naya."

She raises her eyebrows, half in surprise at his honesty. Maybe that's why Lucas likes him so much, it must be exhilarating to always hear the truth. "So you'd take it?" She's not really considering it just because he thinks she should, but it's always good to hear an unbiased opinion.

"In a heartbeat," he says. "And I wouldn't think twice about it. Besides, it's not like you're giving him your life — it's just a job. If you don't like it, you quit."

They leave it at that. Lucas is more than happy when they do, but so is Naya. Later, when she is trying to fall asleep, she keeps thinking back to the conversation. It prevents her from closing her eyes, until she finally turns around, figuring that she won't get any answers from sleep deprivation.

Not more than twenty-four hours after her last meeting with Julie, her friend suggests meeting again, this time to actually catch up. The motive for the meeting becomes clear after half an hour, and Naya's on the edge of her seat when Julie speaks.

"So, have you seen the mysterious hot guy from the alley ever since?"

The nickname is not Naya's choice, but once Julie sets her mind on something, she can't be budged and Naya has long since given up on trying. She guesses it's her way of brightening up an already messed up situation, especially considering Naya's reaction to it all.

She hates being the one that needs special treatment, but she does have to admit it helps.

Naya shakes her head. "I don't even know if he is involved somehow. It could just be a coincidence."

Julie tilts her head, clearly unimpressed, before she picks up her almost empty glass of wine and speaks again. "Coincidence my arse. I think we've already covered that last time. You and I both know something else is going on here, and we need to get to the bottom of it."

Leave it up to Julie to treat this as another puzzle.

When Naya doesn't respond in any way other than to finish her glass of wine, Julie continues, "I think you should seriously consider talking to my guy."

Naya tries not to disregard the idea straight away, but her eyes seem to have a will of their own, and she can see Julie scowling when they roll.

"Or, you could just try to wait and see if you see any of them again?" Julie offers instead. "Seems like for now, neither of them mean any harm, and maybe you can ask them yourself what's going on. Since we have ruled out Joshua, why not Aidan?"

"Yeah, why not Aidan?"

The male voice that intrudes on the conversation leads Naya to look upwards to see no other than the man in question. He pulls out a chair and joins them at the table, unannounced and not entirely welcome. Julie raises her eyebrows, checking him out. Then, with her mouth curling upwards, she turns to look at Naya. There is no need for telepathy to help Naya know what Julie is thinking, which makes her want to wipe the stupid smirk right off her face.

"Julie," the blonde introduces herself, and Naya is partly thankful because she hadn't even thought of doing it. "I suppose you're Aidan?"

"Yeah, alleyway's mysterious hot guy at your service." He holds out his hand, and Naya can see a trace of ink in between his fingers when they shake hands. She thinks she can almost make out the shape of a tattoo when he withdraws his hand, placing it on his thigh. Not that there is anyway she would be interested in checking it out.

She thinks he's doing it on purpose.

He was also eavesdropping on their conversation, which is enough to rule him out, to use Julie's approach on the matter.

"What are you doing here?" Naya asks, the annoyance clear in her tone.

He is holding a pint of beer and smiles as an answer. Julie is gushing at the gesture, but Naya is not fooled. She had chosen this pub at random, and London isn't a small city so she couldn't have possibly run into Aidan by chance for the second time in two days.

"I was just thinking about our meeting the other day," he gives her an answer, but doesn't elaborate.

Julie, however, is happy to contribute. "When you pushed her against the wall?"

Aidan has the nerve to laugh, and Naya feels like Julie has finally found her match. "Did she actually say that?" Aidan queries.

"Yeah, after describing your strong hands."

Naya groans, swearing that she will kill Julie by the end of this encounter. "That is not what I said."

"Right," Julie chuckles. "She might have said something along the lines of how she couldn't breathe because there was a ridiculously muscular hand trying to meld her to the wall."

"I was actually just trying to rip her head off," Aidan jokes.

"Of course you were, sweetie," Julie is practically cooing at him as she takes her final sip of wine. "I'm going to get another one, do you want something?"

Not waiting for an answer, she leaves Naya alone with Aidan. He looks at her expectantly, daring her to spit it out. She knows she won't last long, especially when he throws the challenge effortlessly at her.

It takes her exactly one and a half minutes before she breaks.

"Okay. Seriously, what on earth are you doing here?"

Aidan smiles, holding his beer in the air again and says, "I'm having a drink."

Naya wonders briefly if he is so self-confident to think that she would accept his answer, but then she realises that he doesn't know her at all. The obvious stalker-like chracteristics of this encounter have not gone unnoticed, and she raises her eyebrows, waiting for a better explanation.

When he says nothing and just takes a sip of his drink, she tackles the subject herself. "How did you find me?"

The man holds her stare again, only breaking it to look at Julie. She is by the bar, the bartender chatting her up, while probably trying to think of an excuse to leave Naya alone with him.

"Your friend seems nice," he changes the subject, gauging her response.

"Stay away from her, or—"

Aidan puts the drink down on the wooden table and folds his hands, giving her more than enough time to come up with a proper threat; she lets the sentence hang instead, leaning back in her seat.

"Oh," his mouth curls upwards, like he's holding back a smirk. "Jealous, are we?"

"You wish."

They're silent for a few long minutes, and Naya is trying hard to ignore how easy it is to just be with him, with no need for idle conversation or trial and error in small talk; she can just relax for a moment, and pretend everything is normal again.

Then he chooses to speak, and the illusion disappears. "I want you to have my number."

The piece of paper that he slides her way is actually a napkin, and she wonders if he sat down prior to joining them and scribbled his number. The writing is messy, like he was in a hurry, and it's almost illegible, but she's happy to know it's just numbers.

"What?" She finally finds the word.

"Just in case," he casually explains. "Please resist the urge of using it to ask me to go out with you," he pauses, trying to add the light tone again but Naya isn't fooled. "It's just... If you ever find yourself in danger or something."

She ignores the first part of the sentence, and focuses on the latter. "Should I expect danger?"

"You shouldn't expect anything, Naya." He uses the same easy-going tone again, as if they were not talking about troublesome situations. "But I would keep your friends as close as possible if I were you."

"Is that a threat?"

The question is meant to come off half jokingly, but instead her tone is demanding. Aidan, however, does not seem too concerned and just shrugs.

"I'd never do anything to hurt you," he swears, and

it's on the tip of her tongue to tell him that it didn't look like that the last time they met. "Look, it's important that you have someone to call, just in case, okay?"

Naya, not quite understanding his meaning, only nods. She has already figured out that she is not going to get an answer in any case, so she refrains from repeating herself.

He only moves to leave when she accepts the napkin, making sure he sees her tucking it into her bag before nodding at her and at Julie from across the room. He doesn't say anything to signal whether he's upset or disappointed with her reaction, but she can feel the tension in the air, and it scares her.

When Julie returns a few seconds later, she tries to lighten the mood, once again.

"Let's get you home," she says after a while, tapping on her cellphone to call a cab for the both of them.

Naya doesn't object, and lets her friend guide her to the exit of the pub and then onto the street. She swears she can sense that Aidan is out there, maybe watching them as they enter the cab, but she doesn't say anything to Julie, who she feels is involved enough as it is.

If she has to sum up the next few days, she can only focus on the fact that she's not getting much sleep thanks to her nightmares. It is always the same one, with slight changes, yet it doesn't throw her off anymore, nor does the fact that she hasn't seen or heard from Aidan or Joshua either.

The days flow hazily, and she finds herself lacking in wanting to do anything other than to keep up her normal routine as much as she can. So she changes her shifts to work only mornings, that way she is able to make constant plans with her friends and minimise her alone time. Having the same schedule every day helps tremendously, and this is also the excuse she uses for her co-workers.

It doesn't change the fact that it feels like a futile attempt, but she's anything if not stubborn.

It's about two hours into her shift on Friday when she feels the change in the air. A quick glance around promises her everything is fine for the moment; Anna and John are serving tables, there's the usual hum of customers speaking and even the weather is turning out to be better what with the sun shining through the tall windows overlooking the street.

All is well until she reaches the bar and looks at her boss.

All it takes is for Charlie to change his posture for her to understand something is wrong and it's not just in her mind. She follows his stare, and for a moment can't find the reason for his discomfort until she spots him: Joshua Adams is just about to sit down near the entrance to the restaurant, looking sideways wearily and muttering something to John.

It doesn't go unnoticed by Naya that he's not seated in one of the tables she's supposed to be serving.

"Naya—"

Without listening to Charlie, she jumps at the chance to confront Joshua, even if she's not sure what about. She moves past her boss's outstretched hand, most likely there to hold her back, and positions herself next to Joshua, just after John has taken his order.

When John exchanges glances with her on his way to the kitchen, she realises two things: the first one being how suspicious she looks, stalking a customer who has just arrived at the restaurant and the second — maybe even more important, is that Charlie has no reason to feel uneasy by Joshua's presence.

"Miss Tellus." Joshua's words avert her attention back to him. She feels tongue-tied; all of her earlier resolve leaving her as he looks at her calmly.

She begs her mind to function properly, not to look into things that don't exist, but it's on overdrive due to the many questions, doubts and insecurities. But most of all it is shutting down because she hadn't counted on the fact, that even in her comfort zone, Joshua is still supposed to be a threat, or at the very least someone who intimidates her.

She lets her instincts take over, but she knows she'll have no filtering of her words and will blurt out the first thing that comes to mind.

"What are you doing here?"

No filter usually results in her saying something stupid like that.

Joshua gives her a pointed look, but doesn't comment on her rudeness. He takes the napkin that is neatly folded on the table and puts it on his knees, which strikes Naya as too casual, as if they were not about to have a deep discussion on what he wants with her at any moment.

"I came to apologise," he says after a while, and Naya feels her courage melting away by the way he hangs his head.

She thinks he looks ashamed.

When he doesn't elaborate, she urges him on, "Apologise?"

"Yes," he nods, and stops for a moment while John brings his order of black tea, a jar of water and a croissant. He speaks again only when John is out of earshot. "I believe I may have scared you away."

Naya wants to tell him that she would have used a more extreme term, but refrains from it.

"I simply thought you needed to hear the truth," he continues, which makes her think that she does not really want the truth he's talking about. "Given your curious nature I thought you would like to see all the pieces of the puzzle before making a decision on how you want to assemble it."

"Do I wanna know what the hell you are talking about?"

He smiles as a first response, as he places two cubes of sugar in his beverage. "Nothing I've told you has been a lie. I do believe we can work well together, but it seems like you choose not to. Which is, in my opinion, the wrong move for you, and I do hope you will not see this as a dead end."

She moves to fold her arms, deliberately showing her displeasure. "Are you threatening me?"

"Never. It is something to bear in mind. A warning, if you will."

Her mind is quickly wrapping up their conversation, getting sick and tired of his mysterious character. "What are you warning me from?" she asks.

Joshua moves to stand, but freezes. His eyes fall on the full jar of water that John had on his table not too long ago. Naya catches what's wrong even before it actually happens. For a split second, everything around them seems to be in the ordinary.

When the liquid in the jar shakes, it's the only indication both of them have before the ground shakes below them. The first impact causes her to lose her balance and fall back.

Then chaos erupts.

Her instincts put the pieces together and however unlikely it is, she knows the earth is releasing its fury upon them. It's a mess of screaming and crying; she tries to find a hold onto anything solid — anything that can promise her safety.

Behind her, a table slides her way and the ground opens itself. It is a dead end — the probability of death seems closer than ever, before a hand moves in front of her, and grabs her sleeve just in time before the table crashes and falls into the sudden pit where she had just been standing.

"Are you alright?"

Joshua's concern sounds weirdly vivid above all the noise, and she silently watches as her workplace succumbs to ruins, with only Joshua Adams by her side.

CHAPTER EIGHT

As the ringing in her ears mellows down, Naya is able to once again think clearly. The strong urge to close her eyes and ignore everything around her is still very much present and nagging, but she's doing what she can to keep the anxiety at bay.

There's no time for that, she manages to convince herself.

"Are you alright?" Joshua asks again, as he moves in front of her, most likely looking for any visible damage.

Unintentionally she does the same and finds a sharp cut on his left cheek that thankfully doesn't look too deep. He had discarded his waistcoat and jacket; his dress shirt is stained with dirt and teared a bit by the neckline.

When she starts to look around, he tries to stop her. "I wouldn't do that," he advises.

She assumes that they both know it's a futile attempt, but she considers the fact that he's making an effort to spare her. As she examines her surroundings, she only then notices how difficult it is to draw a proper breath. The dust is so thick in the air she can see it through the dim light of the emergency lights Charlie had insisted on installing previously.

It's probably for the best that she can't see too much. Nothing can quite prepare her for damage of this magnitude; no pictures or movies can equal seeing it first hand. The side of the restaurant they were on, seems the only area to be somewhat intact, but it had collapsed a few floors down. To her left she recognises the storage room in the basement with all sorts of furniture flipped over and a few dripping pipes.

They're alone, however, and it seemed like they had quite a climb above them.

"We need to wait here for rescue," Joshua breaks the silence, but his words sound unsure, like he's hesitant in asking for her cooperation.

"There could be aftershocks," Naya says, and quite frankly was a bit surprised he hadn't mentioned it, being a seismologist himself. Perhaps just like her, he was not prepared for anything like this.

The thought is both comforting and distressing.

In any case, it seems his mind is a few steps ahead of hers, as he gestures upwards. "The only way out of here is up, but we need to move these flanks there," he points in front of them. "There's always the chance that moving them will cause the ceiling to collapse, but..."

He makes sitting and waiting sound like a dream idea, but it leaves Naya completely out of control and she can't have that, so she takes out her phone. Other than a large gash in the glass of the phone, it seems fine, and while she didn't think she would have reception, she's partly discouraged. Her brain is working relentlessly, thinking there must be another way out that wouldn't be risking being buried alive.

"I'm not waiting," she says offhandedly, filling in the definite silence. She feels detached from everything, and she knows it's a coping mechanism — her own psychiatrist had explained it to her years ago. However, it doesn't stop from catching her off-guard as to how eerily everything feels. It's like being inside a nightmare, although this time she knows screaming and kicking won't force her mind to succumb to reality.

Focus, she repeats in her head again and again, like a mantra.

The restaurant had been semi-full when the earthquake struck, so if she needs to estimate, there must have been ten other people there with them. Although most of them had not been close by, she still thinks that they should have heard something or someone by now. The fact that they hadn't, can only mean that the two of them are at the lowest part of the collapse.

This also means, and she knows this from too much free time watching TV shows, that search and rescue teams would get to them last. That could take hours, and there's a solid chance of air running out.

Of course, she could be all wrong, but with no way of making sure, she's not about to sit and find out.

Naya looks at her phone again; sixty four percent battery should be a good sign, so she turns on the flashlight to further examine the site.

"Do you know a little physics as well?" She asks after a while. Her voice sounds different down here, and she clears her throat a bit hoping for it to get back to normal. Still looking at Joshua, Naya begins to walk around the small space.

It's a survival instinct, hoping he will follow her.

"As well?" He echoes her question. Much like her voice, Joshua's voice resonants from within the fallen walls, and sounds off too.

"You're an expert on seismology," she offers an explanation, even if he didn't ask for one directly. "I googled you."

He chuckles, and for a second she's relieved to hear that it sounds like he is following her as she continues looking for a way out. "I know a bit of physics, yes. However, I'm afraid it is not something that would help us to keep the place from collapsing on us while we climb out," he answers nonetheless.

Naya pauses to look at him. He gives her a pointed glance that is a clear question to her coming to a sudden halt. It seems odd to her that he answered her idea without her even forming a question, but she does not explain herself.

It makes her think back to their meeting a week ago. Some of the things he said ring a bell now. How he spoke of natural disasters as if they were man-made.

"Some events are so unnatural they must be made up", he had said then, which makes her think for the first time in a few days about the implications.

"London doesn't have earthquakes," she says and turns away again, determined to get answers from him. People talk more freely when they're not feeling watched over, and it also gives her a chance to continue looking.

"True," he hums out the word. He doesn't have to raise his voice too much as the echo gives their words the volume they need. "The last one was less than ten years ago, but London is situated over a few fault lines, so it's not extremely unlikely. This one, however, feels too precise to be a mere earthquake."

Naya thinks about it for a few moments. "So, a terrorist attack…?"

"We cannot be sure the damage done here was designed to be a planned attack against your workplace. However, if that is indeed the case, I suppose in order to cause this much accurate impact someone would have needed to place bombs directly below the restaurant in the same manner used to dispose of old buildings," Joshua says thoughtfully, as if he's mapping out his thought process simply to entertain her. "I suppose it could be considered an option. Do you think your boss has upset enough people for this to happen?"

"Charlie doesn't seem the type," she says immediately. Knowing Charlie so well and for this long leaves no doubt in her mind that he wouldn't be the one to be involved in such things.

"People rarely are what they seem," he offers her a different way of thinking, and she wonders if they're even talking about Charlie anymore. "A wolf in sheep's clothing, is that the phrase?"

Their discussion is momentarily pushed aside as Naya finds a crack in the ruins, but one she won't be able to reach without Joshua's help in boosting her up. She wonders out loud whether she would fit or not, since it seems pretty narrow, but Joshua believes she must try.

"Perhaps just your hand, then? You can wave with your flashlight and there is bound to be someone out there."

Naya looks at the gap again, this time more closely. It seems like it had been the small shaft the kitchen used to deliver food and dishes. So that must mean they are right next to the kitchen, or at least what is left of it.

"There should be a staircase outside somewhere," she says, and a strong sense of direction fills her as she begins to realise that there might be a way out. "The kitchen is to the left, I think, and right through it there's an emergency escape to the street. Charlie — that's my boss — he insisted on clearing everything from the door there, so if we're lucky..." she trails off, sure Joshua has caught on to her intention.

Joshua's not saying much, but she hears his footsteps as he follows her to what she believes is the kitchen. The hallway that they are standing in gets so tight that they must move sideways to fit in between the broken furniture and concrete. She can feel the walls scraping her forearms through her uniform and catching on to her hair, but she doesn't stop, and neither does Joshua.

Luckily the earth seems quiet, yet despite no aftershocks, it doesn't mean they should slow down and rest. She tries to calculate how much time they spent looking for the correct hallway, and while it feels longer, she knows it couldn't have been more than an hour. This means that if they manage to leave the ruins through the fire escape in the kitchen, emergency services should be right there.

The more they advance, the less light they have, and she hopes she's not leading them into death; the amount of blind trust Joshua has put in her sets her on edge when she should be flattered.

It takes a few minutes to see, considering how slow they move, but she can make out a few glints in the dark and her flashlight's beam catches on to the metallic kitchen counters. As the gap opens to the area, she lets out a sigh of relief at seeing it.

Out of excitement, she walks too quickly to the space and feels the tremor in the ground, a little too late. Once again, she's pulled back just in time from certain death as one of the overhead extractor hoods falls down. She looks at Joshua, his hand still clutching her apron; he looks just as alarmed as she is, and she mutters her thanks as she moves past it.

"The exit should be there," she tries to make as little noise as she can. "If it's not blocked, we can squeeze through."

Joshua doesn't ask for an alternative, and Naya hopes they won't need to find one.

"I think it was an earthquake," Joshua sounds eager to let the words out, as if he had thought them through before. It takes her a few seconds to understand he's referring to their earlier speculation. "I don't know if one should assume that it was a natural occurrence, but it was an earthquake. Undoubtedly."

They're almost in the clear; the red neon with the words EMERGENCY EXIT looks like a blessing, and she finds herself focusing on it instead of on Joshua. He must notice her lack of attention, since he doesn't say anything else or trigger any reaction.

The door is stuck on its hinges, but thankfully there's enough space for both of them to slip out. They move one by one, helping each other as needed to hold the door. Once Joshua is through, Naya climbs up. She's happy to see one thing has gone right, and the stairway is in place and reliable enough to walk on.

As they make their way up, the sounds of the outside world make sense again. She can hear screams to help people, sirens and, if she's not mistaken, rain.

There's another door at the end of the stairs which is the only barrier between them and the street, but it's stuck.

"Shit," she mutters, and looks back at Joshua. "Help me get it open?"

He moves to stand next to her, and counts to three before shoving their bodies against the door. It doesn't budge, but she hears some commotion from outside and in no time, the door is opened from the other side, causing her to fall forward.

From then on, it's pure mess. She can barely grasp what's going on as she is being led to an ambulance. Both the paramedics and the firefighters try to get answers she does not have about other survivors.

"I don't know," she says again as she's being seated

at the back of an ambulance. "There was just me and someone else, he was right behind me—"

The person examining her pauses, and orders her to look her way as she checks her head for a concussion or any other injuries. Naya takes the time to look for Joshua, but cannot find him. Seeing as there are a lot of people around, it does not surprise her. Once the paramedic leaves her for a few minutes, she manages to spot him.

He's still by the fire escape, but no one seems to be noticing him. He seems to be talking to a woman — the same woman Naya believes she saw in his office the day she was there. While she can't hear them or see what they're doing, she can clearly see the smile on Joshua's face when they depart.

What causes her stomach to turn however, is that the person who leaves right on their tail — is Aidan.

Eventually, things start to calm down around her. She was questioned by the police and interrogated by the firefighters in the hope she could help them figure out another way in or the number of survivors, since there are at least seven people missing.

She can't make much sense of the earthquake site, but she hears the paramedic treating her relay that the only street that got hit was the one Charlie's restaurant was on. They exchange theories when they think Naya isn't paying attention, and go over the same theories she and Joshua had.

"Naya!"

Logan's voice floats through the crowd. The last police officer to talk to her gives her the clear to leave, but clarifies that she would need to stay in London as they were not ruling out foul play. He doesn't spell it out, but she can read between the lines: everyone's a suspect.

Either way, the only thing she can think about right now is to get home. She jumps at the option to do so and squeezes past people to reach the other side of the street, where Logan is waiting and waving at her. He's unable to cross the red lines the police have set up, but she doesn't care anymore. It's a huge relief to see him, and she crushes into him the moment she can.

"Thank God you're alright," she hears him say as he tightens his arms around her, and for a moment it muffles everything else. "Come on, Lucas is waiting in the car. Let's go home."

CHAPTER NINE

Reality doesn't relent, even if Naya wishes it would.

Over the next few days, Naya is summoned on and off to various police stations to give sworn statements all of which ensure her that, just like her and Joshua, the police also suspect that something else is going on. Despite that, she suddenly has way too much time on her hands and it feels like, for the first time in a while, she can focus on her own career; albeit nonexistent at the moment, but still a career in the making.

She tries to reach Joshua in hopes he can shed some light on what happened, but he either dodges her calls or is simply busy, according to his secretary.

She also hopes to run into Aidan and confront him about his connection to everything, but even that falls behind as she spends most of her days at home in front of the computer. She thinks more than once of using the number he gave her, but she always comes up with a good enough excuse not to.

She speaks to Charlie a few times; he assures her that he is physically fine and will do what he can to restore his restaurant. Thankfully her co-workers are doing well as well and they all express the same sentiment. Charlie promises them all in their group chat that as soon as he is able, he will call on them for help.

Lucas and Logan try several times unsuccessfully, to get Naya to look for jobs through websites — anything to get her out of the house. But she is already aware of the mystery that she needs to solve which is not going to change if she gets a new job.

It turns into somewhat of an obsession, knowing there's something going on, thinking maybe her theories aren't as crazy as people liked to believe they are, and she dedicates too much time to it.

It is a cloudy Thursday morning when she almost loses her mind, as she sets off to a meeting scheduled for her at the Paddington Police Department. She was told over the phone that she should find an officer Merton in order to speak to her about what she saw happened five days ago.

Halfway there, while sitting on the bus, her phone lights up with an incoming message from Julie.

"*Do you wanna speak to the private detective?*" The message says, and it is not as out of the blue as Naya would have thought, even if it was almost two weeks ago that they spoke about the man. Julie doesn't wait for a reply, however, and immediately sends another text.

"*I have just spoken to Andre's secretary and he has a cancellation for tomorrow. What do you say?*"

Naya is tempted to say no, but she kids no one with how quickly she replies back, "*Yeah. Let me know what time.*"

Naya appreciates the effort Julie is making on her behalf. Quite frankly, Julie is the only one who supports her fully, despite how insane she might sound to someone on the outside.

Even the twins have drifted somewhat away. They are always seem to be on the brink of saying something and then perhaps collectively decide against it, but it drives Naya mad, and she knows the situation could easily turn explosive.

Before long, she pushes the button for the bus to stop, and when it does, she steps outside, moving quickly between the buildings until she arrives at Harrow Road.

The place, as she had expected was not too well kept; just a regular industrial brick building with a sign showing that she was at the right place and with nothing much more than that.

The receptionist looks at her briefly before he hands her a form to fill out stating that she had arrived and then shows her to a small sitting area. She doesn't have to wait too long before her name is called.

Officer Merton, is a tall and well built woman, who manages to look both intimidating and comforting at the same time. With her dark curls nestled into a tight bun and a round face, she greets for Naya with a warm smile as she introduces herself.

She leads Naya past a long corridor until they arrive at her office, and she gestures Naya to take a seat in front of her desk.

"Good morning, Miss Tellus," the officer says, as she sits down.

Even with a desk separating them and her utmost attempts to seem friendly, Naya holds back. She greets her and then takes in the office. It is plain and shallow with nothing too personal or decorative — just a desk with a computer and a few storage spaces scattered around it.

"I suppose you know you're here to give another statement."

Officer Merton's tone is quick and to the point, and Naya gets the feeling that, despite her welcoming attitude, she wants to get it over with just as much as Naya. Naya nods and then relays to her exactly what she had told the two other officers who asked her the same questions.

It is all the same, at least until they get to the part about Joshua. The officer stops for a moment to consider what

Naya is saying, and then asks her, "Do you know what happened to Mr. Adams afterwards?"

It's a new question, Naya notes. She had assumed that the authorities had contacted Joshua as well, considering it had only been the two of them down there.

"I've no idea," Naya replies anyway.

The woman looks at her for a long time before questioning her again. Naya is not sure if it's intended or not, but all of a sudden she feels guilty, like she's aiding something forbidden.

"Are you sure? He didn't try contacting you in any way?"

"Why would he?" Naya answers the question with a question, not able to understand why she is expected to have any connection to Joshua. "We don't work together, or talk on a regular basis."

"But you do know him," Officer Merton says, and it sounds like an accusation.

Naya scoffs. "I know him, I know other people as well. Do you want to ask me about them too?"

The officer doesn't even blink when she talks. "No, just about him. How well do you know him?"

Naya pauses, and then sighs as she leans back in her uncomfortable chair. She has nothing to hide, so she might as well play along. When she had spoken to her father about it, he had told her the same thing — just be yourself, you have done nothing wrong. It's all just procedure. Naya supposes he's right, as usual. It is the police, after all.

"I met him at the beginning of the month. He came by where I, uh, used to work... offered me a job—"

"To which you said?"

"I refused, but only afterwards, when I went to the actual job interview."

The officer writes everything down in an expensive looking notebook, and signals Naya to keep talking, which she does. Naya tells her everything she knows about Joshua — where he works, what he does, how he speaks, what he looks like, his offer to her and about their third meeting, just before the earthquake.

"I googled him, before we met," Naya says as she concludes and the officer is still silent. Naya can't help feeling judged even though there is no real reason for it. "I didn't just go to meet, a random person without knowing who I was meeting."

The officer doesn't seem impressed, but the look she sends Naya is almost consoling in a way that manages to upset her.

"Do you google all the new people in your life?"

Immediately her first thought was about Aidan. It doesn't take a genius to know that her previous statement doesn't apply to him, and even if she didn't go to meet him willingly, he still found her. She doesn't know anything about him, but she thinks that she may not need a private detective when she has the police by her side.

"Can I ask you something?" Naya asks quickly instead, before changing her mind. When the officer nods, she smiles. "Have you heard the name Aidan Hall? In connection with Joshua, I mean."

Merton squirms in her seat, but it's out of curiosity more than anything. She narrows her eyes, eventually looking at the computer on her desk. "No, do you think they're related?"

"I think they might be, somehow. I met him around the same time I met Joshua — he seemed to be following him around..." Naya trails off, second guessing herself. "This is going to sound crazy, but I think he might have been following me around, too."

This causes the officer to stop messing around with the computer; she puts her hands on the table as she looks at Naya once again. "What makes you say that?"

"He's just — everywhere. Well, not everywhere, but we have bumped into each other occasionally, and he seems to know Joshua. Can you look him up?"

"Why didn't you google him?"

Naya lets out a dry chuckle, which makes Merton laugh.

"I'm sure it's nothing, Miss Tellus. Perhaps this person has just been at the right place and at the right time for you to meet. It doesn't sound like anything was done on purpose."

Naya is tempted to say that she hadn't even given the officer any details, or provided her with any information that might lead her to reach such a conclusion with such finality, but she feels she needs to keep it to herself.

She has a gut feeling that something is not right.

When the meeting ends, Naya goes straight to Julie's workplace near Liverpool Street with Officer Merton's words still ringing in her mind.

Julie agrees with her, which leads her to make the right decision of meeting with Andre.

It's Friday afternoon when Naya finds herself standing by Victoria Underground Station, following the GPS application on her cellphone to find Andre's office.

The application brings her to the front of a dodgy looking building. She can't help but double check the address Julie had given after way too many heart emojis, claiming how proud she was of her. When Naya sees that she is indeed in the right place, she pushes the door open to enter.

It is not much — just a small reception hall with an office desk that looks like it has seen better days, with plain walls with creaky wooden floors to match. The blonde woman sitting by the desk watches her eagerly, and Naya almost stumbles trying to tell her why she's there.

"Third room to the left," she tells Naya and holds up a delicate hand to show her the way. "He's waiting for you."

Without hesitating, Naya walks the distance in a few seconds. Her nerves are getting the better of her, and she worries about what awaits her.

She almost expects to find Andre's office in a shaded corner, with only one small window covered by a dysfunctional blind and crowded with a beaten-down sofa. The look of surprise on her face is probably evident when she takes in the tall windows and the uncharacteristic sun that shines through them.

She totally blames Hollywood for her unrealistic expectations.

Andre is standing by the time she glances at him, and he gives her a crooked smile. He is taller than both her and the twins and is wearing a suit that fits just right. It is now evident to her why Julie insisted on sending her to him. He looks professional enough as he gestures to the chair in front of his desk.

Without lingering in the doorway, she does as he suggests and takes a seat, finding the chair a lot more uncomfortable than it looks. Either people don't stay very long ot the tanned-skinned man in front of her does not want them too.

"You must be Naya," he says, and she understands it's only to start up a conversation.

"Yeah." She plays along. He takes it as a good sign and resumes his seat. It looks far more comfortable than the one she's sitting on. When his gaze falls on her again, she tries to push all irrelevant thoughts from her mind.

"Julie said you would be able to help me with—"

His mouth curls up in amusement. "Yes, the case of two stalkers."

Naya contemplates his choice of words, and while she would have chosen a better nickname for them, she guesses it's as good as any. Just like she thought — Julie spared no details when recruiting him.

Andre's smile grows bigger, and he scratches his stubble thoughtfully. "Well, firstly, tell Julie she owes me big time. You do realise this whole ordeal is pretty strange, and that's coming from me."

It's not really judgment. It's purely analytical and strictly a way to ask her without words if she's involved in something illegal. He gives her time for a confession, and even without her being at fault, it is making her anxious, but she swallows the feeling and focuses on him.

She nods, when she understands he is looking for verification.

"I'm afraid there's not much I can tell you about them," he begins slowly, his tone a mixture of sympathy and pity. "Whoever these people are, they are very good at staying off of the grid."

"What?"

When Naya dares to look at Andre, she sees his frown. He doesn't show too much emotion, and she wonders if he's just putting up a show for her benefit. The silence in the room is almost unbearable, and she finds herself stuck between nerve-biting annoyance and an overall feeling of being overwhelmed.

"I've checked everything I can," he tries to reason with her, thinking that he should explain before she gets mad. "They don't have a bank account, any insurance or anything registered in their names. I even tried social media — nothing came up. These people are ghosts."

"I don't understand. How is that possible?"

Andre seems to share her suspicions, and he almost looks concerned before he brushes it off. "I don't know who they are, where they came from or what they want with you. I do know to tell you that you shouldn't try and engage with them."

She automatically shakes her head. "The police already know about them."

"They do?" It catches him by surprise. Julie must have not had time to update him on that.

She nods. "The earthquake about a week ago? That was Joshua and me."

Andre lets out a sigh. "And what do the police say?"

Naya tries not to go into too much detail, but she explains the situation as best she can, especially the latest encounter with Officer Merton.

"They're useless," Andre ends up saying. "Can't believe she brushed you off like that."

Naya doesn't say anything, because there's not much to say. The fact that Andre thinks the same doesn't comfort her, and even if it's the only emotion she has gotten out of him, it just increases her understanding that she is way in over her head. The situation feels too out of reach for her to handle, and as anxiety peaks within her she struggles, just briefly, to breathe.

"I have Aidan's phone number," she blurts out after a few seconds. "That would help, won't it? You'll be able to link it to something."

She doesn't know if it actually would help, it's just something she saw in a TV show some time ago; but Andre seems to humour her as he nods. She pulls out the crumpled piece of napkin from her purse and gives it to the man.

She's half thankful when he gives it back after copying it down.

"Look, Naya, I know it may come off wrong, but I honestly don't think you should mess with them."

The advice, however reasonable, falls on deaf ears.

She wishes it was that easy, and truly, if she believed all she had to do was back down, she would. She had tried letting it, yet reality keeps coming back to push her. So what else can she do other than push back?

"Would you, if you were me?"

She assumes that it was his curious nature that led him to his current occupation, and so she can lay the question without fearing his answer. If he's anything like her and Julie, he wouldn't back down from the challenge.

But he doesn't answer, not directly. She's not even sure why she is seeking his validation. His small smile at the corner of his lips says it all. It must be a professional tendency to not give his personal opinion on matters.

Maybe that's where they're different.

"I will admit it's a first." He folds his arms. "The fact that I was not able to find anything on such a large scale."

She knows he wants to elaborate, so she waits patiently.

"People leave traces of themselves all over. Heck, the entire city is wired with enough CCTV to find someone even when he doesn't want to be found. No one can use only cash and not go into a bank or withdraw money at least once in their life, especially not in a modern city like this and without help."

She knows what he wants to say. She also knows why he pauses before actually saying it. It was her suspicion after all, but for the sake of hearing another person say it, she asks anyway.

"What do you mean?"

He's thoughtful again, and she can't help but pressure him into speaking. "I think you're dealing with an organisation. Whoever this Aidan is, or Joshua for that matter, I don't think they're doing it all by themselves. I feel like there must be something bigger at work here."

Naya is dreading asking her next question, but once again, she has to know. "Do you think they're working together?"

Andre shakes his head. "If they were, why would they go through all the trouble of coming into your life when they only needed one of them to do so?"

She's about to give her opinion on the matter, when he speaks again. "From what Julie said, they seem to have different agendas. Good or bad, I don't know, but I think you are going to find out soon, whether you want to or not."

He stands up again, and Naya hurries to follow his lead. She recognises her cue to leave, but not without asking for his guidance on how to proceed.

Andre chuckles, and she has to applaud him for being so calm about it. "Be careful, I guess. There's not much else I can offer. I will keep investigating what I can though, and will keep you informed."

Naya's not certain whether she should be happy with that or not. The man clearly has a reputation, according to Julie, and the fact that he seemed troubled shouldn't make her feel at ease. It should alarm her and make her reconsider her decision about not going to the police. It should basically have her running in the opposite direction.

However, there is a small part of her that is content; the small part of her that loves taking risks, is itching to explore.

Naya thanks Andre as she bids him goodbye. Once again, he promises to stay in touch. Her legs carry her of on their own accord all the way back to the underground station.

CHAPTER TEN

The days come and go, and it is early November by the time she hears about Andre, and not in the way she thought she would.

Naya and the twins are engrossed in what Lucas likes to call 'flat meetings', This meeting though, revolves around Naya's situation and not their usual bickering over who gets to clean the kitchen or who gets to speak to the utilities companies.

She's just about to ask for a break to refresh their drinks when her phone rings from the bedroom. Crossing the living room to get there, she asks Lucas to be in charge of drinks and answers the incoming call from Julie.

"Hey, Jules, what's up?"

"Naya," Julie's voice sounds strained, like she's rushing through something in a panic. Then she hears her sigh and knows that whatever this is — it can't be good. "Andre is dead."

Without even realising she's halfway back to her seat on the sofa, Naya stops in her tracks. "What?" she says, and the urgency in her voice causes the twins to pause — as she had.

"Andre, the private detective you went to see? He was found dead. Watch the news, it's on all the channels."

"Loggie, turn on the TV," Naya requests, while Julie waits with her on the line, although Naya is not sure what for. Naya can only imagine that Julie is on her way home, but everything moves to the back of her mind as she looks at the screen.

The news anchor is talking about the murder Julie has just mentioned, Andre's name is printed in white letters over the red *breaking news* sign.

"—He was found dead in his office by his assistant early this morning, and even though currently we don't have too much information, the Met Police can confirm that they are treating this as a homicide."

"Do we know him?" Lucas asks, coming back with cups of tea for Logan and Naya and a bottle of beer tucked under his armpit.

"Nay?" Logan asks.

"I'm on my way," Julie says to her and hangs up, leaving Naya to deal with the twins.

Slowly, she explains everything that has happened since the earthquake and has not yet filled them in on. It's not that she hadn't meant to do it eventually, but she was worried they would think she was spiraling out of control on the subject, and give her that pointed look that clearly means that she is way in over her head, or she is about to make a huge mistake.

That same look mirrored in their expressions right now. She had been on the receiving end only once in her life, which was enough to remember, even if she had only been seventeen and stupid enough to date someone they deemed unworthy.

In hindsight, they were right, but she won't rub it in right now.

"Okay, look, I know how this sounds—"

"Do you really?" Lucas starts, and she knows she can't stop him, so she may as well just let him have his moment. "You go and talk to this Joshua bloke alone, without even knowing much about him. Then when you know the police is looking for him, instead of getting out while you can, you sink in deeper by going to talk to an investigator like we're in the fucking fifties and now, guess what! He's bloody dead!"

"Like I said, I know how this sounds, but I swear I had nothing to do with it!"

Lucas looks outraged, as if Naya had come up with the most horrible conclusion ever. "I know you're not, idiot! I'm worried you might be next!"

The words resonate with her. She hadn't even considered the possibility of someone after her. Her heartbeat is slow, but it picks up and she finds it slightly harder to breathe.

"What?" Her voice is shaky. Lucas sits on the coffee table, facing her, with Logan on the other side, and as they touch her, she realises that she is shaking. "You think I got him killed?"

"No," Logan says quickly before his brother gets the opportunity to talk. "He doesn't, and neither do I. We can't be sure about anything. This guy was a private investigator, so I'm sure he found out plenty of secrets beforehand…"

Naya wants to believe that, but Lucas's perspective on the matter seems more likely. Guilt overcomes her, and she can't stop thinking that Andre's death is on her. The feeling is momentary though, as the front door opens and there is Julie, enveloping her in a hug that speaks for both of them, and helps her think a little clearer.

Sometime between that and her sitting down again, one of the twins turns off the television and they settle down into a conversation about everything. Julie fills in whatever Naya forgot and two hours later, she is exhausted.

Once Julie says her goodbye, everyone settles into their nightly routine, and Naya is grateful for something to take her mind off everything, even if it's something as petty as sleep.

As per Julie's suggestion, Naya does everything she can to cleanse her mind and think clearly about her moves going forward. Even though they still don't know much, Julie tries to calm her by pointing out that if the police thought she was in danger, she would already have been contacted by them.

Covent Garden tube station appears as usual, although, even busier, mostly given to the city's nature of becoming much more of a tourist attraction the closer it gets to Christmas. It takes longer than usual to even get off the train and she has to navigate the busy platform to avoid bumping into someone or worse, having her worst fear fulfilled by falling down onto the tracks.

The air from the tunnel is a nice relief, however, as she makes her way through it and up via the lifts and into the street.

Something catches her eye as she swipes her card at the exit barrier. It is subtle, yet enough to put her on edge, so she moves with the crowd until she's standing right by Covent Garden before she takes a proper look.

Nothing looks out of the ordinary; just tourists and locals doing their Christmas shopping. The decorations for the occasion are already up on the walls of the stores around and there are a few drunks outside of the street's pubs.

It comes over her slowly, but she can definitely tap into the feeling that she is being watched, but she can't see by whom.

She starts to think maybe Lucas is right, and perhaps she should have not gone out alone. Her decision to escape is made swiftly, and she turns around to go back home with her tail between her legs, figuratively speaking.

Naya nearly falls backwards from the force of crushing into someone, but they manage to catch her, and it's a sigh of relief to see Aidan, of all people, holding her in place.

"You alright?" he smirks.

He looks exactly the same as the last time that she saw him, with that demeanor that screams of over self-confidence. She would have commented on it, had her mind not been messed up and she not being slightly out of breath.

"Are you alright?" he repeats, this time more seriously.

Maybe she imagined it. Maybe it was Aidan who she thought was looking at her, and he came by to say hello. She could have gotten away with thinking this, except the feeling would not go away.

"Yeah," she breathes out. "Sorry, I wasn't paying attention."

"Clearly," Aidan says. "I guess you're just as shocked as I am to see you here; third time's a charm and all, yeah?"

"You do realise a third time is not a charm when you act like a stalker, right?"

He chuckles, unaffected. "Naya, you should be flattered that I'm looking to spend time with you."

"No, really," she says and folds her arms. "How do you keep on finding me?"

"Fate," he shrugs, and then to Naya's unconvinced look he smiles and adds, "Look, can you just appreciate the fact that I'm interested in your company?"

She tries to think of saying something witty in return, but the same feeling from before returns and it's almost crushing her in its presence. By the looks of it, Aidan isn't completely unaffected by her lack of attention.

She traces his line of vision to look at two men, staring directly at them — or at Naya more than Aidan. They look extremely alike, even though she can't really see more than their height and dark hair colour.

"Do you know them?" she asks, trying to push the ominous feeling aside.

"No, but they seem to know you."

Without even touching her, Aidan maneuvers her to stand behind him. It's clear he sees the men as threat just as much as she does, and his body is one fine line of tension, like a spring ready for action, radiating defensiveness. She frowns, worried by his posture.

He looks ready for battle.

Then the men move, undoubtedly towards them, and Aidan turns to Naya, silently asking for her trust. It's subconscious, but she nods. He takes her hand and leads her in the opposite direction. As they pass through Neal's Yard, Naya tries to excuse themselves from the people Aidan bumps into in order to move through the crowd.

Even if she doesn't know Aidan well enough to question him, there's a clear sense of danger from the men pursuing them. She tries to keep up with Aidan as he pulls her quicker, and their steps morph into a quick jog.

If it was a more appropriate time, she would have joked about finding herself in an alley with him again, and that the feeling of the solid wall behind her shouldn't feel so familiar. This time, however, it's for her own protection, and she can tell the difference in Aidan as he positions himself as her human shield.

It sends a direct jolt to her spine, and she shudders. Suddenly Joshua's words become clearer.

My world has its own rules.

She now understands that it was a menacing threat, and she shivers thinking Aidan belongs to the same world. Nevertheless, she can't help but demand answers.

"What the hell is going on?"

Her voice comes out cracked, and she mentally curses herself for not clearing it before speaking. Aidan doesn't seem to mind, though. He is checking the alley, like Naya did when they first met, and rubs his hand on his face, looking frustrated.

She almost sees the trails of the ink again, before he lowers his hand and looks at her. "I'm not sure I can tell you."

She's outraged, not even bothering to hide it. "People are chasing after us and you're not sure you can tell me what's going on?"

"To be fair, people are chasing you, not me."

Maybe he thinks that should make everything better or clearer, but she is not persuaded. However he folds his arms, refusing to say anything else.

"Why?" The question comes out as a short breath, but he avoids her glance.

He lets out an exaggerated sigh, as if they have already covered the subject. "Would it help if I told you these people are your enemies?"

She wants to say no and hit him in the face, but she surpresses the idea and leans against the wall. Now that they are out of immediate danger, she can somehow think straight, although her heart is not yet settled.

"I don't have enemies," she sums up her thoughts after a while.

Aidan arches an eyebrow, and the will to hit him again resurfaces. "Well, news flash, miss journalist, but people usually don't randomly want to kill someone."

"They want to kill me?"

The question shouldn't sound so weak, but it does, and she hates herself for feeling like it diminishes her. Once again, she feels like she is in a dream; the fear that strikes her core shakes her even more than Aidan's words.

It's a fight or flight mode, and she feels that whatever choice she will make, will be the wrong one.

Aidan must realise he's out of line because he moves closer to her, his hand hovering over her shoulder, unsure if his touch will be welcomed. "Hey, no — I'm sorry, that's not what I meant."

If he's about to tell Naya what he really means, a scream from the street away from their own little sanctuary interrupts him, and he pushes her away from it, and they resurface together in a different street.

"Okay," he says, and she wonders if it's to himself or to her. He holds up his hand, and a black cab pulls up next to them. "Look, I know you're scared, but you need to go home now. I promise I'll explain, but only when you're safe, alright?"

Naya doesn't know what she wants to say. She thinks she's in shock, because her body is running on automatic, so she finds herself just nodding and getting into the car after he opens the door for her. She watches as he takes out his wallet and hands the cab driver a few pound notes, and then he turns back to the alley.

She thinks she must be hallucinating when she thinks she sees a sharp weapon in his hand.

"Where to, darling?" The cab driver snaps her out of her reverie and she mutters her home address, hoping that the few words will help regularise her mind.

The drive passes in a haze, and the cab driver has to shake her into reality when they stop at West End Lane. She's so puzzled by everything that has happened, she barely manages to take out her keys and scramble out of the cab.

She's so caught up in her thoughts that she misses seeing her neighbour and almost runs into him on her way upstairs. When he stops her, his face is as friendly as always, the dimples in his cheeks visible as he smiles, but his expression soon turns into one of concern.

"Hey, are you okay?" he asks.

Naya nods, forcing out a small grin that means nothing. She doesn't talk, not trusting herself to and without waiting for his approval, she sprints up the stairs, quickly opening up her flat's door, disappearing behind it.

It is when she smells the familiar scent of her home and recognises the lay out of it, that she allows herself to break down.

CHAPTER ELEVEN

By six in the evening Naya knows her time alone is coming to an end. One of the things she has in common with the twins is their ability to follow a strict routine, so that even them arriving home at specific hour is to be expected.

Logan is the first to come home, just as the clock turns quarter past. The layout of their flat is such, that the kitchen is to the right side of the door, so it takes just a few short seconds from the moment the front door closes softly for Logan to notice her there.

He stops by the small kitchen island, puts his bag and coat on one of the barstools and sits on the other. He takes her in before commenting. "You're cooking," he lets out carefully, like she might snap at him for saying something.

She feels she may just, so she focuses on her cooking instead.

"Yes," she replies, muttering something under her

breath before adding, "Good thing you've got eyes that can see and a mouth that can talk."

Naya has her back to him, but she can hear as he touches the ingredients on the island, most likely to figure out what she's cooking.

"What happened?" he asks.

Naya loves being in the kitchen. Growing up, Dom would pick her up from pre-school and school and take her to his grocery store. He would make her choose whatever she wanted to eat and they would cook together in the evenings. That was back when it was only his store on Chiswick High Street and not a few major supermarkets chains, and he had the means to hire help. Most of the times, these evenings would be about Naya and her father, making some of his Moroccan heritage recipes.

However now, both her and Logan know that the only reason she's cooking by herself is because she wants something to do instead of thinking, and cooking usually does the trick.

Involuntary, Naya's hand pauses and the wooden spoon she is using to stir the soup falls to the bottom of the pot loudly. The sound makes her flinch, but also strengthens her decision to avoid looking at him at all costs.

Nervously and anxiously, her mind wanders back to the afternoon and she thinks about what Aidan said.

Then she thinks about the recipe she is cooking, what her friends will say about it — anything but to face Logan.

It won't last long, it never does with him. Logan has a secret ability to draw out the truth from everyone, especially when they aren't interested in talking.

After a while she surrenders, unable to take the silence any longer. She puts a lid on the pot and turns to face him with her hands hugging her body. "Sometimes I wish you didn't know me so well," she says.

Logan smiles gently at her, and she recognises the expression as the one he reserves for whenever she's caught in a lie. Knowing each other goes both ways, so when he doesn't say anything at first, she knows that he is giving her a chance to ignore the subject.

It's one of the qualities that differentiates him from his brother; Logan would never force someone to be honest, even if he knows it's for everyone's benefit. Lucas, on the other hand, usually pleads his case to get people to tell the truth, or says something that might trigger a repsonse. Logan, in his kindness, gives her a chance, for her sake, to tell him that everything is fine. She's a private person, and Logan knows that she'll keep him in the loop on what she feels he should know, and no more than that.

Naya sighs, deciding that she is not going to ignore the issue any longer. He takes the sign for what it is — giving her another full minute before he tackles the subject again. He tries to be as gentle as possible, which usually she wouldn't mind. However, now it was putting her on edge.

"What happened?" he repeats.

She wonders for a few moments how to respond, opening and closing her mouth several times in the process, simply because she did not know how to express her distress and worries. They don't know Aidan personally, and while him saving her is a good thing, the fact that she has no idea what he was saving her from disturbs her.

Her mind is a mess, and she takes a breath to try and calm down.

Eventually her thoughts form into a somewhat coherent structure of sentences and words and she explains to the best of her abilities.

He holds his tongue throughout her whole ramble, and when she stumbles over complete words, which he would usually joke about it being the problem with bilinguals — now he remains silent. The twins have picked up on a few words in Hebrew, but not enough to hold a conversation. Frankly, she doubts she would be able to explain properly in any language.

She is not entirely sure she's making much sense — which is fine by her, since nothing seems to be making sense in her life anymore. After talking for quite a while, she lets out a sigh of relief, happy to have gotten it out of her system.

She doesn't expect him to say anything, and he remains silent, even when he stands up and pulls her into his arms. Briefly she thinks about the fact that this may be the third time since knowing him that he has been completely speechless, and while usually she would have jumped at the chance of it, it now feels burdensome and dangerous.

When Lucas comes home not long after, he finds them both sitting in the shared living room, with Naya holding a mug of steaming hot tea and Logan beside her. While the scene was not so rare, they did spend most of their time tucked up on the sofa, it must be the atmosphere in the room and Logan's look of concern, that catches him off guard.

So he does the only thing natural to him and sits down on the coffee table, the one Naya always warns him about sitting on or putting his legs on, and puts his arms around Naya's forearms, mimicking his brother's hug from before.

"What are we going to do?" Lucas asks not long after.

Naya wants to tell them they shouldn't get involved just for her sake, seeing that she was the one who put herself in the situation, but she remains silent. It's a hopeful prayer, albeit a selfish one, to not be left alone in this situation.

"You already went and talked to the police, yeah?" Logan muses. "What did they say about Aidan?"

"Nothing," Naya replies, which looking back on now, strikes her to be somewhat odd. "The officer said that she was sure that nothing had been done on purpose, or something like that..."

"And that sounds okay to us?" Lucas fills in for both of them. "Naya tells a police officer about a stalker of some kind, and the police officer says, 'Hey, don't worry, he's just alright'?"

It's Logan's time to speculate, and it's not surprising he catches on quickly. "Do you think that the two of them are connected?"

"I mean, don't you?" Lucas asks "Joshua is all the officer was interested in. Maybe she is covering for Aidan?"

Naya lets it sink in, as do the twins. It's plausible, she supposes; she doesn't know much about Aidan, and she did see him leaving after Joshua when the whole earthquake scene was behind them.

"If Aidan controls the police it complicates things a bit," Naya says. "Do you think they have something against Joshua and Andre got caught up in the crossfire?"

It gets them thinking, causing the atmosphere in the room to take a turn for the worst. Naya knows, of course, what it means — she's not stupid. If Joshua and Aidan are on different sides of the same fight, and Andre was right in the middle, where does it put her?

"One thing doesn't make sense," Logan speaks after a while. "If Joshua and Aidan are fighting each other and Naya's in the middle, why would Aidan go through the trouble of rescuing her? Wouldn't it be easier to let nature run its course and... you know..."

A buzzing sound from the kitchen cuts off their thoughts, and Naya stands up to retrieve her phone. The call is from an unknown number, but she answers anyway.

The voice on the other side is formal and slightly familiar. "Miss Tellus?"

"Yeah," the word comes out as a breath, and she waits.

"It's Joshua Adams," he pauses, perhaps taking the fact she doesn't hang up as a sign to continue. "My assistant told me you have tried to reach me. I apologise for not being properly available... Things have been, chaotic, unfortunately, for the lack of a better term."

Naya holds the phone a bit further away to take a deep breath and puts him on speaker for the twins to hear as she returns to the living room. She mouths Joshua's name and they turn attentive in a flash.

"Yeah, no, I completely understand. I've been... overwhelmed lately too."

"It sounds like you're alright," Joshua says, and Naya can hear the relief in his voice. "I'm certain you undoubtedly have questions about what happened, and I believe I have some answers, if you would be so kind as to listen."

She looks at the twins as he speaks, and Lucas gestures a definitive no with his head, while Logan indicates go on with his hands.

"I'm listening," Naya tells him, ignoring the look she gets from Lucas.

"Not over the phone, I'm afraid," Joshua says just as fast. "I think it's a conversation we should have face to face. Have you considered my offer? I have a few leads, all of which involve the earthquake and, well, now that the police investigation is behind me, we can move on."

Ask about the police, Logan mouths, and Naya does just that.

"You were questioned by the police?"

Joshua pauses, like he's unsure why it matters. "Of course, I was told you had been too, Miss Tellus. I believe they thought we were directly involved or had some absurd notion that I was behind it. Either way, it's over now and that leaves time for proper work."

"Why would the police think you're behind it?"

"Must have been something I said, I suppose." It sounds vague enough, like there's something there, but Joshua doesn't let her think too much about it before he continues. "What do you think, then?"

Naya's mind is still preoccupied with what Joshua might have possibly said to the police that she doesn't quite gather what he means. "About what?"

Joshua, to his credit, doesn't sound aggravated or upset that she hasn't kept up. "About meeting in person to discuss our work together?"

When she looks up to the twins she is mirrored with the same expression of *no* that she had only got from Lucas before, and while it feels wrong to pass up the opportunity, she sighs. "Do you think it's possible to think about it and get back to you?"

"Miss Tellus—"

"In light of everything that has happened, I just need some time to figure out if I want to jump right back in it, you know?"

She tries to be as professional as possible, but she knows she must be coming off as a spoiled child with commitment issues.

When he talks again, Joshua sounds as collected as always. "Of course, I completely understand. I'll give you a couple of days and we'll discuss this again later."

He doesn't bid his farewell or wait for her approval before hanging up the phone. Naya thinks he's either disappointed or mad, but she can't really help it. Even if the twins were on board, she doesn't know if she has the energy to go back and work on natural disasters.

"You did the right thing," Lucas says, though Naya has a feeling he's only talking to avoid the silence.

She gets it, really.

"How about we watch some TV?" Logan suggests a minute later, and while it doesn't help to ease any of them, it does distract them, and while Lucas chooses some trashy reality show that won't make them think too much, Naya finishes her cookings.

Later that night, she texts Julie to let her know about the newest development, and after the initial scolding process of why she didn't go directly to her flat, Naya puts them right back on course on what they should do next.

Julie thinks that, at the very least, Naya should hear Joshua out, even if nothing comes of it. It is one of the things she likes about Julie — her never-ending optimism.

"I can go with you if it will make you feel better." Julie texts and adds a smiling emoji.

It would make Naya better, but she knows that if she decides to go through with it, it's something she needs to do alone. Not less important — her friends are already involved enough, and she will not purposefully put them in harm's way if she can help it.

After that, their conversation ends and Naya is left alone in the darkness of her room, with her thoughts.

The easiest choice would be to tell Joshua to shove it and put the whole thing behind her.

The problem is that Naya has a feeling that wouldn't work. She knows she's in too deep already, and she wouldn't be able to back down now that she is so close to a breakthrough — being in her career or in what's going on lately. She also circles back to what Andre had told her — about how she would be forced to find out the truth one way or another.

Her mind wonders back to the earthquake and Joshua's connection to it. He had made it seem like the police genuinely thought he had caused a natural disaster, which was absurd, and too close to her theory for comfort.

She still remembers the first time she had thought seriously about natural disasters, before it became her desired profession. It was when Julie had said something about how the world had gone mad. It had been on a night like this — two versions of their nineteen years old selves tucked into bed at their dorm room at university. Julie was on about her fear of lightning and thunder, which in a way she knew was irrational, but she had never fully embraced the fear either.

Julie had explained to her way to deal with fear — how to subject the mind to a simple chore to takes its attention away from the fear. She explained how she would count down the time between the lightning and the thunder, in order to calculate and anticipate the next set, giving her mind a marginal job to focus on.

It took forever before Naya understood that she had implemented the same system to deal with her anxiety attacks.

At the time, she hadn't thought about it as a professional career, even though they had spent that night talking about the world climate changing till the storm had passed. The idea itself only full on brewed by the time she finished her third year of university, but she still deems Julie responsible for it. Of course, she doesn't remember Julie's exact words since as far as memories go, they get distorted with time. She does, however, remember that it had been Julie's idea for Naya to turn her back on her degree in economics and management by the time they graduated.

Julie was also the one to convince her to jump head-first into the abyss and start working freelance for a few websites and in turn, become a cast off, as far as the Society of Professional Journalists was concerned.

She never stopped thanking Julie for that.

It is also gave her a new and profound motive to see the whole thing through, no matter the consequences.

CHAPTER TWELVE

Anxiety doesn't let go as much as Naya had hoped it would — on the contrary. Paranoia had set itself in her mind, and she has a feeling it will not agree to leave anytime soon. Her friends point it out, much to her displeasure, although at the very least, it makes her feel like she's not alone in it.

She is not so sure how smart it is — but she'll take comfort over loneliness anytime.

Time moves on as always, and the world doesn't stop just because she's anxious. When rationality stomps in, her worries turn into the form of having to find a way to pay the rent soon. Considering the fact the she was out of a job, the first thing that comes to mind is Joshua's job offer. She still hadn't given any answer, although she had promised Lucas to exhaust any and all means for money before accepting.

Her last resort is in the form of a loan from Dom and, while she supposes there are worst things in life than asking a loan from her father, it doesn't help to ease her mind.

It's eight in the morning when she finds herself standing in front of her father's small grocery store right off Chiswick High Road. She knows he's bound to be there at this hour, despite the fact that the store's opening is only at nine.

It's not much, but it's Dom's greatest treasure, and as a child she spent most of her days helping out in the small space. She remembers the rainy days when the twins and her used to play hide and seek in between the aisles, amid Dom's constant warnings not to break anything.

She uses her spare key to open the shop, and calls out for him.

Nothing seems out of the ordinary and, on a cloudy day like today when the main lights are off it almost looks haunted. She decides it's best to associate the feeling with the fixed state of paranoia she's in, as she ventures into the storeroom.

"Papa?" she calls out again.

She is not entirely surprised to find him sorting out new stock at the end of the crammed room, smiling about his usual routine. The boxes are stacked behind him, and he's holding a clipboard, marking something on it.

He turns to her just before she calls out a third time, and looks mildly out of focus.

"Oh, hey," he says after a beat. "What are you doing here?"

She scoffs in response. "I'm great, thanks for asking. Can I help?"

Dom seems to contemplate it briefly, before he hands her the clipboard and wordlessly gives her the task of counting the contents of the boxes with him. It's a practiced task, in reality, and she's happy for the distraction.

More than an hour later, she is behind the counter, gazing at Dom and his first customer. Her mind is reeling, while the customer leaves without buying anything.

She's about to ask her father about the state of the business, when the front door opens again, letting some of the rain in. The man who steps inside, is dressed in an all-white suit, and is much taller than both her and Dom. She raises her eyebrows at the odd clothes on such a day, and watches as he puts his umbrella near the door and then takes in the store. He's blonde, like Dom, although his hair is slicked back, and his beard is well-groomed.

"Dominic," he says, and Naya catches a hint of a German accent. It takes her a few seconds to understand that he is looking for her father, since she doesn't hear his full name often.

Dom gives the man the same look Naya undoubtably wears on her face — he is frowning and his lips curl slightly downward. Suddenly, the man's attention moves from Dom to Naya and his piercing blue eyes immediately cause her to feel threatened.

"You must be Naya," he says to her, and she has to force herself to hold his stare.

She is aware of the dare he is presenting, and in the back of her mind, she remembers a younger version of Dom telling her to keep her fear to herself. If it worked when he taught her self defence, it might as well work now.

She keeps her head held high, while clenching her hand to stop it from trembling. "Who are you?" she asks, is happy to acknowledge that at least her voice is steady.

The man doesn't take too kindly to her harsh tone and ignores her. He walks over to Dom, and the look they exchange between them seems to hold a bigger meaning that escapes Naya. Then, surprisingly enough, the stranger pats him on the shoulder, and moves to stand in front of Naya.

His smile is anything but gracious, as he holds out his hand to her. "Walter," he introduces himself, and doesn't seem fazed when she does not reciprocate. "Have a nice day you two."

And with that he turns and walks out of the store with his umbrella, leaving a very confused Naya in his wake.

It takes a while for her to snap out of her thoughts, and when she does, she finds that the rain outside has stopped and her father's on the other side of the store, fixing some homeware that was already in place to begin with.

The questions are endless, and she's not sure she'll get answers, even if she asked the most common questions. She must try, though, and waits until he's near her to speak again, even if it does take some time.

"What are you not telling me, Papa?"

Dom studies her, his eyes narrow and his expression guarded. It makes her feel odd, like he's looking at a problem instead of his own daughter. If she had her suspicions before, they are ten times worse now.

The journalist in her is burning for the truth, but she's not sure anymore.

"Surely it's safe to assume that we both have secrets, no?"

The necklace he gave her a month ago feels heavier for some reason, and she knows she is not going to get any answers from him. It amplifies her resolve to figure the whole thing out, even without his help.

She gathers her bag and coat, and despite her not hoping he will stop her, she still feels disappointed.

The fresh air outside soothes her, but only a little. She makes the ten minute walk to Chiswick Park Underground Station in silence, doing her best to steer away the thoughts from her mind, but fails.

She's so preoccupied that she doesn't notice someone falling into step with her, until she feels a hand stop her near the entrance to one of the larger store's parking lot. When a car rushes by, she realises that she was being saved from almost being run over.

Once again, he didn't even need to touch her to do it.

"Now now," she hears the condescension in Aidan's voice before even seeing him. "Don't tell me you're so wrapped up in thinking of me that you can't even see where you're going?"

With everything going on, her automatic reaction is anger, which comes easily. So, through gritted teeth, she says, "Get over yourself, you arse, not everyone goes around thinking about you."

"Really?" he has the audacity to sound genuinely surprised. "Must be terribly boring."

"What are you doing here?" She decides to change the subject before throwing him into the road.

"I was in the area," he says as they resume walking. It's extremely ambiguous, and she has obvious reason asking, especially when he had said that he would explain everything once she was safe.

"A rare coincidence," she says, and if he picks up on her sarcasm, he doesn't bite back.

"Well, good thing I was here, as I have a reputation to maintain as your knight in shiny armour."

That's fair, she supposes, and the banter seems oddly familiar — she'll give him that — for now.

"Considering you're now officially my stalker and manage to find me anywhere, I shouldn't worry about such mundane things as traffic."

He chuckles, like he's surprised at how well she's adjusting to his presence. They probably both are and thinking back to the last time she had seen him, when they were both running from someone, she would have expected, at the very least, to feel concerned.

But she isn't, which is shocking in itself, but what is more is that she is feeling somewhat safe — safer than she had felt in a while, actually.

Aidan doesn't reply to the accusation even as they cross the entrance to the station. She walks in front, holding her Oyster card against one of the station barriers and steps inside.

Aidan does the same, though he seems slightly unfamiliar with it. She wonders if he usually takes public transport.

When they cross the tunnel leading to the Eastbound platform, he speaks again. "I'm not a stalker."

"Really?" She gives him the shocked tone that he used before. "Then what do you call this?" Naya points to them both, emphasising the fact that he had found her — once again.

"A rare coincidence," he throws the words back at her, and even coming out of his mouth they don't sound genuine.

The oncoming train stops them from continuing their banter, and they settle into a comfortable silence as Aidan finds them both seats. Naya counts twelve stations until Westminster Station, and leans back.

She knows she should ask Aidan about what happened, but the train is packed and it doesn't feel like the type of conversation she wants to have in public. So she waits, knowing in her heart that he will most likely follow her anyways. Instead of changing platforms to the Jubilee line that would take her back to West Hampstead, she chooses to exit the station and, as she expected, he moves one step behind her, trusting her to lead the way.

The embankment overlooking the London Eye is one of her favourite places in London, and growing up she'd find herself spending a lot of time by the river. For the first ten minutes, they only look at the water, but she knows even Aidan can't stand the silence anymore.

"You said you'd explain, after I'm safe," she cuts straight to the chase.

Aidan nods. "Unfortunately I did."

It's an infuriating answer to such a simple request, and the calmness the water usually brings over her is dispelled quickly. "Tell me what happened," she demands. "Why were they after me? Who were they? What did you mean when you said I have enemies?"

She has plenty of questions, and the stream of them doesn't stop there; she could go on, but the resigned look on Aidan's face tells her she has to stop if she wants to get an answer.

He rubs his cheek, seemingly out of frustration, but other than that he refrains from doing or saying anything. While she doesn't know him that well, she still feels on edge with how grim the situation looks. She wonders briefly and not for the first time, what she has gotten herself into, and why no one will tell her the truth.

"I can't really say," he speaks after a while.

Once again, the answer annoys her more than she cares to admit. "Meaning you don't know or you just can't talk about it?"

"I can't tell you," he splurts. It sounds like he actually wants to tell her, but something is stopping him. In all honesty, if she wasn't irritated she might have even sympathize with him.

But she's beyond caring at this point.

"You can't tell me," she repeats. "You can't tell me why people want me dead. You can't tell me why someone I just met and who was trying to help me died, and you can't tell me why I'm in danger."

When he hums in agreement to everything she says, she feels her blood boiling with anger. How is it possible he knows exactly what's going on and is deliberately keeping her in the dark?

"Why?"

"Why what?" He answers her question with a question.

If Naya didn't know better, she would think that he was stalling. "Why can't you tell me?"

"Look..."

"Are you serious?" she asks, when it's clear she is not going to get the truth out of him. Julie's plan for her to ask Aidan failed, just as she thought it would, but at least now she has someone to blame, which is enough in the meantime, especially with how hopeless she feels.

"What do you want me to tell you, Naya?"

But it's not really a question, since he knows exactly what she wants to hear; neither is it an excuse or an 'I can't tell you'.

"I want the truth!"

"You can't have the truth." He doesn't rise to the bait of yelling like she does, and looks less concerned that people may be watching them now. "You can't have the truth, Naya, you just have to trust me."

Naya lets out a breath and makes an effort to give him her best relentless stare. "Trust is earned," she says. "Thank you for saving me the other day, but I can't just go on blind trust. For all I know you're a murderer that wants to kill me."

"All you need to know is that I can and will protect you, so you need to let me do it."

Naya scoffs, "I can fight on my own, thanks."

He has the audacity to smirk. "You can fight?"

"Yes," she says, and the look on his face is priceless enough to change the tone of their conversation. "My dad taught me," she answers proudly.

"Your dad taught you?"

She wonders if she has spoken in Hebrew without realising, because she can't see a reason to have to repeat her words. "Yes," she says again, slowly.

"Why would your dad teach you how to fight?"

"Uh..." She is at a loss of words for while, never having to question herself about it, but she gathers herself to successfully produce a sentence. "He wanted me to be a strong, independent woman...?"

The more she speaks, the more her words turn in to a confused ponder rather than an actual claim, and she immediately finds the humour and irony in her tone in contrast to the words themselves. But Aidan's glare is enough to show her he isn't amused, and she tries to understand why it matters so much.

"When was that?"

She feels like she's missing a crucial piece of the conversion, but answers nonetheless. "Some time after my twelfth birthday, but it's been two years since the last time we've trained together. I guess I do remember some things from it, though."

"Yeah," he grits out, and she doesn't understand why he looks so angry. "It's called muscle memory. Did he happen to mention what type of martial arts it was?"

Oh, yeah, there was definitely something she was missing, and it was time to try a different tactic. "He never said. I don't know why it's such a big deal. Are you mad because you just found out that I am capable on my own, because..."

"Trust me, Naya, you being capable on your own is just another thing to admire about you," he says, and the compliment is thrown so nonchalantly that she's not sure whether he meant to say it to begin with or if that's just how he is. He continues with a straight face. "Really, twelve?"

She really tries to think back to something he might have said in the past that could help her understand why it holds such a significance to him, but she fails. When he doesn't offer anything in return, she bristles.

"Why are you mad at me?"

The puzzlement is so clear on his face that Naya almost takes joy in managing to confuse him before his usual demeanour returns and he folds his arms. "I'm not mad at you."

"Right," she stretches the word as far as she can. "Well, I don't think you're going to tell me what this is all about, so let's move along, yeah?"

She is not fooled. She sees the relief on his face; it's brief and subtle, but definitely there. His emotions must be defying him today, since nothing is stopping at the barrier of his usual mask. Everything is penetrating through, even if it's just momentarily, yet it's enough for her to pick up on.

He's lucky she's kind enough to offer him a way out.

"Are you pouting, Little Bear?"

His childish tone and his half mocking frown makes her take her last thought back, and everything stops when she turns to look at him. He's not affected by her accusing glare, and she decides to give him a chance to take the nickname back.

"Little Bear?" she repeats.

"Well, you kinda look like it." He decides to answer her unspoken challenge, even though he doesn't give her a real reason. Naya is sure that there is something he is not telling her, but she is focused more on taking it the wrong way, than diving into it.

"Like a bear?"

"A little bear," he corrects.

Naya purses her lips into a thin line. "You're calling me fat."

Aidan stares at her, baffled. "What? No! Little Bear, it's, uh, it's a nickname — it's cute!"

Naya looks at him, unconvinced. She might have taken pleasure in the fact that he's flustered just by the thought of insulting her, but she decides that it is not worth paying it much attention at the moment.

"It is not cute," she settles on saying instead.

"Maybe you should google baby bears to see that you're wrong."

She rolls her eyes, but doesn't say anything. He smiles, content with leaving it at that. Naya is slightly alarmed by how easily they go back to the norm, despite her feeling that everything is crumbling around her.

CHAPTER THIRTEEN

Despite thinking she may have a proper handle on the situation, Naya knows she's not fooling anyone and the true testament to that is how quick Julie is to accompany her to meet Officer Merton again, even though they both know that she most likely has nothing new to add.

On the way to the police station, they are both mostly silent. Julie most likely does not know how to drift around the subject, causing the whole ordeal to seem more serious than it probably is.

Either way, it helps that Julie is there with her, and Naya is grateful that Julie took the day off for it.

Naya's not sure what prompted her to want to meet the officer again. She supposes it could be viewed as boredom, or as her delaying the inevitable, which is to work with Joshua and properly get to the bottom of everything, if she can.

Once they change trains at Baker Street, Julie breaks her silence, and by the time they board the train to Paddington Station, she is talking away.

"Have you told Logan and Lucas?"

It's not much, but it eases Naya just a little, even if her question is rhetorical. "No," she replies as they sit down. "I figured they would somehow turn it around against me."

It takes a while before Julie responds. "You know that they are only looking out for you, same as me."

Naya scoffs, since she knows it's the truth, yet somehow Julie's way of looking out for her feels much more comfortable. "Well, you don't look at me like I'm insane every time I suggest working with Joshua."

"No, because I know you'll do it anyways, so I might as well support you."

"But you don't think I'm insane—"

"Naya," Julie interrupts her, and she knows it's serious, since she never uses her name like that unless she's about to scold her. "I may not know you as long as the twins, but even I know you wouldn't do something reckless just for the sake of it. They know it too, okay? They just need time to wrap their heads around everything that's been going on."

Somehow Julie's speech helps, even if it's not the answer Naya was looking for.

"Things have been crazy," Naya admits after a while.

"I know, sweetie, and we'll work it out, the four of us."

Naya almost feels confident, but she knows there's

danger lurking around the whole situation, and she knows Julie feels it too, even if she is working really hard to hide it. It's the reason Logan and Lucas didn't know how to approach her lately, and it's the reason she can't seem to get her mind off thinking of Joshua and Aidan.

She tells Julie the latest development a few minutes later, especially about her father and Walter. The blonde listens attentively, not asking too many questions because she knows it causes Naya to sidetrack, and by the time they arrive at Paddington Station, Julie speaks up once again.

"Do you really believe he's a friend of your father?"

"No, of course not," Naya replies just as quickly. "It just made sense, because if he's not a friend, he's an enemy, and I don't know how to feel about that."

Julie chuckles. "If he's an enemy, I don't think he would be as polite as to introduce himself like that."

"But that's what villains do, isn't it? They start off by being friendly and polite."

"Okay, fine, maybe," Julie says. "But that would make Joshua and Aidan villains too, wouldn't it?"

Naya thinks about it while they walk. "Maybe they are; Aidan did say I apparently have enemies."

Julie laughs and uses the moment they have while waiting for the traffic to clear, to grab Naya's cheek and squeeze it, all the while saying in a baby voice, "Who would want to harm such a cute little bear like you?"

Naya immediately regrets telling her about the incident, and takes a step back so Julie can't get a hold of her again. Despite herself, she laughs at the face Julie makes and hurries to cross the road once they have a green light.

Both of them lose all humour when they arrive at the police station. The doors to the place feel as heavy as they did the last time she was there. Julie takes the first step for her this time, and goes to ask for the officer at the front desk.

Naya didn't tell anyone other than Julie that she was coming, and, following her instinct, she didn't let the officer know either. But before Julie manages to approach the front desk, the door behind them opens and Officer Merton steps in, along with a red-headed woman.

"Miss Tellus," the officer says, sounding as surprised as she looks. "I didn't know we had scheduled a meeting."

"We haven't," Naya says. "I was wondering if you have time for a few more questions?" It comes off as a question itself, and Officer Merton turns to look at the stranger, appearing to seek her approval.

It feels awkward and Naya has a feeling she's not as welcome as she thought she would be, but thankfully

Julie is there, and she's quick to introduce Julie to both women.

It snaps Merton out of whatever she was thinking, and she straightens her back, shaking Julie's hand.

"I'm Addison," the red-head offers, and it gives Naya enough time to scrutinize her.

She's impressive. As hard as Naya tries to come up with a different word in her mind, she cannot think of another way of describing her than that.

In spite of the fact that she does not have enough time to do what she loves and analyze her properly, the woman standing in front of her is definitely one of a kind. She holds herself with such self-assurance it must be imprinted in her genes and when you add a full blown smile framed by full lips and a curved face, Naya knows anyone else would be jealous, yet Naya is just in awe.

"So you're a friend of Officer Merton?" Julie asks.

Addison smiles as a first response. "You can say that. We mostly work together."

"You needed to ask me some questions?" Merton says too quickly for Naya's taste, and begins to walk towards the narrow hallway Naya went through the last time she was there. Naya has no choice but to follow the officer and wait until they are in her office to ask anything else.

"So, what can I do for you, Miss Tellus?"

Naya takes the same seat she did the last time she was there, and suddenly all queries she had fly out the window.

"Joshua contacted me," she says to start off the conversation.

"Joshua Adams? And you're… concerned about that?"

"You can say that," Naya says. "Last time I was here it sounded like you were sure he had something to do with the earthquake."

Merton pauses before replying, as if she is thinking how to phrase it. "Joshua Adams has, for the moment, been cleared of all suspicion against him, taking into consideration that an earthquake is not something that is made, but a part of nature."

It bothers Naya how rehearsed it sounds, almost like it's something she heard or was told to tell anyone who should ask.

"So the case is closed, then?"

"For now, yes."

Naya nods and then gets a sudden urge to ask about Addison. She knows it's improper and will probably be brushed aside by the officer anyway.

"Is that all you wanted to ask me, Miss Tellus?"

The hint doesn't surprise her; she is sure that Merton has plenty of things to do, so she stands and pushes her chair back slightly.

Just before leaving, Merton stops her. "May I say something?" she asks.

"Anything you want," Naya says, hoping it will shed some light for her.

"It may not be my job to say anything and of course it is completely off the record, but perhaps you need to be cautious and stop to think about what you are trying to do."

Naya wants to ask more about it, but two officers step into the room requiring Officer Merton's attention, so she just nods and moves out of the room, back into the hallway she came from.

Julie is alone when she gets back, and she offers her a small smile as they leave the police station. "Let's go drink something hot and get out of the cold, alright?" Julie says, and it's not really a question.

On the way there, Naya fills in Julie about what happened, which leaves Julie quiet enough to think of what she wants to say.

As they sit down by one of the windows in a coffee shop, Julie asks, "Why would she warn you?"

Naya shrugs. "Who knows? Maybe she knows something I don't. Maybe she just has a hunch — I have no idea."

"Well, we have some sort of a solution."

"We do?"

Julie sighs. "Clearly Joshua and Aidan know what's going on, or at least some part of it. Just get close to them to see what you can extract from them."

"I thought we were against the idea of me going to work with Joshua."

"I never said that," Julie says. The conversation stops when the waitress takes their order, but Julie jumps right back on it once they have ordered. "I think Aidan cares for you, despite you being annoyed with him, and I think Joshua genuinely wants to cooperate with you. Maybe, instead of playing into their hands, you can take the game into your own hands?"

"And do what? Play the damsel in distress to make Aidan care more and tell me the truth?"

Julie smiles, and Naya doesn't need words to know that is exactly what Julie is thinking. She rolls her eyes, because there's no way it would work, and most importantly, it wouldn't help with Joshua.

Not to mention the fact that the last thing Naya would call herself is a damsel in distress.

Julie must feel her discomfort by that so she offers a different way of thinking. "We just need to find what makes them tick, and once we find that, we'll be able to hold it against them and maybe make them spill the beans."

The only thing that is probably making her feel better, is Julie's constant use of the term *we*.

"You make it sound so simple," Naya complains. "The only thing I know about them is that Aidan doesn't appreciate Joshua very much, but clearly they both know each other."

"Okay, then let's start with this. Meet up with Joshua and start working with him, and we'll see how Aidan reacts to that. Maybe Joshua's work offer might help with everything. Or at the very least, it'll help your bank account."

Naya laughs, sadly because she knows how true it is, but also because it's a plan, and it's better than what she has so far.

CHAPTER FOURTEEN

Naya is only half kidding herself when the first thing she does the next day is call up Joshua to set a date for her first day of work. Truth be told, Julie's approval means a lot, even if she doesn't acknowledge it wholeheartedly, or even if it may not be for the right reasons.

When the line rings and he doesn't answer, it causes Naya's demeanour to change drastically.

It comes as no surprise how disappointed she feels, even if it doesn't mean anything.

At least that is what she tells herself when the day ends and Joshua still hasn't called her back; She hates that it feels like a wasted opportunity, but more than that, she hates how the twins love it.

"It was a bad idea to begin with," Lucas tells her when she takes up the courage to let them know she wants to work with Joshua. "The bloke is either delusional or downright mentally ill—"

"Luke," Logan tries to warn him, but Naya has already heard him and before the situation turns explosive, she takes a deep breath and focuses on the television still playing in the background.

Lucas immediately becomes silent, and it's enough for her know that the expression on her face can't be good.

It's a difficult subject, but they have discussed it dozens of times in the past, so Naya's not quite sure what makes it heavier this time. She knows, even if they don't say it out loud, that they're concerned. That they must talk about it amongst themselves — how her anxiety has been acting up and that her mental state has not been this bad since she was diagnosed at seventeen.

She knows these things because the room goes silent each time she walks in earlier than they anticipate, or when they're in the car by themselves, waiting for her. Even with the way they look at her now, she can see it on their faces.

Their concern is mixed with fear that she could lose control again and succumb to her darkest thoughts, reaching rock bottom once again.

It's not a scenario she likes to think about, even if she understands where they are coming from.

"I'm fine," she mutters, but for all intents and purposes, it doesn't matter.

It's not that they don't care, it's that they are walking on eggshells around her, and it is driving her insane; it is always on the tip of their tongues to say something, and it shows. Frankly, it's a matter of time until it blows over.

"Nay—"

"I'm fine, and Joshua's fine too, and so is Aidan and everyone involved, so if Joshua doesn't want to answer, that's his problem and his loss, or whatever."

Her rant ends, but she's not fooling anyone. Being good friends, they give her the benefit of the doubt by not saying anything. Naya doesn't know what to say either, so she turns up the volume on the television and allows herself to relax, even if it's forced.

Seems like all good things end eventually, and her anxieties even follow her in her sleep.

In her dream she is walking slowly through snow, and even if she has never actually had the chance to see real snow, the sensation is all too familiar for her liking. The road she is following is inside a forest, and it gets thicker and thicker the more she walks. It is haunting how eerie it is, with no sound of nature — only her own footsteps in the snow.

She doesn't know how to gauge how much she has walked, but that is all she can do. It's as if her body is being controlled somehow and she's just there for the ride.

Eventually, the forest turns into marble-like pillars that upon closer inspection build a complete arch around her as she leaves the trees and snow behind her.

"Naya," her name is being echoed from behind her and in front, sending chills down her spine, even if she doesn't recognise the voice or know how to process it.

There's a blinding light that stops her movements and she turns to cover her eyes, but something isn't working — she can't seem to move her hands or close her eyes.

For a while, everything remains the same, until slowly the light fades. She is in new surroundings now. The path before her is bordered at the sides with a dozen black pillars and ends with four steps and a shrine, of some sorts. She sees someone there and, like magic, everything becomes closer and she is at the end of the stairs, reaching out to the person.

She can't see their face. She cannot even tell if it's a woman or a man, but she's filled with joy by the prospect of being close to them, so she smiles and they take her hand.

It's clear that she knows this person, and they know her.

"I am so proud of you," the person tells her, and the voice is like music to her ears. "You have come so far, Naya Tellus."

She wants to ask from what, or who they are, but there's applause and some sort of music around her, so she stops questioning it. In the hindsight of the dream, she wishes she had continued asking, because she sees the knife far too late, and by the time it pierces her chest, she wakes up.

Surprisingly, the first thing she becomes aware of is her phone ringing on the other side of her window pane, and it gives her just the distraction she needs to shake the nightmare off and answer it.

It's still dark outside, but her small clock shows the time of seven forty-eight in the morning, so she slides her finger across the screen without even checking who's calling.

"I apologise, did I wake you, Miss Tellus?"

Her *hello* must have sounded half asleep, but she clears her throat and her mind snaps into action at the sound of Joshua's voice. She takes the phone away from her ear to verify if it is indeed him, and replies.

"Yeah, sorry. How are you?"

"Well enough; hope you're doing the same." It's a courtesy he's not allowing her to answer and carries on, "You called yesterday, but unfortunately I was in a few meetings and therefore was unable to return your call."

Naya sucks in a deep breath as she waits for his next words.

"I hope you called with a positive answer, regarding our working together."

Somehow, knowing he still wants to work with her, despite the gap of almost a week since their last phone call, is both thrilling and intimidating. "Yes, I did. I was hoping to start this week…"

She trails off, but thankfully he's prepared. "Of course! I would love for you to come by today — any time you can."

Her heart beats irregularly as she confirms the full details of his office again, just in case, and lets him know she'll be there by half past nine. After he hangs up, she jumps out of bed to get ready. All thoughts of troubling dreams and anxieties behind her.

Naya doesn't really know what to expect when she returns to the same white lobby she ran out of the last time she was in the area. This time, however, Joshua is waiting for her by the entrance to the lift.

He's not alone though — he's with a black-haired woman whom Naya recognises from the last time she was here. They almost seem excited at seeing her — if Naya can even call the forced half-smile she receives from the woman as excitement.

"Good morning, Miss Tellus," Joshua greets her and turns to introduce the woman next to him. "This is Theresa, she's my assistant, so if there's anything you need, please let her know."

Naya's first thought is how not assistant-like Theresa looks, but she remembers her manners and stretches out her hand politely. "Naya," she says, but Theresa doesn't shake her hand.

"I don't touch strangers," she says as an explanation. Reckoning she is a germophobe, Naya nods in understanding.

"Sorry, I'll keep that in mind," Naya says. The sentiment surprises Theresa, and she looks like she doesn't know what to do with Naya's consideration. She's about to tell her she knows how it feels to be judged by others, when Joshua seems to notice the interaction.

Perhaps he just wants to hurry up and do some work, but Naya has a feeling he doesn't want them to interact much, because of the way he slams his hand against the lift's call button. When Naya sees the flinch Theresa tries to hold back, she promises herself to get to the bottom of it.

They don't talk at all on their way up, and it's pretty uncomfortable, but when they get to the fifth floor in no time, Theresa bids them goodbye. Naya notes the office she disappears into, thinking maybe she can go over there on her break to chat.

"I am glad you've decided to join my cause," Joshua says as he opens the door to his office. "We will do great work together."

Naya only nods in agreement, since she's too

overwhelmed by the huge board with paperwork and newspaper slips to strike up a conversation.

She's familiar with presentation boards, having needed to make several of them for her degree, but she takes a closer look and finds how everything is connected by dots and markers in a way that doesn't look cluttered and is considerably more understandable than anything she has ever come up with.

It's a mind map, of sorts, of any and all disasters and everything related to that field from the past ten years.

The first thing out of her mouth is a gasp, and then a slight exclamation of *wow*. Joshua, in her personal opinion, is pretty apparent about not commenting, and responds only once she talks again. "You've been busy."

"Well," he says, making an effort to look as sheepish as he can. "I have been waiting a long time for this."

His words catch her attention not because of their content, but because of his tone. It has an odd kind of longing, like one between two lost friends and not two strangers who, in a way, have been pushed together due to circumstances.

He doesn't let her ponder too much on it. "You believe these are... coincidences?"

Naya looks at the board again, this time focusing harder to find a pattern. Of course, Joshua already knows her opinion on the matter, since she has stated a few in her past articles, even though they had got her banned from a few websites and newspapers. So she is still learning to share them all over again.

"On average, there have been two major, natural disasters per month in the past year — sixty-five percent of which involved the earth itself," Joshua says, and his tone is all business-like again. "One might consider it as *nature rebelling against humanity*."

Naya's own written words echoing through his voice is chilling, ominous and exciting all at once. She had figured that Joshua wouldn't beat around the bush, but it's still quicker than she would have liked; it makes her feel unbalanced and at a disadvantage, even if she doesn't really have a cause.

"Some might consider it a conspiracy theory," she tells him exactly what she's been called.

"Some are extremely narrow minded, don't you think?" Joshua responds to the challenge pretty easily, and it makes her wonder about what is going on.

"You want answers," Joshua says. "To why everything's happening, to why you've been chosen, to why it is all going to hell."

It sounds specifically infuriating, as if he knows what's going on in her mind and more importantly, as if he knows about everything else that has happened to her — which is absurd, because she has never told him.

"Do you know what's going on?" She finds herself asking, without even meaning to.

Joshua is right; she's so desperate for answers, and he knows he's won by the smile on his face. He invites her to sit in the same chair she sat in last time, and she goes willingly, hoping to battle her demons once and for all.

She tells herself what Julie said to her — *If it will get you answers, take it.*

"Why don't you tell me how you've been?"

It's a diversion, yet despite her knowing that, she still tells him what she feels, even if it comes out in a sarcastic tone. She tells him about how people are chasing her for no reason and how Aidan is the one who is protecting her.

When she tells him she doesn't know why her — he sighs.

"Perhaps you're exceptionally important."

Naya resists the urge to roll her eyes. "I'm sure I am."

"You do not believe that? Surely, considering everything you've been through, some part of your mind agrees that you are unique; that you are powerful and perhaps they are the ones who are afraid of you."

It makes no sense, but his words seem genuine, and it causes her mind to scramble for answers she might be able to use to dispute his claim.

"It sounds like I should be afraid of myself."

Joshua gazes directly at her, his grin widening as if she has just said the funniest thing. He sits down in front of her before actually bothering with a reply. "Well, I would say that we should all be afraid of you, but the fact that you are oblivious to what is within you is what is most dangerous. Not to us, to you."

"Why?"

"I wonder if the question refers to why we should fear you, or why you should fear yourself?" He pauses, and it's enough time to make Naya reevaluate her choices. The conversation is foreboding enough, even without her not knowing what the hell he means. "Or, would you rather we discussed why you are unaware of the real you?"

Not quite knowing, all of a sudden, what she does want to know, or what might benefit her the most, she shoots him her best glare, in the hope of intimidating him.

It feels like a game — one she knows she is losing already.

Maybe Lucas had a point.

"I am unimpressed by that," he dismisses the attempt, but not in a condescending way; it's more like a scolding. "Let us talk some more then, since we finally have the time. I can answer your darkest questions, Naya Tellus; I can tell you exactly who you are, and why you are needed in this world. I can share with you the secret of who you are… I hold the key," he stops again, just to chuckle and look at Naya's key necklace, shining brightly over her green sweater. "To everything you wish to know."

The chain against Naya's chest suddenly feels on fire, but the sensation ends as quickly as it comes, making her wonder whether she imagined it.

Joshua takes one look at her and leans back in his seat. He moves one leg across the other and smiles fondly at Naya. His next words, however, leave her with nothing but apprehension.

"All you have to do is ask."

CHAPTER FIFTEEN

Naya is aware of two different things all at once — her heartbeat pounding in her ears, and how dry her mouth is. She swallows to try and help, but her throat feels swollen and her mind is racing with thoughts she can't even start to piece together.

Of course Joshua picks up on it, and leans forwards with his elbows on his knees and his head supported by his hands. He doesn't talk though, letting Naya process the last few minutes peacefully.

The only thing Naya can tell for sure, is that something doesn't feel right.

She can't put her finger on it, but her intuition is begging her to leave and never come back. It is the same feeling she had the last time she came here, however, this time, she is not so sure she can escape.

"Tell me something," Joshua says, and his tone is too casual for Naya's taste. "Is there not a single part of you that knows you are… not of the norm?"

"Should I be insulted?" Naya asks, despite herself.

Joshua scoffs. "Let the sarcasm be, Miss Tellus. This isn't a place for doubters or deflectors."

Naya wants to challenge that. She wants to tell him, sarcasm aside, that she might as well not be her; she wants to convince him that she deserves the truth and prove to him that she is more than capable of handling whatever he wants to throw her way.

They're playing a game, she feels, and the only way to get answers is to win.

"Who am I, then?"

It's a simple question, in an innocent tone, and it probably moves something within Joshua, since his expression turns soft, or at least the softest it can be.

"All in due time," he replies. "We've got work to do first."

Joshua gets right back to business after that, but Naya isn't focused on her theories anymore; not now that she knows her initial feeling wasn't insane, and that there's truly something else going on.

She knows it all connects somehow to her mother, and she knows it's a puzzle she can't wait to solve. Joshua may hold the answers, even if he is keeping them annoyingly close to his heart, but she knows he needs something from her, and is maintaining his leverage while he can.

That's why she'll play into his hands for now, and will use whatever resources he can give her to find out the truth.

Throughout his speech about the connection between humanity and natural disasters, Naya lets her mind wonder, only contributing when she absolutely needs to.

Sometime around lunch, Joshua dismisses her home, telling her that they will regroup tomorrow. While it strikes Naya as odd, he doesn't let her ponder too much on it as he asks his assistant to escort her out.

Theresa looks less than happy to run the errand, and it makes Naya feel there may be a crack in the relationship she might be able to use, so she tries to hold a conversation with her when they leave Joshua's office.

"So, how long have you worked for Joshua?"

Theresa doesn't acknowledge the question at first, and turns to look at Naya only when they're in the lift, completely alone. "Mr. Adams and I have been working together for a while now."

It's not only ambiguous, but also a brief contradiction to how Joshua had introduced her. Naya knows how to look for details in what people say, and it doesn't sound like Theresa thinks of herself as Joshua's second, but more like his equal.

"Are you involved in the whole natural disasters hypothesis as well?"

Naya knows people find it easier to answer closed questions, so she tries that tactic instead.

Theresa smirks, and Naya is pleased to find she got a real emotion out of her, even if it's just spite. "You can say that."

When they arrive at the lobby, Theresa leads her out, once again changing her behaviour to being professional enough, and Naya thinks it's for the sake of appearances more than anything else. If she didn't know any better, the look of relief on Theresa's face when they step outside would have been almost laughable.

She obviously is not the happiest working there.

Naya decides to tackle the subject head on before leaving. "So how's it like, working with him?"

Theresa looks at her sharply before considering her response. It turns Naya's blood cold, and she knows she has asked the wrong question. Perhaps Theresa is like her — thrown into a situation she's unsure how to get out of.

"I hope you know what you're doing," Theresa tells her, and it feels very important — like Naya is missing something here. "I hope you know you'll need to pick sides soon, and you'd better make the right decision."

"Is that a threat?" Naya's on high alert now, and nothing matters, but the both of them.

"On the contrary," Theresa answers, and her words are surprisingly honest. "Loyalty is important, as well as your biggest virtue. Don't let it be your downfall too."

"You don't know me," Naya tells her, and it's a weak argument to a conversation that has gotten out of hand. She doesn't know what Theresa is getting at, and the secrecy is driving her mad.

"I know your mind," Theresa says and steps down the three stairs that lead to the street. She gestures at a black car and holds the door open for Naya. "Make the smart choice, not the easy one."

Up close, Naya sees the crack in Theresa's expression, but she doesn't know what it means exactly. The cab driver, however, asks her to hurry up and the last thing she hears Theresa say before she closes the door for Naya is to "put it on the bill".

The next few days go by in a haze. Joshua is still particularly ambivalent about whether or not to share his true motives and beliefs with her, and is intent on her being there for not more than four hours of work.

He doesn't let her ask too many questions, mostly just asking her opinion on some matters, and Naya is starting to get suspicious. He does give her unlimited access to his records of anything relating to natural disasters, but she puts it aside when he sends her home for the weekend.

"I hope you'll have a wonderful weekend, Miss Tellus," he concludes their work day on a Friday, slightly later than usual.

He hands her a folder with her usual homework, as the twins calls it, but this one feels heavier. She is tempted to ask him about it when he starts talking again.

"I've left you things to go over, when you have some free time. Let me know if you find anything irregular or something that might be relevant to our cause."

Once again, Joshua is ambiguous; he never tells her what exactly he wants her to find out, and she feels like it's one giant test for him. The problem is that Naya has no idea whether she passes or fails each time, and he acts too professional around her, trying to make her think and not think at the same time.

The only good thing to come out of her new job seems to be her new way to commute. Her driver is usually waiting for her an hour before she needs to leave her flat for Brook Street, and is always outside waiting for her when she's sent home, regardless of the time.

However Theresa is nowhere to be seen, and it's starting to alarm Naya.

She makes up her mind to ask Joshua about it when she comes back to work on Monday.

The drive back is heavy with traffic, considering it's rush hour, and the sky, already dark by the time they get close to West Hampstead, brings a downpour of rain.

Though Naya knows that the tube would be much quicker than a car, she still enjoys the luxury, even if it means sitting in traffic for almost an hour. It's her downtime before she arrives home and has her ears chewed off by the twins, yet again.

Things are not settled down with them yet, and she hopes to keep the flames as low as possible with them. Julie told her that they had asked her for help, when she met up with them without Naya, but she told them to support Naya as much as they can.

Naya knows they try, but they worry too much, so she had come to expect that the usual banter becomes too upsetting to deal with. Still, she engages with them, hoping that they will both understand her choice and go with the flow, instead of unconsciously making it more difficult for her.

What she doesn't expect, however, is for them to be waiting for her on the terrace that leads to their building. It's sheltered from the rain, at least, and she thinks Lucas is just finishing his cigarette by the time she gets out of the car.

She greets them with a hello, figuring that they both just got back. They exchange a few details about their day for some more moments before Lucas puts out his cigarette and they move to go inside. Neither of them ask her about Joshua or Aidan anymore, not since the last time they talked about it and got into an argument.

On hearing Naya's name being called, they stop their conversation and Naya turns to see Aidan smiling, with the same white umbrella, at the bottom of the stairs to the street.

"Who's that?" Lucas asks, and although they have never officially met Aidan, she assumes it might be adding fuel to the fire.

"Aidan," she tells them. "Please be civil," she adds, glaring at Lucas.

Without replying, Lucas moves past her in a flash and stands in front of Aidan. Naya knows that she can't really prevent him from doing anything, but she might as well try.

In his defence, Aidan just stands there, with his arms folded, looking smug, while Lucas scrutinizes him. Naya takes the silence as a sign to look at Logan whom, to her surprise, is watching the two men's staring battle and looking amused.

Naya knows Aidan too well by now not to notice the twitch in his lip before he speaks, and decides to take one more step towards them to try and take control of the situation.

"Like what you see?" Aidan asks.

Lucas scoffs, "I'm way above your league, you twat."

"Ah, the British manners I've been hearing so much about," Aidan says, and he sounds way too pleased with how the conversation is going. "Sorry to disappoint you, but my league consists of brains rather than looks, though I seem to have both, so—"

Naya's cue to intervene has to be at this moment, so she holds a hand up to Aidan's chest to shut him up. "Alright, we get it, you're not going to be BFFs."

"I see no introduction is needed," Aidan says, his eyes still glued to Lucas.

Naya murmurs in response and does her best to keep the peace, especially since they're in the street and it might attract unneeded attention. With neither of them willing to break their eye contact, she forgets about the stubborn drizzle and moves to push Lucas away slightly.

"Okay, that's enough testosterone for now."

"You're defending him?" Lucas is surprised, but does as he's asked and takes a small step backwards.

Aidan smirks, an arrogant gesture that means much more than just humour. So to stop Lucas from saying anything and in an attempt to wipe the expression off his face, she slaps his chest. Aidan gives her a disapproving look, but much to her delight, does not say anything.

"What are you doing here?" she asks him.

Aidan shrugs. "I was just in the area and saw you, so I though I would say hello since you undoubtably have missed me these past few days."

"I've been busy," Naya replies, and though it wasn't what she was asked, she's dying to know what Aidan thinks about her working with Joshua.

"Yeah," Aidan's expression turns tight. "I know. But we'll talk about that later."

Lucas takes the opportunity to pull Naya inside with him, and as much as Naya wants to know what Aidan has to say, yet not in the presence of the twins, she goes willingly.

They remain silent all the way up, and only when the flat's door closes behind them, does Lucas allow himself to let off the steam and blurt out how she should just go to the police.

It is irrelevant as she has tried that, and they know it.

"Yeah, you know, you sound like a bloody broken record, Lucas—"

"And I'm going to repeat it until you get it into your fucking head, for God's sake!"

She looks at his brother for help, but it's futile. Logan seems to take his side, folding his arms in frustration as he observes the scene. As usual, he prefers to keep his hands clean and she would appreciate him staying in character, since it usually helps soothe Lucas, although that doesn't seem to be the case, this time.

"When will you get that he's dangerous? That wherever he is, there's trouble?"

The only retort she can think of comes off as being meek, "You don't know him like I do," and even she realises it's not her best case.

Lucas scoffs. "You don't know him! Listen to me, Naya, he's an egotistical arsehole who's looking to manipulate you—"

"To do what, exactly?"

Naya is willing to humour this line of thought, but she knows Lucas has no place to lead to. She knows, because she has had the same discussion with Julie a few times, while they were brainstorming together, only to come to the same conclusion that Lucas will probably arrive at once he is finished his calculations.

"To make you think he's irresistible; to make you feel something so strong for him that you'll kick logic in the arse if it means you get to have him."

She was not expecting that however, and it irritates her how little he must think of her to come to that idea. In any other scenario, she would have contradicted his view, or at least turned his own thoughts against him.

But coherent Naya is long gone, and so she can be sure the only words that will come out her mouth will be complete trash. So, she really should not have been surprised at that point, when she hears herself speak.

"I'm not seventeen anymore, so get over yourself, Lucas. Not all of us think with our dicks."

She sees the warning signs before he has a chance to say anything. He's fuming, and there's the slight twitch to his left eyebrow that only means trouble. He's silent for a little while longer, and it's only a matter of time before he will open his mouth to say something she knows she will not like.

"You're not Lois Lane, Naya, and he's not bloody Superman."

The words are thrown at her, their meaning a bit harsher than she thought, and she watches as his brother visibly take his side, slowly rising to show his loyalties.

She shouldn't have expected anything else. They are, after all, in sync on everything else.

It doesn't change the fact that it hurts deep down, when they team up against her. As if there's anything she can do to change the way things are — as if she can help it.

"I don't understand you," Lucas continues, and Naya would rather not be listening. "You're the most rational person I know. You don't meddle, you don't look for danger and you don't go out of your comfort zone."

She shouldn't take it as an insult, she reminds herself.

"What's your point?" She forces out the words, though she already knows.

"You shouldn't ask how high when he tells you to jump. You should ask why instead."

She knows he's not talking just about Aidan, anymore.

If they weren't in the middle of a fight, she would have applauded him for the way he chose to articulate himself. But after all, she's not sure he wouldn't have taken the same course of action if it was him in her shoes. They must think it's so simple. They must deem her actions careless and reckless without even looking to see what she is really facing.

She hates how easy it is for them. At times like these, she hates them.

The sounds of Logan's sharp intake of breath and Lucas's jaw snapping shut in an audible click, bring her out of her reverie. It takes her a while to control her senses again and to understand what she had done.

It comes after a while. Oh! She had said she hates them out loud. It's not their first real fight, and probably will not be their last either, but they had a vow when they were small children to always show love and appreciation, and most importantly, to never say they hate each other unless they meant it.

Her thoughtlessness embarrasses her, and she's disappointed with herself. She's too angry to take it back and apologise, even though she should, but she can't take being there for another moment.

"Naya—" Logan starts, but she's way ahead of him.

She is turning around to gather whatever she can, which is mainly her coat and scarf. She hopes to God her wallet is somewhere there with her flat's keys, because the next thing she does is mutter something at them about needing some fresh air and slams the door behind her.

CHAPTER SIXTEEN

Naya doesn't know what makes her seek refuge in the one place that still plagues her dreams. Yet, here she is, standing on the embankment overlooking Tower Bridge, sighing heavily as she takes in the structure.

Her mind wonders as she moves to sit on the concrete step behind her. Usually, she would try to settle her mind, fixate it on one thing at a time just so she wouldn't be overwhelmed. Now, however, with the sound of the water below the embankment and the steady hum of people in the street above her, she allows it to be just so.

Her thoughts are so scattered as they build up into anything and nothing at the same time, all the while colliding as they race in different directions.

It's a trick her psychiatrist, Dr. Howard, taught her. He would say that instead of constantly fighting anxiety and losing, just to let it go. They both know that it may not be the healthiest thing to do, but it helps alleviate some of the tension and the horrible sense of a losing battle.

When she looks up at the bridge again, this time with what she hopes is a clearer mind, she feels breathless and she's reliving her nightmare — except this time there are no passersby to warn her or accuse her.

She clenches her hands in her lap until she can feel her fingernails digging into her flesh, and it's the only thing that anchors her back to reality. She can still see the bridge starting to collapse, and can't tear her gaze away. It's not real, she insists repeatedly in her mind, even if she is struggling to come to terms with it.

Nothing helps, and all she can do is watch as the grey stones before her fall out of their place. The columns, which are holding both towers, twist with a sharp noise and the bridge itself caves into the river. Naya abruptly stands and walks over to the railing to get a better understanding of what is happening. She strains her ears, expecting to hear screams at the very last moment, but there's absolute stillness; she then feels the earth beneath her shake as well, only to realise that something had bumped into her.

Reluctantly, she looks away from the sight before her and notices that it's not something, but someone.

It is a man who seems clearly drunk. His steps are out of sync with his mind as he stumbles ahead, almost collapsing on top of her again. Something's wrong, her mind gauges, for her, and she can't tell if it's anxiety or the way the man's eyes are taking her in with a wicked glint, and she freezes.

She looks far enough to the bridge to find that it's perfect and intact, with not a single stone out of place, and she realises that she had imagined the whole thing.

Fear usually triggers her flight or fight mode, and she's more inclined to flee than anything else, especially when the vision — or whatever it was, is still at the back of her mind, beckoning her to look for sanctuary. She lets apprehension win, and tries to look as casual as she can while backing away, into the street above her.

The steps behind her convince her that the drunkard is on her tail; she doesn't know why he is following her, or what he's about to do, yet she feels like she is too weak at this stage to even try and fight back.

She's almost at the stairs leading to her escape, when she feels his harsh hand wrap around her forearm, pulling her back. Something is definitely wrong, even if not in the way she initially thought. Naya groans, feeling helplessly miserable and something snaps when he presses her into the stone rail, blocking her chance of escaping.

"Come now, Trouble," he says in a drunken frenzy, "Don't go yet, we can have some fun—"

She does her best to show that she is not interested, and pushes him off her. Thankfully he is unstable, since she doesn't think she can outmaneuver him otherwise. He is taller and bigger than her, and she's still recovering from whatever she just saw to be on top of her game.

Nevertheless, she knows she can't just give up. Her father always taught her that when it comes to self defence, it's not a bad thing to let her opponent underestimate her. It's next to impossible to loosen her body to make it seem like he has the advantage, but she's had enough training to know how.

She also knows to be aware of the element of surprise, and when the man has the audacity to smile hazily at her as he closes in on her again, she finds that element in the shape of a different voice joining the scene. It's a deep and too well-balanced voice to belong to the drunk man.

"I don't know what it is about you — you just seem to be some sort of magnet for trouble."

The statement is directed at Naya herself, but it does the trick and catches the drunk man's attention. Naya can't look to her left, where Aidan's voice is coming from, but the drunkard does, and she's not about to waste the edge she's been given. She thrusts her knee upwards and watches as it hits the mark. Naya fights a smirk of self-satisfaction when the the man staggers backwards, clutching his crotch in a cry of pain.

It's definitely a victory, even more so when Aidan moves quickly to grasp her attacker's forearms and twist them backwards, effectively caging him in against his chest. Naya can see he's holding back, even though it is clear that if he would add any additional force he would seriously injure the man.

His intention is pretty straightforward — he means to restrain him, not to incapacitate him.

The man grunts in pain, but manages to push back against Aidan and break free. Aidan doesn't go for another hit, but the drunk aims a poorly directed fist at Aidan's face that would have almost landed around his neck, if Aidan hadn't caught it.

Aidan says something in what Naya is almost certain is Spanish, though she can't tell what it means. Aidan pushes the man away with his fist still caught in Aidan's hand, and it looks like for the moment he is relenting, too busy nursing his wounded hand.

Aidan looks at Naya with raised eyebrows, as if he just remembered she was there, and scoffs. "I would joke about the whole knight in shiny armour thing, but it seems like you actually know how to fight," he says.

Naya thinks he sounds highly impressed, and it triggers a sense of pride within her; men usually don't react that way when they find out — on the contrary, it usually sends them the other way.

She can't help but smile. "I told you."

Aidan opens his mouth to say something, but is interrupted by the drunkard returning for another round. Naya starts to warn him, but it is unnecessary as Aidan sees the movement before she does, somehow anticipating it, and dodges to the side, causing the attacker to stumble forward, clearly thinking he would collide with Aidan, but instead finding nothing.

Aidan doesn't give him the benefit of the doubt anymore, and huffs as he moves to grab his shirt, pulling him backwards and wrapping his arm around the man's neck, keeping him below his armpit in a seemingly effortless headlock

"Well, I'm glad I was here to witness it first hand," Aidan says, and his tone is way too controlled for someone who is holding another captive with only his hands. "I can't wait to see in what other ways you'll surprise me, though I wouldn't expect any less from you."

Aidan seems too fixed on something, but knowing she won't get a proper answer if she asks this head on, she decides to put Julie's theory about him caring for her to the test. "Maybe you're just a bad influence and it has nothing to do with me."

She tries to sound as dismissive as she can, but by the way he rolls his eyes, she knows she failed. They can't have a decent conversation with the man being held Aidan's arm, and so in what looks like a calculated risk, Aidan lets him struggle enough to once again break free. Naya knows the meaning of it — Aidan will conserve the energy needed for a fight, while tiring his opponent out.

It seems to work, because the man doesn't try to attack again, and Aidan uses the momentum to push him backwards against the stone rail he had pinned Naya to. "Are you going to leave us in peace, now?" he asks.

The man tries the same move Naya used, but it's useless — he has nowhere to go under Aidan's tight hold. "Didn't think so," Aidan mumbles in disappointment and bashes the man body's against the railing.

"Go back to fucking Spain, you—" the man spits out, his drunkness turning into fury now.

"I'm Mexican, you idiot," Aidan says, and without letting him say another word, he pushes him upwards and over the edge. It's not high enough to permanently harm him, as he will undoubtedly land on one of the small shores.

"Are you kidding me," Naya mutters and looks over the edge. Just as predicted, the man collapses on the pebble, untouched by the water, besides most probably waking up in the morning with a terrible headache, he seems otherwise unscathed.

"He's fine," Aidan brushes the whole thing off and gives her a pointed look. "Are you?"

Naya's not sure whether he's referring to her having been attacked or just in general, so she gives him a non-committal smile and starts to walk.

He follows, and it may be the adrenaline still pumping inside her, but she feels the need to talk. "Mexican, huh?" Naya says, needing to occupy her mind on something.

He chuckles as a response. "Born and raised, yeah."

They walk in silence afterwards. He seems to be letting her dictate the tone of their conversation, and she's grateful. She doesn't really know what to say to him, besides the fact that she didn't think she has anything in common with him, but that sounds like a terrible thing to say.

"I went to the police," Naya confesses after a while, and by the look on Aidan's face he's neither surprised nor insulted. So she continues, and he doesn't stop her to ask questions in between. It's like he knows he needs to let her finish her piece so she doesn't get distracted.

She talks about how the whole affair is making her anxious and feel completely out of control, and she explains the exact moment Julie and her came up with the idea of asking him, bluntly as it may have been, what was going on.

Especially after matters with Andre took a wrong turn and furthermore, she feels that she is in danger, and not for the first time since this all started.

"What do you expect me to tell you?" he asks, and it speaks volumes, even if he didn't mean it to. His tone, if she has to analyse it, sounds different than their previous conversation, and she's sure that at the very least, she has managed to convey her worries. Now that she knows he cares somewhat, it's easier for her to carry on.

"I can't hear you say again that you can't tell me." She pours all her vulnerability into her words and, despite not looking at him, she knows he's attentive in a way people rarely are. "I get it, you know? Whatever it is you're hiding, it has everything to do with me, and you think you're protecting me, but you really are not. I can't trust you to protect me without knowing what I'm up against."

He sighs deeply, which is the only indication he's close to crumbling under her pressure. Regardless, he doesn't reply.

So she continues talking, even if she knows it's the opposite of the truth — anything to get a response out of him and maybe lure him into telling her the truth. "I know you and Joshua Adams are working together."

Aidan scoffs and stops. For the first time in what feels like hours she looks at him, really scrutinizing him. He seems uncomfortable, but not because the accusation is precise. Quite the contrary, actually. He looks offended.

"You think I'm working with that..." he stops to exhale, like he's looking for the right word. "That— *puta madre*?"

Naya knows just enough Spanish to recognise the phrase and the obvious swear words. The anger in his tone isn't directed at her, as such; it seems everything involving Joshua strikes a cord within him that he can't contain.

It's the opening she is looking for and, while she knows it's not fair, she pushes on.

"Seems like it," she lies, hoping Aidan's too upset pick up on it.

She moves to the edge of the embankment, hopping over the barrier to sit on the stairs leading to the coast line. It's been a while since she has done that, but the water relaxes her enough to be able to ignore the huge sign: *No Passing This Point.*

Aidan joins her just as fast and sits next to her. They are quite close, considering how narrow the stairs are, and, unintentionally, she takes comfort by his proximity.

"Last I checked, I have a higher rate of being your knight in shiny armour than Adams."

Naya scoffs. While the semi-accusation is true, she doesn't really know who came after her and why they were specifically after her. She wishes she could categorise all the incidents under the wrong place, wrong time criteria, but anyone can see that is no longer the case.

"Well, Joshua isn't stalking me — you are."

Aidan chuckles and shrugs. Naya would be shocked to learn she was right, if it had happened two months ago. Right now, though, she's relieved to know she's not crazy.

"To be honest," Aidan says carefully, as if he is measuring his words. "It's not stalking."

Naya, despite herself, rolls her eyes. "Oh really? What do you call it then?"

"Looking out for you," he says.

Even if his words are final, it's his tone that catches her unguarded. He speaks as if it's his one true calling, and he is so certain that she is in danger to begin with. They sit in silence for a long while, and it seems more for Naya's benefit than his, but he endures, and as much as Naya wants to hate it, the stillness of the world is comforting.

She doesn't know how long they sit there, but after a while, she can sense that Aidan wants to say something. She has no idea how he deals with silence, but even without the need to fill it with words the question is on the tip of his tongue.

Naya gives him five more minutes before she sighs and looks his way. "Alright, spit it out."

It shoots out of his mouth in no time. "What were you doing out there anyway?"

The question, Naya concludes, is pure curiosity. She had expected some judgment there, but she supposes she should take it without thinking too much about it. Instead, she shrugs, and despite how childish it sounds, says, "I had a fight with Lucas."

"Your flatmate?"

Naya mumbles in reply. "One of my best friends. I said some mean things, he threw some accusations, and..." she trails off, not sure it's important anymore. Somehow, just the mere presence of Aidan and the water below calms her, and she can't really remember her anger anymore.

"What did you fight about?" Aidan's voice is soft, and she tries hard not to meet his gaze. She honestly is not sure she'll like what she sees there, so she keeps her eyes on the water.

"About Joshua, about the new job, about—"

"About me?" Aidan guesses. "About you going to a private investigator?"

If he seems surprised or angry, he doesn't let it show. In fact, when Naya gathers her courage to look at his face, she finds only a mutual feeling. She knows Aidan well enough to see it as his mask, and she wonders if she'll ever be able to fully break it.

"Who is dead — probably thanks to you," the statement flies out of her mouth before she has the chance to rethink it.

If she thought he looked offended before, his expression now is even worse. "Is that what you think of me?" he asks, sounding so vulnerable that she has to surpass her immediate need to hug him. "I would never harm an innocent," he says with such conviction she actually believes him. "I have my own speculations about who murdered him, but I swear to you, Naya, it wasn't me."

Naya's not sure she wants to know who he thinks did it, but it comforts her to know it wasn't Aidan. He may be hiding a lot from her, but she does not think that this is one of them. She feels the need to comfort him, to assure him she believes him... The only thing that makes sense is to hold his hand, so she does.

It causes him to smile so gently, it warms her heart. "Thank you," he says. It's completely free of embarrassment, and is genuine gratitude for her believing him.

"For what it's worth," Aidan speaks again, "I can't believe you went to a private investigator and to the police to try and dig up some dirt on me."

"If it makes you feel any better, most of the dirt was on Joshua."

Aidan actually laughs at that. "Well, you didn't have to pay any money for that — I could have told you he's a fishy guy and you shouldn't work for him."

It's the first time he's mentioned her working with Joshua, and though she's not entirely surprised he knows, it's still hits an open nerve, but she's too tired mentally to try and analyze it.

Naya smiles, and they settle into silence once again. It's odd how comforting it is, not needing to fill the blanks in between topics, and also terrifying how easy it is to just sit with him. Her mind is spiraling with questions; how he knew where and when to find her, what he knows about Joshua and who Aidan actually is… But she remains silent instead, and can't seem to figure out why she cherishes the quiet between them.

She is still holding his hand.

"You shouldn't be too angry with Lucas," Aidan breaks the spell after a few minutes. "He's just worried about you. He's an asshole, but at least he's got your back."

It makes her chuckle, and she appreciates the use of humour to lighten the situation. "I guess you're right," she says after a while. "I should probably apologise to him."

"Yeah," Aidan nods and gets up, using their interlocking hands to pull her up. "Come on, I'll take you home."

CHAPTER SEVENTEEN

It's close to midnight when Naya closes the door to her flat behind her. She tries to be as quiet as possible, and is semi grateful that both her flatmates seemingly decided to call it a night earlier than usual. The guilt, however, settles as if there is the weight of a small iron ball in her stomach, and it makes her sick with apprehension. It is the thought of actually hurting her two best friends that makes her pause by her bedroom.

The decision to tackle the problem at that very moment happens subconsciously, and her legs carry her automatically to Lucas's bedroom.

Logan will be easier to convince, so she settles on leaving him for tomorrow.

Knocking is irrelevant, since he usually makes it perfectly clear if he doesn't wish to be disturbed, so she pushes the door open and steps inside, but not before discarding her coat and scarf at the entrance.

She knows the layout of his room almost as well as

she knows the rest of the flat. It's more spacious than her own, and since Lucas is extremely tidy — a fact she always knew yet still surprised her when they first moved in together — she does not encounter any obstacles on the way to his bed. Just like her own, his bed is shoved against one of the walls, although he opted for the one away from the window. He has a closet and a dresser right across from it, with a second-hand armchair near the window that they didn't have space for in the living room.

At first she doesn't move, and she catches her breath when she realises she has no idea what she should even say or if she should even wake him up.

"Nay…?" Lucas's voice comes out as a muffled whisper, probably because of the sheets.

She mumbles a reply and then moves across the room to stand by his bed. She has done the same thing so many times in the past that it has become routine by now. She always comes to seek him or Logan out when one of them is troubled.

He reaches out for her hand, hissing slightly at its coldness. "What the hell happened?" His voice is still laced with sleep, but he's starting to come to.

Her guilt resurfaces as the only thing he can think of is her safety.

"I'm sorry," she says quickly, before the courage to try

and approach the subject fails her. It makes her visibly cringe, because she hates how much she struggles with words sometimes.

Lucas doesn't say anything for the longest time and, just when she's about to turn tail and run, he tugs on the hand he's still holding and pulls her onto his bed. It's part of their ritual, and she takes it as a silent peace offering. He tucks her in by his side, wrapping his arms around her and holds her there.

Even after ten minutes, she can tell by his breathing that he is not asleep. She knows he's waiting, and while she would love to push this evening into her *things I don't want to think about* folder at the back of her mind, she also recognises the need to let him in.

And she does. He lets her talk, only pushing her away slightly to give her some breathing space. The more she talks and explains about what that happened, including how she didn't mean any of what she said, and how she feels she is being constantly judged by them, the more the weights lift off her shoulders. She tells him about tonight as well, although she leaves out the part about how Aidan made her feel. Some things, she thinks, are better left unsaid.

"God—"

"I know," she mutters, interrupting what he's saying, because she's not sure she wants his comment.

"This is some messed up shit," he says to summarise, and she can't help but agree.

"I know," she replies, although it comes out in shattered syllables that only show her anxiety. Usually the comfort of being with someone she feels safe with does the trick, and she should have calmed down already. But her heart is hammering in her chest like it is sure she's still in danger.

She wonders if Lucas can feel, because he tightens his grip on her and pulls her closer again, caressing her hair gently with a silent promise that things will get better.

Sleep doesn't come easy for her, even with how exhausted she is, but Lucas's arms around her and his slow breathing, manage to soothe her down long enough for exhaustion to finally take over, and she is at least content to have a nightmare-free night.

She wakes up some time in the morning — her body stiff and her muscles aching. She and Lucas are an array of tangled limbs, and she has to be extremely careful as she detaches herself from him.

When she feels awake enough, she glances at the clock. It occurs to her that both brothers will be up fairly soon, and she's not sure she can face Logan just yet. So she manages to grab her scarf and coat from the previous night, in record time, and slip into her bedroom.

She checks her phone out of habit, finding a text message from her father sent sometime around two in the morning, stating that he has something he needs to do this weekend and will not be able to meet up with her as per usual.

It's not disappointing, as such, as these things happen, but it still upsets her.

Now there is no chance of going back to sleep, so she resolves on getting some work done. Usually she'll choose the living room or the small island in the kitchen to work on, but her options are very limited for now. She pushes the blanket out of the way and settles into the comfort of her own bed, more than happy to keep her mind distracted.

Eventually, sleep beckons, and she surrenders, barely even bothering with the blanket.

In the fine line between a memory and a dream, she's fifteen again, and the younger version of Dom fits perfectly in it, so much so that it doesn't feel like a decade ago. She remembers this was the last time she had seen her mother's grave, deeming her too selfish to have left the love of her life behind.

It's eerily silent, which is probably the only indication that this is a dream rather than a trip down memory lane, but it's still accurate to the bone, and feels very vivid. With the light breeze on her face and the sound of the high grass crumbling beneath her feet as they walk through Highgate Cemetery, she brings up the inquiry of her mother's death like she had done all those years ago.

When they are standing over the grave, Dom answers, and she thinks how funny it is that she has never thought of asking who else visits Kaia, because there are fresh flowers every time they are there, and she knows they are not from her father.

But then he talks, and she can't focus on anything else other than his face, void of any emotion as usual, whenever they discuss difficult issues.

"Sometimes it's funny how monsters wear the same faces as humans."

Those words stuck with her, and she knows there's not much she can do to try and block them out. It was probably the only truth she had ever received regarding her mother's fate, and it was then that she bitterly decided that a quiet tombstone on the other side of London was not worth her time.

It's not a nightmare by any standard, but when Naya wakes up from it she feels drained, like it took a mental toll on her. Outside the sun is shining brightly, but her room is freezing. She hears the twins talking amongst themselves, probably trying to keep as quiet as possible for her.

As much as she would prefer to evade the subject, she knows she owes Logan an apology, so she pulls the sheets off her and gets up, suddenly realising that she is still in her clothes from yesterday.

With the *now or never* mantra, she ignores the twins' looks at the state of her clothes, and goes directly to sit next to Logan.

"Loggie—"

He just smiles at her, taking in her expression and reading everything she wants to say before she tries to articulate herself. Then he nods, pulling her closer into a hug.

"I know," he says, and it's perfectly parallel to her and Lucas's conversation.

She needs to say it, though. "I'm sorry, I never meant it."

Logan nods again and takes a deep breath. "I know," he says again. "And you know we just worry about you, is all."

She feels the sofa sinking behind her, as Lucas sits down and lays a hand on her back. "It drives us crazy that we can't help."

Naya's not sure what to say, so she just nods.

"But we're here for you," Logan says. "And we're in this together, so you have to trust us enough to let us take some of the weight off you. The situation is messed up as it is, and we can't fight between ourselves if we want to see this through."

Naya is speechless; it's not new to her that her friends are as loyal to her as she to them, but in between everything that happens, it's a constant reminder that she is not alone, and it makes all the difference.

The only thing that worries her is whether or not she is putting them in danger.

Sometime around noon, after her lunch with Logan and Lucas, Naya gets a call from an unidentified number.

"Little Bear," the voice on the other side says, and she doesn't have to associate the nickname with Aidan to know that it's him. "Are you up for a little field trip?"

Truth be told, her entire body is aching for some rest, but she supposes she'll still have the following day to rest before Monday, so what's the harm? Perhaps today will be the day to get some answers. For the moment, she doesn't bother asking him how he got her phone number.

"Okay," she says. "Where are we going?"

"St. Dunstan," Aidan immediately replies. "I'll be at your place in ten minutes."

He hangs up without saying anything else, and Naya looks at the twins. "Aidan," she explains. "We're going to the east, to the church Julie was going on about."

"What for?" Lucas asks, and she can tell he is being careful with his tone.

Naya stands up, "I guess we'll find out soon enough."

Neither of the men say anything to that, so Naya thinks she should take it as is and goes to her room to change her clothes. The temperature has dropped significantly over the past few days, so she dresses warmly enough and is out the door in under ten minutes.

Aidan is already leaning against his motorbike by the time she steps outside — this time with a pink helmet in his hands. The other helmet is on the handle of the bike, and Naya eyes it hesitantly. The previous night when he took her home and explained how precious his bike was, all she could do was roll her eyes and think how very Aidan-like it is for him to own a bike and to treat it as if it a living being.

He had given her his own helmet, taking the risk of driving without one himself.

"This is for you," he says, handing her the helmet. "So you won't complain about me endangering us."

"Do we really need to use this?" She is refering to the black motorbike itself.

Aidan chuckles. "You'll get used to it, eventually."

Naya really wishes she won't. It's not that Aidan drives recklessly, in fact it's quite the opposite. He drives extremely carefully, but she assumes that it's just for her benefit. The problem is that it's bitterly cold and she's not looking forward to the chilling wind she can already feel, despite her thick coat. Aidan is either not too bothered or just oblivious, and gives her an expectant look once he ignites the motorbike.

Aidan stops the bike just outside the gates of St. Dunstan Church and helps her off before doing anything else. He takes the helmet from her and leaves it on the bike, along with his own. Naya wants to ask if he is not worried it will get stolen, but he moves away.

"You're going to tell me what's going on?"

He stops at her words, and is silent long enough for her to start getting worried.

The longer he takes to answer, the more Naya gets to scrutinize him. It is odd seeing him this nervous, almost hesitant. She has spent her life picking up on other people's anxious habits, sometimes in attempt to make hers less intimidating and more normal, other times out of boredom and on rare occasions such as this — out of fear.

She knows people tend to turn edgy when they are hiding something.

Aidan's habit is surprisingly simple — he licks his lips and narrows his eyes. She almost lets out a hysterical laugh at how banal it is, but what stops her is how resigned he looks, like he is preparing himself for something much worse and just can't summon up the energy for it.

"You needed proof," he says, slowly like it should explain everything.

"Proof of what?" she asks.

Aidan glances at her before tilting his head in the general direction of the church. He starts walking towards it, without waiting for her to catch up, which she does. It is obvious to them both that she trusts him, and now that he is finally starting to trust her too, she can't find it in her to push him on the subject.

Whatever he's hiding from her, he needs to tell her on his own terms.

He leads them through the main grounds of the church in silence, and she can see a few other visitors there. She had heard of St. Dunstan a long while ago from Julie, but can't remember for sure what she has told her about it other than how beautiful and worthy of Instagram it is.

Naya is sure that Julie has never been here, despite her love of architecture and culture. She makes a mental note to come back here with her once things have settled down.

Aidan turns a corner, causing Naya to nearly collide with him when he finally stops in front of a solid door. It looks firm and completely non-functional, and she's about to comment on it when he shoves a key in the keyhole and twists the knob.

Leaning heavily on its hinges, the door creaks open and clears out a path for them. Aidan lets her take the lead down a narrow stone stairwell and makes sure to seal the door behind them.

She wants to throw at him some cheesy line about closed spaces and serial killers, but words escape her as she takes in her new surroundings. They are right beneath the church's alter, or what's left of it anyway. Her lungs take time to adjust and she hears Aidan coughing beside her; the dust taking its toll on both of them.

"This is where your ancestors lie," he says, his voice bouncing back and it sends her body on edge. She looks closely. The ceiling is low, but most of it is cracked and it lets whatever sunlight there is outside filter through, giving the space an eerie feeling. What's worse, however, are the stone boxes that take up most of the room.

It only takes one more look to understand that it is a graveyard.

The stone the tombs are made out is plain, polished and most definitely ancient, but other than the words *Anax Demands The Best* written in dusty silver letters, there's no indication to what it is.

"What the hell is going on, Aidan?"

CHAPTER EIGHTEEN

"I knew you wouldn't believe me unless you saw it firsthand," Aidan explains, somewhat defensively, like he's protecting an act that he shouldn't have done in the first place.

Naya looks again at the tombstones. The names scattered there don't ring any bells and, despite not knowing her grandparents on either side personally, she's sure he doesn't mean them.

"Who are my ancestors?" she asks.

Aidan looks at her, and his eyes look different. In the sheer light of the place, he can't wear his mask anymore. He looks tired and completely drained, and Naya is not eager to know what is causing this.

The crypt is too quiet without any of them talking, and though silence is a mandatory part of a burial ground, there's nothing comforting about it. The spell of their last few meetings was broken the moment Aidan opened the door to this place, and Naya can't be certain of the cause for it.

"Have you heard of Goddess Gaia?"

The name sounds familiar, even if she's not sure she can connect the dots just yet. It does, however, manages to strike a cord within her, even if she's not sure with what to associate the feeling.

She knows Aidan is close to telling her the truth, and his approach feels much softer and safer than Joshua's. He doesn't leave her much time to compare, as he resumes talking, turning away to look at the tombs.

"Gaia was the creator of this world in Greek mythology," he starts in a somber voice. "Alongside the other initial gods, she basically ruled the world and all that was alive belonged to her. Some would say that she lent life to this world, and when life forms end… they return to her."

He gazes briefly at her Star of David necklace and then sighs, looking back at the tombstones. "It's the equivalent of '*for dust thou art, and unto dust shall thou return*', in a way. But Gaia is gone now, so we don't really know what happens at the end of life form."

"I don't understand how this connects to me," she says, folding her arms.

"You're not here for a history lesson about life in general, Naya, you're here to learn about your heritage." His words are short, well-rehearsed and unkind; it's a juxtaposition to everything he has been so far. "Gaia created a ritual before she perished, and with it, she gave a portion of her blood to a female human, in the hope she would continue her legacy. Since Gaia created this world, she has the ability to change it and, while the version of the story has changed quite a lot during the course of history, in its core it remains the same. They who succeed in bringing her, the goddess, back to life, get to dictate the way of the world, and all that it entails... And all they need in order to do this, is to use Gaia's blood, and in extension — your blood."

"What?"

"Please don't tell me I have to repeat this monologue again."

She really tries to form a coherent sentence which would explain what is going on in her mind. However, nothing comes out, and she knows she must look comical opening and closing her mouth again and again. Her thoughts are so disorganised that she can't even make sense of what he is saying in her own mind.

Aidan seems to brave it, and offers her a smile. "I know it's a lot to take it—"

"A lot to take in?" she repeats, the words themselves tasting odd on her tongue. "This isn't a lot to take in, it's bloody impossible! You're saying I share blood with a Greek goddess. That is insane, you're insane! I'm the most normal person there is, honestly, and I just..."

She trails off; her rambling dying when she understands there's no rational explanation to everything that is happening, and there is a small part of her that is terrified that he is right. Her words bounce back, echoing themselves, and she feels so detached from the situation.

Aidan lets her take it out on him, and once he's sure she's done, he speaks again. "You can't trust anyone else, Naya. There are people out there looking to get close to you to get your blood, and we can't let them have it."

"People like who?" Naya dares asking, even if she's not sure she even wants to know the answer.

"You remember these people in Covent Garden? They're the disciples of Joshua Adams."

"Joshua Adams, the renowned Seismology expert? The one I'm working for?" She is doubtful, and she knows Aidan can't really blame her. Still, he's patient enough for now.

"It's bullshit, Naya. Anyone can forge papers to apply to some rule," he says. "Joshua Adams and the rest of his followers — they're after your blood. They are looking to destroy the world and create a new one using Gaia's powers — the same powers that were used to form this world out of the void that was Chaos."

The sincerity written on his face is alarming, and for

the longest time, he does not push her for an answer. She can't say that she believes him one hundred percent, or that it sounds even remotely logical, but it's the only explanation she has gotten, and she's not sure why anyone would go to these lengths to lie.

Still, even if the aura of safety she gets from him isn't wishful thinking, the whole prospect of belonging to an ancient bloodline of a goddess feels out of this world and unfamiliar.

Eventually her thoughts succumb to a simple "*no*," and she's happy to end it at that.

Aidan sighs, his exasperation written all over his face, before he mutters a tight, "Excuse me?"

"I refuse to believe it."

"See, that's the fun part," he says, and Naya has a feeling he actually sees the entertainment in it. "You don't have to believe me, you just have to let me do my job and trust me, and no one will get their hands on you, or your blood for that matter."

She keeps quiet for a few long moments, and Aidan makes no effort to try fill in the silence. Quite frankly, it's a comfortable one, much less charged with tension than the previous one — now that most of it is out in the open. Still, his explanation sounds insane. Her first instinct is to deny whatever he claims; maybe even question his mental health or just to get the hell out of there.

"Naya?"

She has to give it to him — he managed at least ten minutes without speaking. She nods in his direction, hoping to convey that she had, listened and was now analysing his words.

The only thing she can think, though, is how she had not drunk enough wine to start processing this information.

"*No mames*," Aidan mutters, and even without knowing Spanish she can tell she didn't just think the words. "Maybe we can work on your alcohol solving problems approach, ay?"

He tries to lighten the situation for her, but it doesn't work. She's still thinking of his words and the tombstones, the whole Joshua affair and the fact that the Greek mythology might actually exist.

Naya glances at the tombs again, and the words on the stone make as much sense as the words that came out of his mouth. She has to consider why he would lie to her, or how he could have actually come up with such an elaborate lie, if he wasn't telling the truth.

"What is Anax?"

Aidan doesn't hesitate with his answer, and when he does, there is a spark of honour and pride. "Anax is who I am, and like so many others, we are all dedicated to the goddess offspring, which is you, and your mother, and her mother and so on. We belong to an Order that has made sure that your bloodline survives until now. So, our fates have been intertwined with one another since our birth and probably will be until we draw our final breath."

"And what is your role in all of this?" she asks.

She suddenly notices how very close they are standing, and he takes his hand in hers, as she had done last night. It makes it extremely difficult to look at anything but him, and the same tone is reflected now in his eyes. It's like his one true calling; like fate has done its thing and the only thing that matters is here and now.

"I'm your protector — your guardian, if you will."

"You'll protect me?"

She means the question to come off as light and mocking, borderline on joking, but instead turns out to be serious. There's so much that she doesn't know, so much she's still missing, and even the slightest hint of truth is giving her no real comfort — if it is even the truth. The cloud of questions above her is ever present, like an annoying buzz that she can't get rid of.

"Yes," he says quickly, cutting her train of thought. "Until death — if need be."

His hold on her hand tightens as he speaks, and when she doesn't reply, he starts leading her out of the crypt.

"What about Joshua?" she asks as they walk up the stairs. "Is he your enemy?"

"Him and his Order are our rivals, but I wouldn't go as far as saying enemies... They're different than us. They have no real rules and for people like Joshua the end goal is everything — he will stop at nothing, spare no one, to get you to sacrifice yourself for him."

Naya considers this. "This is what you meant, when you called me *Mavro*?"

Aidan smiles bitterly, like he's upset thinking back to their first meeting. "Yeah, it shouldn't come as a surprise. I have had far too many bad encounters with members from the Mavro Order..." he trails off, but Naya can read between the lines and gathers how badly these encounters went. "Once I figured out who you were, though, I was so ashamed that I had almost seriously hurt you. It's ironic how the first time we met I did the exact opposite of what I was meant to do."

It makes sense now, why Aidan had never touched her until now without her explicit permission, or why he had been so gentle with her. Every time he saw her, he probably thought back to their first meeting.

"It's alright," she tells him. She assumes that he already knows, but some things need to be said out loud.

"You can't work for Joshua anymore," Aidan says suddenly, withdrawing his hand from hers, as he moves to the door. "He's just trying to manipulate your mind and use you so you will think his cause is worth dying for."

"He said he'd tell me who I am, when I first started there..." She's unsure why she is telling him that, but it's better than to just accept things as they are. It's in her nature to defy and ask questions, even if she knows that it is futile.

"He'd probably spin a lie that comes close to the truth. That's what they do; that's who they are."

It feels much more personal than it should, so Naya tries to make a joke to bring some light into the situation. "Maybe you're the one spinning a lie to make me believe you."

The door Aidan is opening screeches loudly, and he pauses at the threshold. When he turns to look at her, she sees the hurt expression. "I've gone against everyone I know to tell you the truth, so don't think I'd use cheap manipulations to get you to trust me."

She thinks this over as they walk across the grounds of St. Dunstan and out into the side street where Aidan's motorbike is still waiting. She knows in some way, she has to believe him. It may sound insane, but what other explanation is there?

As she is about to take the helmet from the seat, her gaze moves to the main street ahead of them, and she sees the damage before it happens.

The earth is tearing itself open, and the red double decker bus is collapsing into a hole in the ground. It feels detached enough from reality to know it's a vision, or a dream of some sort, but the ruin is still there and she can't tear her eyes from it.

The screams in the street sound real enough, and so is the smoke coming out from the horizon between the buildings. Her heartbeat picks up, and she's not sure what part belongs to her anxiety and what part belongs to the real world anymore.

Then, it all stops, and there is only piercing silence.

She's not aware of much, but she is aware of Aidan's voice, slowly leading her mind out of the cloud of destruction and pain. She doesn't understand what he is saying, but she hears the hint of desperation in his voice. It's a tone that she had yet to hear him use, and he's begging her in Spanish. Naya wants to tell him she doesn't understand, but she is unable to speak.

It gets easier, after a while, and her mind relents to the sound of Aidan's pleading. She can see his hands now clearly hovering over her shoulders, but not touching them. He is speaking in English, now.

"Come on," he pleads. "Come back to me," he continues, his words so weak that she almost misses him adding, "Please, Little Bear."

Naya looks at him; her hated nickname steadies her and Aidan must see it in her eyes, because she feels him sighing with relief. Yet with the way her chest constricting, she is not sure that she is entirely out of it.

At the back of her mind, the voice is still there, the buildings and the earth are still collapsing and her world is still black.

"*Respira*," he says over and over again, and she's not familiar with the word. He must have done it by mistake, since he switches to English at some point. "Breathe with me," she hears him say, and she forces herself to do as he asks. He makes a show of breathing, forcing her to stay in sync with him.

She knows what happened, but she's surprised he knows how to handle it.

Her heartbeat slows down, and she breathes properly without his guidance. He takes a deep breath and smiles, and it's a tentative one, almost shy. In the haze of her anxiety, she allows herself to think it's a nice smile.

"Can I touch you?" he asks. It's an innocent question, but what throws her off is the consideration. Most people don't know how to react after an attack, and they think providing physical comfort helps. It does, maybe, to some people, but Naya only draws comfort from it when its done by one of her close friends.

The fact that Aidan is asking, means he knows, and is thoughtful enough to act on it.

She nods, and Aidan puts his hands on her shoulders, just at the point, where her neck meets her shoulders, and squeezes. It's the most intimate gesture they have shared, when he doesn't push for anything more, it plays on a different cord in her heart.

She doesn't tell him what she saw, and he doesn't ask.

CHAPTER NINETEEN

Aidan doesn't say anything on the way to Naya's place. She supposes he can't talk much with a helmet and over the wind, especially considering how he speeds through London's streets, but she can feel how tense he is, and it puts her even more on edge.

It's always like this — the first time someone experiences her anxiety attack. She knows by now that most people don't really know how to respond, but it doesn't leave her unaffected. She usually feels hurt, even if they can't really help it and even when she knows she would have reacted in the same way.

But Aidan seems different, in that regard, so she knows it's just her insecurity showing.

Before she can think any longer, he parks the motorbike by the side of her building and helps her to the pavement. She is unsure how to proceed from here, so she just takes off her helmet and hands it back to him.

Aidan takes off his helmet and shakes his head. "It's for you," he says and puts his own helmet on the bike's handlebars as he turns it off. Then, he dismounts and looks at her. "About before—"

"It's fine," she tries to reassure both of them. "It happens."

People don't understand, she repeats in her mind, people don't realise how delicate and how serious it is... They brush it aside, sometimes. She doesn't have the energy to explain though.

"It happens?" he repeats.

Why she needs to state the obvious is beyond her. "Yeah, I've got anxiety, so sometimes things are too hard and—"

"That wasn't an anxiety attack," Aidan cuts her off. He leans back on the bike and folds his arms.

She's left speechless; Aidan sounds so adamant that she thinks back to it. Sometimes, her mind blacks out whatever happened and she would have no recollection of what started the attack or how she felt during, but she was told that was natural. Nevertheless, his reaction is slightly different.

It makes her try to think back, and she sees the ruin and destruction again. The words are out of her mouth before registering if she wants to say them. "I have a wild imagination, and I dream and see things that aren't really happening, and really, it's fine, I just don't want to be medicated so…"

Aidan doesn't look at her the way other people would look at her after saying such things. In fact, he does not doubt what she is saying. His stare is pointed, but the slight confusion she sees turning into anger, is not directed at her.

"You need to stop working for Joshua Adams, Naya."

She has never seen him more serious, and it scares her, just a tad.

"Let me do my job," he asks. "I'll tell you everything you want to know, I swear, but you need to stop working for him."

"Okay," she responds weakly, and if truth be told, she had already made the decision on their way home.

"Promise me."

Naya nods, and he holds out his hand for her to take. It's thoughtful, once again — the touch is there if she wants it. "I promise," she says and takes his hand.

"Good," he smiles, and the anger in his eyes settles a bit. "I'll pick you up tomorrow. There is someone who wants to meet you."

She knows Aidan won't volunteer any more information on the subject, and she feels mentally drained as it is, so she just nods and bids him goodbye, moving away out of the cold and into the warmth of the building.

Julie and the twins are both there when she steps past the front door, and she collapses right next to Logan with a sigh. She doesn't beat around the bush, telling them immediately everything that happened.

"That's insane," Lucas is, unsurprisingly, the first to comment.

Naya has to agree with that.

"Are you sure he's telling the truth?" Logan wonders.

"Why would he lie?" Julie asks. Ever the pensive one, Julie knows, like Naya, that there is no real reason why anyone would come up with such an elaborate and unbelievable lie just to gain someone's trust.

Julie also knows that, unlike Joshua, Naya already trusts Aidan.

Lucas scoffs. "So what? Are we supposed to believe mythical gods exist just because some arse said so?"

Julie decides to ignore him, and turns to Naya. "Are you going to do what he asked? Stop working for Joshua?"

"I guess. Even if he hasn't offered to tell me everything, Joshua is…"

She doesn't need to carry on. Somehow, they all know the word she is looking for. They all know that, one way or another, working with Joshua will only end badly, and while the idea was convenient and somewhat easy, it will lead her into trouble.

At least she knows that Aidan is looking out for her, since he did save her.

It's Logan who changes the subject as to how they are going to celebrate Christmas and Hanukkah, and Naya gets into the whole festive spirit for December quite easily.

The next day starts with a phone call at five in the morning, and Naya answers, half asleep. She swears that she will hit Aidan the next time she sees him, even if only for the audacity to laugh at her sleepy tone.

"Rise and shine, Little Bear, we have another field trip, so I'll be at your place in ten."

He hangs up, and Naya looks at her phone to make sure she hadn't imagined the whole thing. The number she saved as *Aidan Stalker* is the last incoming phone call, and indeed occured for not more than ten seconds.

She would be lying to herself if she says that she is not even slightly curious and, that in itself, is enough to get her out of bed and into decent clothes in the eight and something minutes remaining. Her phone pings with an incoming text precisely ten minutes after he hung up, so she gathers her coat and helmet and goes out the front door, as quietly as she can.

Aidan is waiting patiently in the street where he was not more than twelve hours ago, and looks wide awake considering the early hour.

"Not a morning person, then?"

Naya makes a face and shakes her head.

"I didn't think you were."

"I'm an all-day type of person," he replies easily. "Though I really hate how it's still dark till around eight in the morning. You really have the worst days here."

"Seriously?"

"Back home we have sun at seven in the morning in the winter, like any other normal country."

"You must have great use for that one hour's difference."

Aidan chuckles. "Well, there are great many activities for mornings," he says and laughs at the look Naya gives him. "Come on, we don't wanna be late."

Already used to the way Aidan puts his helmet on and ignites the motorbike, Naya does her part and uses his arm for balance as she swings her leg over the vehicle. He must sense when she's settled, since he takes off down the empty street.

It's not a long drive, and Naya recognises the place immediately. They're right next to Regents Park, but what surprises her is that he parks the bike not far from Regents Park Barracks. As he helps her off the bike, she wonders out loud why they're coming to the military.

"We're not going to visit your military. We are going to see mine."

Naya looks at him, waiting for clarification, but it doesn't come willingly. Aidan leads her through a narrow alley and into the back of the street, and only when they're off the street does he speak again.

"Remember I told you about my Order? About Anax?"

Naya nods when she understands he's waiting.

"Our Order is ancient. It was formed a long time ago, and lately we've sort of... well, we took over the barracks at the beginning of the century. Now they belong to us, but we can't really have just anyone know about it, so..."

Without giving her enough time to process anything, he resumes walking. His explanation feels too rushed, like he wants to tell the truth but doesn't have the time to go into extreme details. She supposes it makes sense, since he said they were meeting someone.

They stop before a metal door and once again Aidan takes out a key to open it. "Come on," he says, once it's open. "We're almost late as it is."

Naya hurries after him, and finds herself in a small hallway, almost as narrow as the alley they were just in. Suddenly Aidan stops in his tracks. "Also, we're technically not supposed to be here, so keep it down."

Naya wants to tell him she wasn't about to make a commotion, when they cross the hallway and step into a hall.

There's not much else to call it, since the place is huge, with white marble floors and walls decorated with tasteful arts and statues, all dedicated to Greek mythology, adding another layer to Aidan's story.

Even at half past five in the morning, the hall is bustling, filled with people scattered everywhere, going in one room and out the next. Aidan holds her close by, clearly anxious about losing her in the crowd, as well as worrying about being discovered. She wonders for a short moment who she's about to meet that demands such secrecy, but that thought is disrupted as soon as her companion tears her away from the hall and into a different room.

"Be quiet," Aidan hisses softly before she even thinks of opening her mouth to protest.

As on cue, she hears hurried footsteps stump over the marble floor in the main hall and shouts, of what seems to be orders, to get out of the way by people she can only assume are soldiers.

"Remember how I said we're not supposed to be here?" Aidan says, his mouth right by her ear as he allows her to take a look outside. "He is why."

Even with her short stature she can see the man he's talking about. The aura in the hall ten-fold more tense than it was when she was crossing it. The members of The Order divide themselves into two parts, giving way for the tall man to pass by.

In awe, people move out of his way, though Naya can't tell whether they do it out of fear or out of total respect. He looks oddly familiar, and it takes a few seconds to recognise him. He looks slightly different than he did when he came into her father's shop, but it's unmistakably him. His name is on the tip of her tongue, though, so she can't really ask Aidan about it.

As soon as the man leaves, Aidan resumes walking, past another room, leading up a staircase. Naya counts three whole floors and feels slightly jealous that he is not breathing even slightly as much as she is. Eventually he slows down and knocks on a door.

The door opens and in its way, stands a young woman, probably around Naya's age and with a slightly darker complexion than Aidan's. She looks as elegant as Naya hopes to one day. She reminds Naya of Addison, Officer Merton's friend. The woman is wearing a suit that sits just right, with matching heels and short curly black hair that frames her face. She folds her arms, as she looks at Aidan.

"I hope you know what you're doing," she says.

"He is the one who asked for it — not me." Aidan, in his defence, looks calmer than Naya assumes he would be after such an accusation. Even without knowing what they're talking about, she feels the tension there.

"Naya, meet Mickayla, she's... well, she works with us."

"Nice to meet you," Mickayla says, shaking Naya's outstretched hand. Naya is pleased to see that Mickayla's antagonism is solely towards Aidan, and almost tells him such as Mickayla moves away and they go inside.

As they enter the office, Naya can see that it overlooks the hall they were just in. She tries to stay at the back of the room to prevent being seen.

"It's quite alright — it's a one-way window," someone says, and Naya turns to see another man, extremely pale with blonde hair, in a three-piece suit, to match the elegance Mickayla portrays. Something about him looks familiar, even if Naya can't place the memory just right. He holds himself in the same manner Aidan does, and she wonders if it's something about The Order that forces them to behave like that.

Naya is free to move about the room, but she stays rooted to her place as the stranger moves closer.

"George Hastings," he introduces himself with the same casual handshake Mickayla used. "I've been waiting to meet you for quite some time. Aidan here has been going on and on about you."

Aidan scoffs and Mickayla smirks, and that's the only indication she gets it's probably true.

"You can leave us," he speaks to Aidan, who seems hesitant to follow his order. Mickayla moves to leave, but waits for Aidan at the door. George doesn't look mad, and his gaze is indifferent as he looks at Aidan.

"We're just going to talk," he insists, and it does the trick. Aidan looks briefly at her, ducks his head in a manner she doesn't quite understand and then he does as he was told.

"I must say I didn't think you'd come," George says and moves to stand with his back to her. It gives her time to examine his office, and she's surprised to find such a lack of personality in it. It's bland, with white walls and pale floorboards; she can't help but compare it to Joshua's, which seems much more lived in and well kept. This room looks temporary, like it wasn't meant for this purpose.

But the one-sided window behind his desk must mean it serves as a watchful position onto The Order's main hall, and she can't help but wonder who's watching whom.

"Aidan didn't leave me much of a choice," she finds herself saying.

The blonde chuckles. "Yes, I don't suppose he did. That is his role, after all."

"To drag me to places I don't want to be in? Great."

She knows she has said the wrong thing by the way he abruptly turns round to look at her. Then he raises his head slightly, and arches his left eyebrow, calculating his words. The gesture strikes her as familiar as well, but she doesn't know how to pinpoint it.

"He is a hunter," he says, as a matter of fact, like she should know what he's talking about.

Nothing about The Order makes sense, and she can't tell whether she's fine with it. She doesn't understand the roles and obligations, and has yet to form a solid opinion about her involvement in it all.

"Why am I here?" She chooses the easiest question.

"I'm looking to be your ally," he says slowly. "You remind me of Kaia, you know. Both of you have the same stubborn nature and almost the exact same glare when you have no idea what's going on."

She almost doesn't catch the way his mouth curls in a bitter smile, before he covers it up.

"And let's not forget you both have a terrible taste in men — though personally, I am inclined to agree with you. Nevertheless, I know you won't be easy to convince, so I offer you whatever help I can give you in the hope that you will learn to trust me and rely on me."

And then it hits her that the man before her shares the same features and movements as her father. George somehow knows both of her parents, and that may be the closest thing to the whole truth that she will get.

"Why?"

"It's a jungle out there, surely you've noticed. And as much as I appreciate my place here, The Order's interests don't correlate with mine."

It's a convenient truth if she ever heard one. "What are The Order's interests, then?" she asks.

George smiles fondly, and shrugs. "They're irrelevant, I'm afraid. Just the musing of old men and women who haven't advanced with the rest of the world. I don't align myself with them; as dangerous as it may be — my loyalties lie elsewhere."

With you, he means to say, but perhaps doesn't trust this place enough to say it out loud.

"And Aidan?"

"Aidan is a difficult nut to crack, I'm sure you know. But he'll get there, hopefully with your help."

By the looks of it, she is not going to get much out of him, at least not now. But she also knows she can steer the conversation to a safer topic, since the whole Aidan subject is out of the question.

She finally remembers the name of the person from her father's shop, and she knows it's a good thing to ask about. "You know someone named Walter?"

The blonde smiles again, but it's strained and forced. "Yes," he simply says, not offering more.

"He came by to see my dad a couple of weeks ago," she continues, folding her arms. She had been right to think Walter was a part of her father's past. "What do you know about it?"

"Probably as much as you do," George replies and turns to sit on one of the chairs in the room. "Although I would imagine he meant it as a threat."

Naya only arches her brow at him, silently asking for more information.

"It's a show of strength. If I had to guess, I'd say he was looking to make it known you were out in the open and, as they say — fair game."

Naya's not liking this one bit, so she tries to ask about her father instead. "How do you know my dad?"

"We go way back," he answers, and it's a convenient truth once more; not quite right, not quite wrong. "We used to be friends, I guess, but that went sour a long time ago."

Naya thinks about it. There's no way this man made her come all this way just for alliance. There must be something more there, even if he's not saying it himself. However, it doesn't mean she can't use it, and if he used to know Dom, it means they're somehow connected, and she can play that to her advantage.

The first thing that comes to her mind is the wooden box in her old bedroom.

"You want to prove yourself?"

George nods, but doesn't say much else.

"How about reuniting with my dad and keeping him busy for a few hours?"

Something in George's eyes light up, and Naya knows she's about to get what she wants. Even if she knows Dom's routine, there is always a chance he could show up at his flat in the middle of the day, so perhaps a visit from an old friend might help assure her at least some time there.

"I can't give you more than an hour, if he'll even be interested in seeing me."

It's enough, Naya decides, and is happy to know that with everything that is going on, she can make the best of it and shape her own way.

CHAPTER TWENTY

Naya knows talking to Joshua will prove to be a difficult thing, but she still owes it to him to tell him in person, despite Aidan and her friends insisting that she do it over the phone.

On Monday morning, she walks into his office as if her life hadn't changed over the weekend, and asks Joshua to clear up a few minutes to talk.

He doesn't seem aware of the urgency, but does as she asks.

"I've been thinking about it over the weekend," she starts, hoping to say the same thing she had rehearsed on the way over. "I think I need to quit, unfortunately… I, uh, have been considering my theory about natural disasters and have come to the realisation that I was wrong."

She knows it's wrong to lie, even to Joshua, but what else can she say?

Joshua doesn't respond for a while, and Naya thinks she should just thank him for his faith and time. By the way he looks at her though, she knows he isn't deceived by her lie.

"Think again about who you're allying yourself with, Naya," he says, and it doesn't sound like anything but solid advice. "If I were you, I would not let myself be fooled by good looks and personal charm."

The last part feels like a warning.

"I have no idea what you're talking about," she says, but it doesn't fool Joshua. She decides not to try anymore.

"Very well," he says and gestures to the door. "Do not say I didn't warn you."

Naya doesn't need to be told twice; the calmness Joshua is showing feels like the calm before the storm. She does not look back as she makes her way out of the building. Not even Theresa's disappearance troubles her anymore.

At the entrance to Bond Street Underground Station, she sees Aidan, this time without his bike, and looking less than pleased.

"Didn't we agree on you not going alone?" he asks by way of hello.

Naya rolls her eyes. "Did we?"

Aidan pulls her away from the people and into the station. "I thought I told you that he is dangerous; you shouldn't have gone to see him alone."

"Really? And you would have come in with me like a bodyguard?" Naya says, and regrets it as soon as he tries opening his mouth to respond. "It's a rhetorical question, Aidan!"

It seems to settle him, even if only for the moment. Once his body language seems to relax, Naya moves further into the station and down the stairs that lead into the ticket hall. "Where's your bike, anyways?"

"I've decided to live today as a commoner and use the tube," Aidan answers, and Naya swears that even if he would use different words, he would still sound as arrogant as royalty.

"Welcome to the real world, then."

"It's on you," Aidan is quick to joke and blame her as they move past the barriers and towards the tunnels to the tube platforms.

"Well, aren't I just a bad influence to show you how normal people live."

The train arrives as they reach the platform, and he doesn't comment even as they board it.

Naya moves to the end of the carriage, her own personal haven in any carriage she rides. There she is not affected by the cold or the mass of people. Aidan pulls her backwards, and she turns around just in time to see him shaking his head. It causes her to do a double take to see what she had missed, but the two seats are just as empty as they were couple of seconds ago, so she looks at him again, this time demanding answers.

Besides Aidan moving her to the other side and settling her down in the only empty seat next to the door, she gets no other explanations.

She folds her arms demonstratively.

He does not say anything or even look at her. Instead he surveys the train and the people in it, shifting his face methodically and Naya understands why — he's looking for escape routes, just in case.

"Don't pout, Little Bear," he says, his tone playful enough and Naya wonders if he is doing it to distract or to reassure her.

However, he escorts her all the way home, after helping her with a few errands around West Hampstead. He leaves as soon as he knows she's safe back at home, not before making her promise to tell him before she plans on going anywhere alone.

"It is only for your protection," he vows, and she gives in.

The next few days are a blur of laziness and some proper research about the Greek myths, and while she does not find much about Gaia, she does find one piece of information about a clan, devoted to her, somewhere in Greece.

It's not much, but it's a piece of something that might make her fully believe Aidan.

On Thursday, she gets a phone call from an unknown number, which turns out to be George. He assures her that he will be meeting her dad at three o'clock that afternoon.

It doesn't leave her much time to prepare, but she asks Aidan to come pick her up about half an hour before three, and is happy to know she has got a personal driver now, too.

Aidan's reaction to the address he finds himself at is somewhat comical. "You want us to break into your dad's place?"

He looks as alarmed as she has ever seen him, and double-checks the building that they are standing in front of. It's a semi-detached brick house; the colour on the outer walls as faded as it was when she was last here.

She knows she should dwell on the fact that he knows exactly where they are without her needing to spell it out for him, but George had agreed to keep Dom busy for just an hour, and their time was running out.

Besides, Aidan would probably just smirk and go on and on how it's his business to know. Naya assumes she either knows him too well or his arsenal of answers have dwindled down to only a few anticipated sentences.

She has a strong feeling it's the former.

"We're not breaking in," Naya says to ease his mind.

"I have a key. Besides, didn't you say a few days ago that things have been too settled for your taste?"

What Aidan had actually said was that they should enjoy the calm while it lasts, but it sounded way too ominous for her taste, so she paraphrases it.

"I'm pretty sure I never said that, and even if I did, it doesn't mean we should actively go and look for trouble — Naya!"

But she is not listening anymore, taking out her set of keys and turning the knob of the door to the first floor. It's just the lobby, yet it has a pretty heavy door, so she shouts at Aidan, "Hurry up before I leave you outside!"

She hears the swear word playfully directed at her and something else in Spanish, before entering and shutting the door behind him.

As quickly as she can, she makes her way up the stairs. The stillness Aidan portrays behind her should put her on edge, but it doesn't anymore. Instead, she focuses on the task at hand and leads them past the front threshold, directly into her old bedroom.

She expects Aidan to comment, even if she doesn't know what or why, but he keeps quiet.

The box is still there, and as she reaches for it, Aidan stops her. He still does not say anything, but his eyes are fixed on the initials, and she knows he can deduce who it belongs to.

"What are we doing?" he asks after a few moments.

Naya doesn't have an answer ready, since this whole thing has been instinctive, but she knows this box might contain something important, crucial even, to her heritage.

"I'm finding out who I am," she says.

"You know who you are," Aidan replies. "You don't need some box to tell you."

His words leave her weak, hitting her exactly where it hurts, despite his intention. "No," she says. "I'm an heiress to some legacy that belongs in mythology books, and it is messing me up to know that I have no idea what that even means."

Saying it out loud doesn't help her make any sense, but somehow Aidan understands. He takes the box from her shaky hands and opens it for her, directing the contents towards her.

Disappointment runs through her as she looks at the emptiness inside, and it must show on her face because Aidan looks past the lid, closing it for her.

"Naya—"

"It's fine, let's just out of here."

Truth be told, Naya had been meaning to snoop around some more, perhaps in Dom's bedroom and office, but she feels she's on the verge of crying and cannot wait to leave the flat as soon as possible.

Aidan doesn't say much else as he follows her outside, where she does the first thing she can think of, and puts her helmet on, waiting for Aidan to do the same.

He gets her clear message, and hits the road in no time. However, he does not drive back to Naya's home. Instead, she gets a front seat to London's great monuments and simply enjoys the ride.

Eventually, he stops somewhere around Big Ben, and it's his turn to lead her down the embankment to sit as close to the water as they can. He must have guessed that the water calms her down, for there is no other explanation why they are there.

Aidan sits fairly close to her, and they don't speak for the longest time. She focuses on anything she can, but after a while, she is drawn to his hands. She feels safe enough to ask, so she does.

"What is this?" She takes his left hand in hers, and while the gesture isn't meant to be intimate, her question is. She had always considered tattoos to be a silent story carved into a person skin, and while she never thought of getting one, it always interested her to know their stories.

Aidan lets her fingers graze over his tattoo, tracing the shape of the flame and the arrow coating his middle finger. He almost seems relaxed at her touch, and she finds herself at ease for making him this unguarded.

The realisation hits her instantly, and she almost draws her hand from his, if it wasn't for his next words.

"Those who formed the Anax Order were normal people who sought to help someone in dire need, but to do so they had to leave everything behind. They chose to give up their attachment to the ordinary world by fire — Prometheus's fire, to be exact."

He pauses, looking pensive as if he can see his ancestors following through their decision.

"It's a rite of passage that follows us to this very day, where we choose to devote our lives to the way of The Order, unquestionably and undoubtedly." When he stops, Naya assumes it's because the memory pains him in some way.

She murmurs to show she was listening, and then diverts the subject to what she think is a safe one. "And the arrow?"

However, this seems to have the opposite effect of what she thought, and right before he answers she sees the small twist of emotion, which bothers her even more. It almost looks like regret and guilt, but he pushes it away, not giving her a chance to examine it properly.

"It's my role in The Order. We all have one. Otherwise it would be in complete chaos."

"Hunters use arrows," she wonders, yet feeling bad for forcing him to speak about something he clearly doesn't want to tackle. "That's what George said you were."

Aidan lets out an uncommitted mumble, and she lets it go. For now.

Instead and for his benefit, she chooses a different subject. "He also said he knew my mum."

"What do you know about her?" he asks

No one has ever her that question before. Usually, when she tells people about her mother, they react with empathy or avoid the subject all together. Not Aidan though — he looks straight into her eyes.

She averts her gaze, looking at their hands still joined. "Not much," she confesses. "My dad doesn't like talking about her... It's a sore subject."

"For you too?"

Naya wonders briefly, whether he is considering this just now. Nevertheless, she answers. "Not really. I didn't know her, so it's not like I can mourn someone I never knew."

Aidan considers this, nodding after a while. "She died when you were...?"

"She killed herself," Naya corrects automatically, not even bothering to look at him to gauge his reaction. With everything that was going on, it's the least of their worries, and she reckons he'd seen and done a lot worse than talking about suicide. "When I was six months old," she adds. "I think it was something like postpartum depression. At least that's what Lara says."

"Lara?"

"Oh, The twin's mother."

Aidan doesn't reply for a few moments. Naya figures that is reasonable, since she wouldn't know what to say either. It's a delicate subject, and even if she doesn't mourn her or feel the need to be sad, it doesn't make growing up without a mother easy. She knows that Dom did his best and she will be forever grateful to the man for working hard so that she never feel like she was missing out on anything.

Lara had inserted herself into their lives seamlessly, functioning as a substitute mother during her childhood and onwards — whenever Dom was unable to. Seeing as she never had anything to compare to, she never felt like she was missing out on much.

"I barely know my father," Aidan admits. He is not looking at her anymore, but his voice is steady when he continues. "I was born out of wedlock, to a Mexican mother in the lowest rank of The Order and an American father who was probably much too important... To this day I have no idea how that even happened—"

Naya nudges him, giving him a pointed look as he turns to her. She tries to lighten up the situation.

It works, since he chuckles. However, it quickly

backfires, turning into a smirk. "Don't think of teaching me about the birds and the bees, Naya. I can teach it to you myself."

She laughs, thinking of how she had brought this on herself.

"I don't even know how they met, since my dad's pretty high up in the ranks... but they did, and he kept me a secret for about fifteen years, making sure I train to be his successor for when the role of The Hunter opened up. When I was seventeen, he shipped me off to the UK, where I started officially training for, well, you know, and that's that."

Naya doesn't have much to add. "So you haven't been back home since then?"

"In January it'll be ten years," he says. "But I'm planning on going back sometime, so that's okay."

She knows he's only saying that to try and ease the tension in the conversation and, while she appreciates the attempt, she really wishes he would wholeheartedly open up to her. She leaves it at that, laying her head on his shoulder and sighing softly.

CHAPTER TWENTY-ONE

Even after Christmas has come and gone, there is still peacefulness in the air. Naya had expected something to happen, but instead, nothing. Joshua's warning seems like a far-off dream, and even her nightmares have toned down, ever so slightly.

It's a gift she's not about to throw away and, in her mind, this makes things simpler.

Usually around this time, she would be making plans with her friends to celebrate New Year's Eve. However, Logan will be working at the hospital, giving Lucas more of a reason to complain about his brother's ungodly hours he spends at the Royal London Hospital, where he works as a nurse — and Julie had decided to go back to Manchester for the holidays, so Naya hasn't seen her since the second week of the month.

For Lucas, though, the lack of friends is more of a reason to go out and enjoy.

She waits until two days before New Year's Eve to inform Aidan of their plans. It is perfect timing — not too long before so that he would try and convince her not to go out, and not too close to the date to leave him unaware. He is invited of course, and she assumes that he will tag along, even if she hadn't thought of inviting him, which even Lucas had agreed on.

She waits until the twins leave to visit their mother and then asks Aidan to come by. When he shows up, she doesn't waste anytime telling him the news.

"We're going out to celebrate on New Year's Eve," Naya says.

Aidan looks slightly annoyed and somewhat frustrated, but that doesn't surprise her. "You really think it's a good idea going out with all those people around?"

Naya pauses, not really sure how to respond. "Why not?"

He doesn't answer immediately, but considering how thoughtful he looks, all Naya can do is to wait patiently. She knows they're very similar that way, and that is partly the reason why she is willing to endure the silence.

Eventually, Aidan sighs. "I just have a bad feeling."

"Has something happened?"

Aidan shakes his head. "No, not at all. In fact, things have quietened down with the whole Joshua situation. It's like he's hiding or something."

"Maybe he has accepted it, you know? That I chose Anax, and that you guys are protecting me."

Naya knows it's wishful thinking, and so does Aidan. "Well, it's just gonna be me and Lucas. Logan has to work and Julie's back home anyways, and if anything happens..." She lets the sentence hang there, both aware of the implications.

When Aidan nods slightly, Naya hopes his mind is at ease. Truth be told, she knows it might be a bad idea, but who's to say Joshua won't try and get to her at home or anywhere else. Celebrating New Year's in public shouldn't be different on that front.

Seeing as Aidan doesn't try to cancel her plans, he must be thinking the same thing, or he may just being respectful of her wishes.

New Year's Eve feels just like any other previous year, and Naya, in all honesty, doesn't see what Aidan was worried about. When he promises that he won't be far, and will only join them if he feels there is a threat, Naya assumes it has more to do with Lucas. In any case, she appreciates and knows that Lucas does as well.

It's close to ten at night when they squeeze their way past the bouncer to some dance bar in East London. They move past the lobby to pay for their tickets, which Lucas assured were extremely discounted, thanks to Patrick, who knows someone there. He is supposed to join them, but they don't wait for him.

Naya is happy to hang her coat up in the coat room, even if it is overpriced and sets her back a whole ten pounds, and they then move away from there to get drinks and have as good of a time as they can.

They do exactly what they were planning on doing — dancing, drinking, having a good time, even taking a few selfies to send to Julie and Logan on their group chat. The cell phone reception is horrendous, though, so they know they'll only get a response once they leave the club.

The DJ lowers the volume just for a moment to let everyone know that the countdown to midnight is happening soon, urging them to go and have some more drinks. When Naya looks at Lucas, they both laugh and go and do just that.

"Go get some nice cocktails. I gotta run to the loo," Naya says in his ear to make sure he hears her properly.

"No worries, I'll go and see if I can find Patrick here, too," Lucas replies, or at least that's what she thinks he's says — the bass from the music makes it hard to hear properly.

Naya gives him the thumbs up, and then turns to the opposite side of the dance floor, where she has already located the restrooms.

She sees the end of the queue to the ladies restroom — as usual in public places — but before she gets there, she feels something is odd.

It's a feeling she knows well, unfortunately; the sharp contrast to reality which usually signals upcoming anxiety, yet she knows that is not the case now. She remembers feeling something similar before the earthquake, and she trusts her instincts enough to recognise the signs before something goes terribly wrong.

All she needs to do is to get to Lucas, to warn him, and then get the hell out of there. It's a simple plan, and she silently keeps repeating this to keep the stress from taking over. She still has time, she hopes, but she is almost at the edge of the dance floor when she hears the commotion.

It's starts slow, like most things. Just a few people shouting and hurrying to get somewhere else, but then she hears an explosion and from that point on — it's complete chaos. People scatter all over, eager to take any form of shelter, and she can't fight the crowd to get to the bar, on the other side of the club.

The mob pushes her back against the door to the ladies' restroom, so she locates the closest exit from the club. It is an emergency exit, but it's guarded by two men in black who look alarmingly similar to the same ones that had come after her and Aidan in Covent Garden.

"Shit, shit, shit," she mutters. She doesn't know what happened, but the only logical explanation is that they are looking for her. Aidan's words ring terribly clear in her mind, now. They will stop at nothing, he had told her, and she finally sees the proof.

The other side is also blocked, as the people scramble to leave the club; their screams almost too much to bear. The only option is the room behind her. It can be either a hiding place, or an escape route, if it has a window she can squeeze through. From there, she'll need to find Aidan and get Lucas.

The restroom is decorated all in black, as is the rest of the club, but there are no windows she can see. There are four stalls, for her to check. However, she first needs to block anything that might come through the door. There's no lock on the door, which makes sense, but there's a heavy bin she can use to barricade herself in until... She is not too sure what she is waiting for, but she can't stop to think.

However, before she can do anything, the door opens and closes just enough to let someone in. She turns just in time to see Aidan standing there, his dress shirt soaking wet and a curved gash to his jaw. He has a dagger in one hand, which he shoves beneath the gap at the bottom of the door, locking them inside.

Only then does he turn to look at her; his eyebrows

raised when he realises that she is holding part of the trashcan as a weapon.

"Really?" he asks, and she lowers the metal to the ground. "I'm not sure what I should question first — your choice of weapon or your choice for a hideout."

"It's the ladies' loo," she offers as an explanation. She would have said more, but her gaze keeps focusing on his cut, now noticing the blood on his left hand. "You're hurt," she barely manages, before stretching her arm to him.

He takes a step back, colliding with the door again. "How very perceptive of you," he drawls, and she tries not to take it as a rejection.

Naya swallows the lump in her throat, firmly reminding herself that this is not the time, and folds her arms. "There are no windows here and there are two guys guarding the exit on the left. So how are we supposed to get out?"

"We fight our way out, obviously," Aidan says without a hint of hesitation as he moves across the room to gather a few paper hand towels. He wets them under the water from the tap and then wipes all the blood from his hand. It may not be the time, but if they go outside with him looking so bloody, it might set off some odd reactions.

Naya really hopes that she does not look as scared as she feels, but she knows that it is hopeless, when she sees his face soften and closes the distance between them. He extends his right hand to her, and she takes it.

"We'll get out of here, alright? It's like that night with the drunk man, okay? We're a team."

Naya nods, some semblance of assurance sneaks into her by his words and his touch. Then she remembers, "Lucas is—"

"I know, I've got someone handling it."

Naya forces herself to take a deep breath, and he moves only when she nods, giving him the all clear. He lets her go, just for a moment, to removes the dagger from the door and then takes her hand again. "On me," he says, and opens the door.

The club looks like a mess, and is suspiciously deserted. There is not a soul about, but she sees how hunched Aidan is — he is ready for battle. She tries not thinking too much — not about the gash on his cheek nor about the blood on his hand holding the weapon. As they move quietly, Naya does her best not to step on his heels or make any noise.

When Naya sees that the guards are no longer by the door, she assumes that Aidan had something to do with that. But even once they are behind the doors, outside in the somewhat fresh air, she does not say anything.

When they come to an alley Aidan hides the dagger away in the sleeve of his shirt. "Are you ready to run?"

he asks, indicating to the left. There are three men at the entrance to the alley they have walked into, but the other side is clear.

"Ready when you are," she mutters, and it's the only answer Aidan needs.

Even while running, he doesn't let go of her hand, and Naya is thankful since she doesn't think she would be able to keep up with him if he didn't drag her along. She loses count of how many streets they have run past, or if she even recognises the buildings, but she knows they can't be too far. He slows down at the sight of his bike and pulls her into another alley.

She gathers that the alley is remote enough from the club, since she can hear people in the flats above, talking and laughing aloud — blissfully unaware of what has happened. They are far enough, so she can catch her breath.

When it's just the two of them, it's easier to think. Aidan is panting with exhaustion, although less then her, but she doesn't doubt their run took a toll on him as well. After putting the dagger into the back pocket of his jeans, he rubs his neck.

Everything is still for a moment, until she really looks at him, taking in his dark jeans and tight dress shirt and all she can about is how unfair it is that he looks so good in such casual clothes.

She knows their dynamics well enough to understand that there is no room for words at the moment — there is no room for anything other than themselves.

Naya blames the alcohol for making the air between them thick and heavy; for making his presence almost unbearable. She also blames the alcohol for her shortness of breath or the way nothing matters but him.

Her mind's begging her to say something, and there are endless words on the tip of her tongue, anything to stop him from staring at her like that, but she stays quiet instead, giving him the time to examine her, silently enjoying the way his eyes cloud over as they rake over her frame.

She extends her hand out of instinct, not really sure what's she initiating, but he seems to follow her lead, taking and intertwining their fingers, all the while advancing towards her, pushing her gently to the wall. He gazes down at her, his hand hovering above her hip, and for a moment, while people outside the alley, are counting down to the new year, they snap out of it.

When he looks at her again, all resolve slips away. He grasps her thigh, making her move one hand to his forearm, and the other rests on his arm, digging into her leg like a lifeline.

She puts her hand on his, helping him drag it up her body and forcing it to find its place on her hipbone.

He responds with a sharp intake of breath, making her smile smugly.

If he notices, he doesn't say anything, and only moves closer. His forehead rests on hers, pulling her body tighter to him, and cups her neck with his thumb, briefly touching her bottom lip. He's controlling himself, she muses after a while, and there is a small part of her begging his control to slip, and for her to be the one to cause it.

She lets out a sound, somewhere between a gasp and a whine and twists her free hand in the fabric of his shirt, daring him to close the distance. Naya has no idea if the sound or her touch, has an immediate effect on him, but his hands leave her body, going instead to pin her arms to the wall, and when he looks at her again she sees the control slowly disappearing.

It's a perfect mirror to how they first met.

He waits to see what she will do, but it's not something she's willing to show.

"Midnight," he sighs out the word, as the people above them and in the street yell out *happy new year*, but it doesn't matter in the slightest.

Naya opens her mouth to respond, but the sound of a gun shot pierces the air and any magic that might have been there, disappears entirely.

The shot is coming from the street, and undoubtably

they have been wasting time when they should have been running away.

"Aidan—"

"No, I'm done running," he says, and moves to shield Naya with his body. There is only one man, holding a silver shotgun, but the threat is there, and Naya is more than happy to stay where she is and not engage.

"There's a prize on your head, Aidan Hall," the man says, and Naya sees the bald man, dressed in black, advancing. His features show no emotion, other than malice, and she has no doubt his intentions.

"It is a pretty nice head," Aidan replies, throwing his dagger to the ground. "Why don't we solve this *mano a mano?* We don't need guns."

The other man nods, seeming pretty self-assured. "Alright, *hombre*, why don't we indeed."

Aidan doesn't wait any longer and lashes out immediately. The other man, in all honestly, doesn't stand a chance and finds himself on the ground in no time, pinned down by Aidan. It's so different from how he fought the drunk man on that Friday night, and it scares her to watch him fight to do actual harm.

"Do you wanna talk about my pretty head some more before you die?"

Clearly, it's not a question Aidan is expecting an answer to. He moves his hands to the man's throat and squeezes as hard as he can, so the man under him has no air and eventually is forced to succumb.

Naya remains frozen in her place, not daring to move a muscle, even when Aidan stands and turns to look at her. It seems like he has forgotten she is there; his expression turns sour as he moves directly to the street and to his bike.

She gets the message, that they should get out of there while they still have the chance, but she's too shaky to walk quickly. Aidan catches her just before she stumbles, and uses his helmet for her safety. He helps her put it on and then get on the bike, taking them away from there, as quickly as possible.

CHAPTER TWENTY-TWO

Aidan speeds through London on the bike. Even if their pursuers have probably lost track of them, he is still going as fast as he can. Naya has no idea where they are headed, but doesn't plan on asking anytime soon.

He must feel how tense she is, because after a while he slows until he abruptly puts the brakes on and stops in the middle of the road.

Naya isn't prepared for this of course, but what worries her more is his tone when he speaks.

"Get off," he says, switching the bike off and waiting.

Naya, feeling slightly apprehensive, takes off her helmet and places it on the bike. He comes to stand by her on the pavement. Thankfully, the street still seems deserted, and she is still feeling concerned until she looks at him properly.

Everything about him sends chills down her spine. She hunches over, suddenly aware of how frightening he can be if he really wants to. The fact that he just took another man's life to spare hers, is not justifiable in her mind. For the longest time, she looks anywhere but at his face, until he turns to her, addressing the matter.

"Answer something for me," he breaks the silence, straining not to sound intimidating. "Are you afraid of me?"

She stalls, and then mutters a simple, "What?"

Aidan moves swiftly to stand a couple of centimeters closer to her. His hand hovers over her cheek, as if he was still feeling the same as he did in the alley. In order not to succumb, she has to remind herself that he murdered someone with that very hand, not more than half an hour ago.

He searches her face for something, and as she opens her mouth to answer, he sighs. "Don't you dare lie to me, Naya."

"You just killed a man," she chooses to reply instead, keeping her voice to a whisper. "Am I supposed to not have a fit?"

She sees her own thoughts reflected on his face. He can see, as she can, how different their lives are, how limited her knowledge of his world is and how for granted she takes her normal life. These thoughts had crossed her mind before, though now it is evident. How easy it is for him to kill, to play god and decide to take another man's life. His soul, his mind and his body are those of a war machine and that in itself scares both of them to death.

She's so confused.

"I see," he says.

"You expect me to just accept?" The words just spill out and she immediately regrets it. "No, wait—"

"That man would have killed you, given the chance," he spits out the words, as if the need to explain is beneath him.

It's a moral argument she can't ignore.

"And that makes it okay? That makes it alright? I'm sorry — but that's not normal, and don't give me a hard time if I'm having troubles accepting it!"

"Sorry to break it to you, but I am not normal."

It makes sense now.

She sees his soul even when he doesn't mean for her to see it. She sees the scared child they tried to train into an emotionless creature; she sees how it's not really who he is. She remembers their encounter with the drunk man, or the way he watches out for her and how he asks for permission before doing anything, and it clicks. This is what he has been conditioned into being — for her bloodline's sake.

But that's not who he is, and now is the time for her to comfort him.

In all the time they have known one another she never considered for a second the heavy burden he carries every day. He looks so miserable she can't help but cup his cheek and pull him into an embrace. His arms wrap around her torso in a blink of an eye, and just for a moment, she thinks she feels a tremor through his body.

"I'm sorry," she says. There's so much more to say, but he accepts it, and tightens his arms around her.

Naya loses track of how much time they spend standing embraced, leaving them both extremely vulnerable. For the moment, she lets herself enjoy his close proximity, despite everything that has happened.

A while later, Aidan pulls away, seeming more collected and serene than he did before.

"Where are we going?" Naya asks when he tugs her along.

"My place," he replies. "It'll be safer for you there. My team is watching your friends, but we'll get proper news in the morning. For now, we should probably rest."

Naya feels her weariness as soon as he mentions resting, and she knows she could use the protection and comfort right now.

She lets him take the lead to get back onto the bike, and soon they're driving through London again. She doesn't recognise the area, which makes sense considering how big the city is. Aidan stops the bike in front of an expensive looking building, and he holds her hand as they walk inside.

"I have a feeling you'll like my place," he says as a distraction. "I have the best view in London."

The interior reflects the outside to the point, with silver marble flooring and matching tiles on the walls. There's a sitting area with plush black satin armchairs and sofas, and a hallway that leads to where the lifts are, she assumes.

They go past the concierge, a man, in his mid-fifties, dressed in a black suit, who immediately stands up to protest.

"Mr Hall! This is unacceptable—"

Aidan dismisses the man with the gesture that reminds Naya so much of how he used to be with her, that it throws her off slightly that he can behave like that so easily.

"Yeah, yeah," he says in return, practically shutting the man up as he pulls Naya into the hallway. Somehow she had expected the concierge to have more say in the matter, but instead he sits back down like a dog being scolded. Then, she realises, the look in his eyes is more of awe than fear, as she had originally thought.

There are three lifts in the hallway, and Aidan presses the button to call one of them. One lift is already on the lobby level, and Aidan scoffs in the general direction of the concierge. "Doormen these days," he says as they step inside the lift.

Naya's not really listening though. She is trying to make sense of what could be so unacceptable; she supposes it's quite late at night, and they both looked pretty close when they arrived... Maybe he just commented on what he thought was a reoccurring thing — Aidan bringing girls home late at night. Not that it's any of her business.

"It's not just girls in general — I don't bring dates home," Aidan tells her, and she really has to work on her brain to mouth filter. She can't believe she had said it out loud.

Naya is the last person to judge his preferences and, while she knows he probably doesn't need it, she still smiles reassuringly. "I must be so special, then."

She knows she has said the right thing, because he squeezes her hand in gratitude.

The lift stops and the doors open to another identical corridor. Aidan leads her to the door on its left, and doesn't pause as he unlocks and pushes it open. They enter a narrow hallway. Aidan leads her to the left, past what she think is a cupboard of some sorts and into an open space, designated as both a kitchen and a living room.

It's spacious, but just enough so it doesn't feel tight like Naya's own flat. Although she would argue how great her flat is, considering it is home, even though it may be lacking in personality.

She's not sure what she expected when it came to Aidan's taste in furniture and decor, but this was not it. It looks like a showroom, with a black kitchen on the left and a small round dining table and chairs right next to it. The living room is the key feature, with a grey fabric corner sofa that fits just right in the space, with a matching carpet on the floor. There's even a TV — Naya is relieved to know it's almost identical to the one she and the twins splurged on — over a wooden console table.

Aidan is still behind her, so when she steps further into the room and takes in the view from the adjacent balcony, muttering, "Are you serious?", he lets out a soft laugh.

Tower Bridge, in all its mighty, is right outside; the water below as peaceful as it gets. The terrace outside the windows is wooden, with two lounge chairs just waiting to be sat in.

He wasn't kidding when he said he has the best view in London.

She must have lost track of time watching the view, because when she hears him calling her name and turns to look at him, he is holding a pile of clothes that look like pyjamas.

"These belong to my friend, Addison," he says, without her saying anything. "She keeps them here in case she needs to stay over."

"Addison? I think I met her," Naya says, the name of Officer Merton's friend still fresh in her mind. She guesses that the clothes are not her size, so she doesn't move to take them. When Aidan looks confused, she assumes it is about her meeting with Addison. "I went to see one of the officers who questioned me... Addison was there. At least, I think it was her... Red hair, really skinny, nice big brown eyes?"

Aidan nods, looking again at the pile of clothes, as he does the math in his head. "Yeah, that's her. She didn't mention meeting you, though."

Naya smiles, raising her eyebrows at his incredulous tone.

"I, uh, just meant that I thought she would have told me, not that—"

"Relax," Naya says, not taking any offence, but comforted to see him as bashful and stumbling over his words like any other person. "I think I interrupted her date, so maybe that's why she didn't say anything."

Aidan nods and waves the clothes, like he just remembered. "Let me get you something else," he says and Naya thinks there is some colour in his cheeks, when he checks out the clothes again.

He obviously didn't give it too much thought and grabbed the first thing he was able to find so she wouldn't be left alone too much.

This time he disappears for slightly longer, but giving Naya time to look around some more. Her gaze falls on a black metal shelving unit that holds books and some mementos. Looking closer, she sees two picture frames. She figures she has enough time to examine them both.

In the first one, she recognises Aidan, Addison, Mickayla and one other man whom she doesn't. They are sitting on the sofa in Aidan's flat. She moves quickly on to on to the other picture, which is clearly of Aidan, except he's a few years younger. Right right next to him is a woman in her mid thirties; they're both smiling widely, and it's the happiest she has ever seen him. The woman is tanned, but her skin is still not as dark as Aidan's. Her eyes are unmistakably similar to his, in size and colour.

"That's my mum," she hears Aidan speak, and he's right next to her. He is holding out black lounge trousers and a hoodie, which she can tell belongs to him. "This was taken the day I left for the UK."

Naya knows that he hasn't seen her since, and she's filled with sympathy for both him and his mother, who clearly loves him and had to give him up to fulfil some obligation to The Order.

"Do you have any other siblings?" she asks.

"I have a half-sister," he says. "She's turning twelve next year... She'll start her training with the Mexican Office of The Order shortly after."

"Everyone trains in your Order, then? Regardless of status and role?"

Aidan nods. "It's mandatory. Most roles in The Order go from father to son or mother to daughter, but there are exceptions, like in my case. The role I'm serving — it belonged to Walter. He's the man we saw at HQs. He never had any children, so our council decided to pick someone else... Luckily, my father's stature spoke on my behalf."

Naya nods as she processes the information. It seems that The Order is more complex than she thought, and while she has plenty of questions, it is beginning to sense now. "Twelve is awfully young," Naya comments, and by the look Aidan gives her, he understands where the conversation is leading. "Is that why you got mad when I told you my dad taught me martial arts when I turned twelve?"

"Yeah," he says, but leaves it at that.

Considering everything that has happened, everything that he has already shared with her, she lets him have his secrets, for the moment.

They stand together in silence, Naya's eyes glued to the shelves and the things it holds. Her dad always told her that there was so much to learn about a man, from his belongings, especially the ones they put on display.

Naya had learned that herself, when she moved and found out how many of the small treasures she had gathered over the years, were important enough to take with her.

Even though while she was growing up and didn't have too much, her dad still encouraged her to collect things and make her room her own.

"Addie and I..." Aidan starts, and he sounds a bit hesitant, like he's unsure whether Naya would care at all. "We're not together, or anything like that."

Naya can't think of any response that wouldn't embarrass her so she nods, a short and curt one. Did he think she was jealous, or that it bothered her? As he takes her hand in his again and looks at her, his sincerity overwhelms her.

"She's like a sister," Aidan says, and he must have misplaced Naya's stare as uncertainty if he felt he needed to clarify.

Naya only nods again, reassuring him with a smile, but she yawns and it loses all the effect it might have had. Aidan chuckles.

"You can have my bedroom. I'll sleep in the office; there's a couch there," he says.

In truth, she wants him to be as comfortable as she is, and so she suggests they share. She laughs when he raises his eyebrows and assures him that she'll be staying on her side of the bed.

Without replying, he shows her into his room so she can change into his clothes. Aidan's bedroom feels more like him than the rest of the flat. It is laden with personal items, trinkets and photos from all over, and while the high wooden bed is impressive, the thing that she looks at the most is the ancient standing mirror at the side of the room, right alongside the window.

After she has changed into his clothes, she asks him about the mirror.

"It is from the 17th century," Aidan replies, going inside another room which Naya guesses is an en suite bathroom.

"Where did you get it?"

"There's an antique shop in Kensington."

Naya traces the lines of the mirror. It's magnificent, and she had always dreamed of something like that in her own bedroom. Not that it would fit, but a girl can dream.

"I didn't think you'd be interested in antiques," she muses out loud.

Aidan chuckles, and there's a slight echo from the bathroom. "Yeah, I don't fit into that category, do I?"

She thinks for a second that maybe she offended him, by assuming and judging him as a certain type of man. But when he walks out in similar wear to hers and smiles, she knows it's alright.

The only good outcome of the night, is that she can fall asleep seeing Tower Bridge before her. Aidan must notice how it entices her, and he does nothing but turn off the lights and climb into bed next to her.

She should be surprised how relaxed she feels about sharing a bed with him, and instead is happy about how at home she feels.

Naya doesn't remember the dream, or what causes her heartbeat to race, but she feels her distress.

It floats away at the touch of warmth against her flushed forehead, and the softness of it makes her smile obliviously. Then the warmth leaves her, and she struggles for breath as the fake reality disappears and her mind's on high alert, obsessively looking for the next danger.

"Naya," she hears Aidan's voice, once again it manages to pull her back from the abyss. He hovers above her, his silhouette clear even through the darkness of his room. She is trying to piece together the information that separates the nightmare from reality.

"You're alright," he says, and it should be funny that he sounds more relieved than her, but instead it helps her mind free itself from what happened and focus on Aidan instead.

When he looks at her, she is not quite sure how to interpret it at first. It comes after a while, in the shape of moving, piercing eyes.

He is scrutinizing her, lingering on the bluish skin below her eyes, which is the only physical evidence that sometimes she forces herself to stay awake to avoid the nightmares. Only when he looks at her hands, does she realise that her fists are clenched so tightly, she is harming herself.

She doesn't release the pressure until his own hands move to glide over them, silently asking her to let go.

Aidan doesn't say anything, and she knows it's because, just like her, he sometimes is also unable to use words properly. He acts instead, and that probably works better for him than for Naya. He pushes her slightly to make room, and lies down closer to her, allowing her to take comfort from how close they are, yet without sending the wrong message.

Now that he is so close to her, looking at the ceiling, she can evaluate him. His shoulders are fixed, and his arms look stiff, like he is so completely out of his element and it is making him visibly uncomfortable.

She takes her hand closest to him and moves it to hold his, looking at their hands, because she knows he will look her way, looking for answers. She can't face him, which he seems to understand. He simply accepts the gesture, intertwining their fingers and pressing their hands together.

Naya is relieved when he doesn't push her for answers, and just finds herself basking in their closeness. Nothing about the situation makes her think that he doesn't care enough to ask, but she can't seem to stop herself from finally meeting his stare.

As she turns to face him, his grip on her hand tightens and it takes her a few long moments to figure out that he is frowning — not because of her though. It looks like guilt which he wipes away, before smiling at her.

"Go back to sleep," he suggests, weakly.

It almost bothers her how well he knows her and sees the question in her eyes. She can only return the courtesy and silently does what she is told, closing her eyes and willing for sleep to capture her.

CHAPTER TWENTY-THREE

It's a loud bang that wakes Naya next; Once she has awakened properly, she associates the sound with pounding on the front door of the flat.

"For fuck's sake," she hears Aidan mutter from next to her and, without even opening her eyes, she can tell they had moved closer together during the night. He groans and gets up, moving slowly not to disturb Naya.

Aidan leaves the bedroom door open, giving her a direct view to the kitchen area, with is how small the hallway by the entrance is. Aidan's sluggish movements in the early morning seeming how human he suddenly looks, almost make her smile. But the serenity ends when he opens the door and almost gets tackled by another man. Something tells Naya to stay put, so she just watches as Aidan pushes back the man.

"What the fuck, Nate!" he almost shouts — all thoughts of Naya forgotten.

"Show me yours." The man demands, shoving a necklace in front of Aidan's face. Naya can't see much from the bedroom, and it looks like a simple silver coin, but it clearly holds significance to the two men.

Aidan's silence gives her time to examine the other man. From what she can see, he has brown hair and is almost as tall as Aidan with a similar body shape. If it wasn't for the striking differences in their facial features and the fact that the newcomer's skin tone is similar to Naya's, she may have mistaken him for a relative of Aidan.

He is the person she didn't recognise from the photo in Aidan's living room.

Neither of them say anything for the longest of time, until Aidan reluctantly gives in to his request and reaches under his T-shirt, pulling out a similar necklace. He waits for the man's sigh of relief, before putting it back where it belongs.

"Do we need to address your trust issues, Nathan?"

The man, Nathan, holds his head in his hands which Naya can only identify as frustration. They stay in the hallway, as Aidan gives him time to compose himself.

It can't be more than a minute before Nathan throws another necklace in Aidan's direction. Effortlessly, Aidan catches it and surveys it almost methodically, as if he can find the answer just by staring.

"This was found at the club."

"Who—"

"I don't know. I've already checked with Addie and Mickey. It's not theirs. We have to do a sweep of our teams."

Aidan goes silent again, and she hears his footsteps as he moves to close the bedroom door. She can still hear him as he says, "What the fuck happened last night?"

She's thankful Aidan doesn't know she's awake, since she doubts he would have asked such a question otherwise.

"I don't know," Nathan says. "One minute everything was fine, Addie and Micky were at the club and the next I get a call from them saying it is under attack and then you text to tell me that Naya — where is she, by the way?"

Aidan probably points towards the bedroom, but Naya can't see them anymore so she can't be sure. She does hear Nathan's very audible sigh.

"Are you bloody kidding me?" Nathan sounds angry, though Naya has no idea why.

"Calm down, *cabron*, we were literally just sleeping."

Nathan sighs again and Naya hears him walking around the flat, heading most likely to the living room. She can no longer hear him, since he's too far away, but there's no time to ponder over what he said because the door opens and she feels the bed dip down as Aidan sits next to her.

She opens her eyes, and if he knew that she had already been awake, he doesn't say anything about it.

"Morning," he says after she blinks a few times. "Figured it was time to wake you up," he adds. "I have someone over. He's, uh, a friend of the cause, in a way."

Aidan hesitates on how to call Nathan, but Naya doesn't think too much of it. She gets up and tries to fix up her hair as much as possible, causing Aidan to chuckle, and then they both join Nathan in the living room.

When Aidan introduces them, Naya politely shakes the other man's hand.

"Unfortunately I'm the bearer of bad news," he tells her when she sits down on the sofa next to Aidan. He doesn't wait for confirmation or anything else to continue. "Your friends are fine, but Lucas is in the hospital."

"What happened?" Naya's voice comes out in choked breaths.

"We don't really know," Nathan admits. "The moment the shit hit the fan, Addison was tasked with finding him... But she couldn't, not with the amount of people there. It was only later that she located him. Apparently someone took him to the hospital where his brother works."

Naya lets the information sink it, though she's not sure how to categorise her feelings. Once she is honest with herself, she knows it is guilt she is feeling. The idea to go out wasn't entirely hers, but she should have listened to Aidan when he said he thought it was a bad idea.

She wonders who knew to take Lucas to the same hospital where Logan works, since it was clearly not one of them. It doesn't seem random, either, considering there are emergency rooms much closer than Whitechapel.

"It wasn't your fault," Aidan says, as if he is reading her mind. Naya assumes that the emotion is all over her face.

"And he's fine, for the most part," Nathan adds.

"For the most part?" Naya echoes.

"I think he twisted his leg, but he's fine."

Before Naya can open her mouth to argue, Aidan steps in. "I can take you to see him."

It sounds like a smart idea, and after Naya agrees, they're out the door in no time. The drive there doesn't take more than ten minutes, especially at half past six in the morning, but Naya's not paying much attention.

Aidan drops her off at the entrance and tells her he'll be right there when she's done. Naya agrees with him about going in alone.

Her anxiety starts acting out, and she feels her fingertips beginning to shake as she approaches the front desk to ask for Lucas. She is automatically assuming the worst, even though she has been told what happened.

When someone calls her name, she suddenly finds herself surrounded by a warm embrace and a scent she is very familiar with and which never fails to calm her instantly. Lara's hugs are the closest thing she has to a mother's love, and even though she knows that Lara might be as upset as her, it doesn't stop her from crumbling down in a broken cry.

"I'm so sorry," Naya mumbles over and over again, and all Lara can do is shush her.

"Lucas is alright, sweetheart." Lara lets her know as calmly as she can, and Naya wants to hit something because it pains her that Lara should even need to comfort her when it's all her fault. "You didn't know," Lara says after a few more sobs from Naya, holding her at arms length to wipe away her tears.

There is no doubting that Lara is the twins mother; They all have the same sandy-blonde hair, with the same face and round hazel eyes. The only difference is their height — Lara is much shorter, almost Naya's height, and she's curvier too.

"Mum, Naya." It is Logan's voice this time, and he's just leaving the room next to them. It must be the first time Lara is seeing him as well, because he's still in his scrubs, and she goes to him immediately, enveloping him in the same hug. Naya might have missed it if she wasn't looking at Logan, but she is paying enough attention to see he is just as affected as she is.

They stay like this for a while, and then Naya moves to the room Logan just came out of.

"He's sleeping, Naya," Logan stops her, and she tries to hide her disappointment. "It's been a rough night, for all of us, but he's fine, just a few bruises and a twisted ankle. We'll leave him here for supervision to make sure he doesn't have a concussion too."

"Who brought him here?" Naya asks.

Logan looks at his mother, and Naya knows it's because he can't tell her much in front of Lara. It can only mean it's someone from The Order. "I don't know him, and I don't think Lucas does either, but if he shows up again I'll try to ask."

"If he shows up again?" Naya asks.

Logan chuckles. "Lucas asked him to, said he owed him a beer or something."

"Your brother is the only one who can be injured and come out of it with a date," Lara says, sounding fondly enough, even though she catches the underlining tension in the words. Naya hopes she knows it's nothing to do with Lucas's personal preferences in partners.

"You would tell me, if something—"

But Logan doesn't let her finish the sentence. "Mum, can you give us a minute?"

Lara looks at both of them suspiciously, and Naya realises that she must know there is something else going on. Lara does as Logan asks, and gives them some space.

"You can't go home," he says in a low voice, so only they can hear. "Aidan's friend, Addison, she was here. She gave me the gist of it — they didn't come after Lucas, and they probably won't come here, either... That's why I'm trying to keep him in the hospital for as long as possible. Here, we're somewhat safe, and I gave Addison a key to the flat so she can check it for us."

Naya can only nod, the guilt eating her away, preventing her from responding properly.

"We're fine," Logan says again. "Addison will help us, if we need it. But right now, you're the priority. You're not at fault, Naya, okay?"

She thinks again about Lucas getting hurt because someone was looking for her, while she was too busy with Aidan...She should have known to go back, she should have begged Aidan to go back...

"Whatever is going on, we knew the risks; Lucas is alright, and that's what matters. But if something happens to you..."

"Thank you," she exhales, and it's not enough, but it is all she has.

"That is what family's for," he hugs her. "I can't tell you much about who brought him in, but I asked Addison. He is not one of theirs."

Naya nods in his embrace. "Why would someone from Mavro bring him?"

Logan lets her go, and shrugs. "Who knows. He didn't seem like trouble, though."

"If he comes back—"

"Yeah," Logan says. "I have exchanged numbers with Addison, so I'll keep her and you updated. Naya..." he starts, then lowers his voice again. "Don't take unnecessary risks, please. I don't want to see you here as a victim."

"Don't worry," Naya says. She's not a vengeful person and, while there's something in her pleading for justice for Lucas, she knows it won't do any of them any good. "You'll tell me, right?" she asks again. "If something happens."

Logan nods and hugs her again. It's not the comforting hug she got from Lara, but more the reassuring one that holds a promise and strength. She lets herself be absorbed in it, so when he lets her go she smiles at him, glad that they are all alright, and then goes to the entrance of the hospital.

Back at Aidan's flat, Nathan is still waiting. He is leaning back on the corner side of the sofa, looking completely drained. Naya doesn't know anything about him, but she assumes he didn't get much sleep the night before.

Aidan makes it clear Naya is part of the conversation they started earlier, and goes straight back to business.

It's a relief for Naya, especially because she knows there's not much to do other than wait and see how Lucas will recover.

She thinks of reaching out to Julie, but she really doesn't want to drag her into this as well.

"So, what do we know?" Aidan asks.

"Not much," Nathan replies. "All that I know is that they've outsmarted us." He's going out of his way to ignore Naya's presence, and speaks directly to Aidan. "They made sure we got the wrong intel. That's bloody brilliant, to be honest."

"What the hell is wrong with you?" Naya interrupts. "They put my best friend in the hospital!"

There's something about Nathan's arrogant smirk — it's infuriating. "The Mavro Order finds ones weakness and uses it to their benefit. They do the same with the trust we put in one another, like they did with you, and that's a great strategic move, even if you can't be expected to understand."

"Nate's our Spymaster," Aidan interjects before Naya gets the chance to say anything. Nathan gives him an exasperated glare. "He has got eyes and ears basically everywhere."

That explains Nathan's self-assuredness. Nathan doesn't say anything, and if he thinks it's rude or Naya doesn't need to know, he doesn't tell Aidan.

The men seem to settle things with a simple stare, and then move on with their discussion.

"Mavro had no way of knowing Naya was at the club," Aidan says.

Nathan murmurs. He sounds thoughtful as he speaks. "Yeah, we made quite an effort to make sure of that." He looks at Naya's necklace, and Naya wonders if he thinks it has something to do with it.

Aidan pieces it together aloud before Naya even has a second to process it. "Do we have a mule?"

Nathan nods. "Looks like it."

"That's fucked up," Aidan says. "Do they know?"

Naya's not sure who *they* are, but she just watches as they talk.

"I can't risk letting anyone else know," Nathan admits. "I don't think we should trust anyone right now."

"Right," Aidan says, slowly measuring his words. "So who is it, and how do we find them?"

They're silent again, and Naya is calculating the situation. Perhaps it's guilt causing her to think it, but she knows none of them would be in this place if she and Lucas hadn't insisted on going out. It's most likely the Anax enemy, and in extension — her enemy, which can only mean Joshua or someone from his Order.

She won't have anyone else getting hurt, if she can help it.

"Okay," Naya says, her expression turning solemn. "Let's find them."

The objection comes from Nathan, surprisingly. The easy "*no*" he says is final, not negotiable and straightforward.

"Why not? It's obvious that whoever they are, they want me," she shrugs. Nathan, as arrogant as he is, seems like a rational man. He must see the logic in her plan. "You can use me as bait, lure them out into the open and capture them."

Aidan sighs. She knows him well enough to know that given enough time, he'll side with her. They don't have the luxury of time, though. Nathan is the one with the least ties to her, so maybe he'll be easier to convince. Once she does that, Aidan is a sure thing.

"It's a bad plan," Nathan says after a moment of deliberation. "The amount of possibilities for it to go wrong is high, and we don't have an army here, just the two of us."

Naya's next argument is already lined up. "From what I have gathered, the two of you is enough."

It catches Nathan off guard, and Naya is happy to shut him up. She sees Aidan scratching his stubble as he considers it, and she looks at him for reassurance. "What other plan do you have? You have no idea who it is."

"It's a bad plan," Nathan insists.

Naya holds her last card and says, "But not one they'll be expecting, right?"

Aidan chuckles at that, and Nathan catches his gaze. They seem to come to the same conclusion as she had earlier, and Aidan gestures with his hands as if to say, *well, there you go,* and there's something akin to pride in his stare.

CHAPTER TWENTY-FOUR

It has just been Nathan and Naya for a long time, and it surprises her, how despite their earlier animosity, they actually work well together. They have tied all the loose ends up of the plan by the time the door to the flat opens again and Aidan steps in, placing two large paper bags in front of them on the coffee table.

In all honesty, Naya is happy to smell burgers and fries.

"I thought you would get Thai," Nathan mumbles, not taking his eyes off the notebook in his hands.

"Naya doesn't like Thai," Aidan replies as he moves to the fridge for drinks. "Didn't really see the point in going to another place."

"You don't like Thai?" Nathan refers the question to Naya, genuinely curious about that.

"Yeah, though I don't recall telling him that."

Aidan returns with two beers and one bottle of water in his hands. When Naya looks at him, he just shrugs.

"You didn't," he answers after a beat of silence. "I noticed you and your friends never order Thai, so I just assumed."

By the sound of surprise coming from Nathan, she can only guess the way Aidan pays attention isn't a given.

Naya insists on them taking a break to eat, and she uses the time to catch up with Logan again, who tells her Lucas is still recovering, but that he's fine and he is being kept there for obseravtion. Addison is there, he promises her, and the man who brought Lucas in has not shown up yet.

When she turns her attention back to Aidan and Nathan, they're in a heated discussion over the identity of the mule. They throw out some names that Naya cannot keep track of, but Nathan seems to be convinced that whoever it is, they are from his team.

It's a lot to make sense of what they mean when they say teams. Naya is trying to understand how it all works, so she inquiries out loud. "So your team is, what, your followers?"

Nathan scoffs at the question, and it's so disrespectful it makes her glare at him, as he is suddenly focusing more on coming up with something to say rather than their mission.

"My life isn't Instagram," he says, the general tone of the sentence coming out as being acceptable, except for the disdain he used for the last word. "I don't have followers or get 'likes'. I myself hand-picked the people I work with. They are meant to be ordinary and forgettable. They are not people you would look at twice at when crossing them in the street. But make no mistake, they are the best at what they do, and whoever this mule is — they will be impossible to find if they don't want to be found."

"And why's that?" she asks.

Nathan looks at her, and it's annoyingly righteous. "Because I was the one who trained them."

Naya thinks back on the words Joshua told her not so long ago. *My world has its own rules* and they are beginning to make much more sense now. It's inevitable, and Naya knows she will learn more about their world whether she wants to or not. Nothing makes this easier, and suddenly, the idea of being bait out in the open as she and Nathan had agreed, sounds less and less appealing.

She understands why Nathan didn't approve, but she also knows she can't back down, and she wants to help as much as she can.

The plan is simple. Choose ten random places in London and start a rumour that she would be at one of these places. Then mention to Nathan's inner circle of followers that she will be in one particular place unprotected and, as George called it — fair game.

That part was Nathan's idea, since they know for sure whoever the spy is, they must be working with Joshua, and so they'd be stupid not to seize an opportunity like this.

Nathan hopes he hadn't trained them too well, and that they will show up alone, if they show up at all. They are counting on the spy's arrogance, which is not ideal, but it's the best they have at the moment.

Nathan leaves Aidan and Naya to get ready, and Aidan seems as anxious as Naya, even after going over the plan a dozen times and going through all the worst case scenarios and outcomes.

Aidan hands her an earpiece, to keep in touch and to know what's going on every step of the way, but her hands are too shaky to do anything right, so he moves to help her.

"This can work from far distances," Aidan explains. "But don't go anywhere other than where we agreed."

Naya nods, letting him take the earpiece from her hand and watches silently as he plugs its cord into a small and slim radio that might appear to anyone else as her own cellphone. Wordlessly, he turns her, stopping at her back and clipping the device to her jeans. She shivers at his ghost-like touch over her lower back, at the way his fingers graze over her skin and below her shirt as he drags the cord over her back and into her ear. She holds her breath, swearing that such a mundane act shouldn't take her breath away.

"Don't worry," Aidan says, probably taking her short breaths as nerves.

"Yeah, I know," she replies. It doesn't feel like a lie. She knows they'll do whatever it takes to protect her, if it comes to that.

Aidan gently turns her around, making it difficult to look anywhere but at him. "Hey," he holds her in place, one hand steading her at the small of her back and the other at the nape of her neck. "We don't have to do this, I can tell Nate—"

"Don't worry," she returns the gesture, feeling his own anxiety. "I'll be fine. You'll be right there, won't you?" As he nods, she smiles weakly, resting both her hands on his chest and using him as a weight to stop her heart from beating so fast. "Besides, if I back out now, how will you stay this impressed?"

He chuckles and arranges her hair so it will hide the earpiece. "You probably will never stop impressing me, Naya."

The place Naya picks is the last place anyone they know would stumble into unknowingly — St.

Paul's Cathedral. It stands as a grey contrast to the uncharacteristic blue sky. London weather's tendencies to change every few minutes is a perfect mirror to Naya's own life at the moment. She can only hope it won't turn sour, whatever waits for her at the cathedral.

She makes her way inside the cathedral, her ticket in hand. There's no need to ask where she's going, the blueprint of the place is already printed in her mind whether she likes it or not.

Naya has been coming here throughout her youth, whenever she could get a chance. Then the cathedral held an appeal that has nothing to do with religion, and she would spend hours just walking around, absorbing the calmness the halls provide.

This time it is different, and she knows it. Her heart is beating a lot faster than it did the last time she climbed the two hundred and fifty seven steps, and she has no idea what to expect at the top. People rarely come here, which means the place is near empty as it is, so she assumes that whoever will come here must be the mule.

She doesn't wait for more than ten minutes, when the the person , standing at the entrance to the Whispering Gallery, makes her gasp in surprise. "Patrick?" she asks.

The gallery is built inside the doom, and so her whisper is loud enough for him to hear from where he is standing. There must be some sort of mistake, she insists on thinking.

But Patrick just walks with purpose, stopping not more than two steps away.

It's the same Patrick she knows as Lucas's best friend, with the same boyish-like charm, blue eyes and dark hair that always falls over his eyes, but most importantly — the same one who advised her to work for Joshua.

Patrick just smiles, and Naya prays to whatever deities there are out there that he has no way of hearing Aidan's voice in her ear, calling out her name in such urgency she knows something is wrong. She does a double-take at the man in front of her, calculating her chances of a physical confrontation and how best to avoid it.

"Just stay where you are," Nathan's voice says, like he can tell her will to flee is too great to overcome. "We're coming to get you."

He's extremely calm about it, or at least that's what he's trying to convey. Naya knows better; she picks up on the way his words have a sharp edge to them.

She thinks she can last at least four minutes before he calls off her bluff, because she knows without a trace of doubt that her distress is evident on her face. Nevertheless, she takes a deep breath and tries to extend that time.

"I haven't seen you in ages," she speaks clearly, pleased with herself for keeping her voice so steady. "Hope you're well?"

It didn't mean to come off as a question, but it makes him chuckle, and a big part of her makes her think she's being played.

"How've you been, Naya?"

His words roll off his tongue easily, and she understands now why Aidan was so reluctant to let her play the bait. It isn't some Order member out of control, or someone out for revenge with no real motive other than bloodlust — this is someone with a strategy, someone who has her right where he wants, and she's starting to realise the plan is going to backfire.

She's at a disadvantage, and she's alone.

"Perfect," she says instead of piecing the puzzle out loud. Her voice sounds more confident than before, a facade she wishes will work. "Aren't you supposed to be at work, though? Lucas said it was the only way for him to take time off for the holidays."

Patrick's smile fades, and something dangerous glints in his hazel eyes.

"Stop talking to him," Aidan demands in her ear, "He's unstable—"

But Patrick's voice cuts him off, and she tunes out Aidan to listen to him instead. "Well, you know, I've had a lot of earth-shattering things to do. Though I'm sure you know all about that," he pauses, and Naya swears he has spent way too much time with Lucas to learn this dramatic effect. "Don't you now, Naya?"

She wants to tell him she hates how he says her name, or that she wants to personally make sure he's punished for exploiting Lucas's kindness, but she's so sure there's something he knows that he's not telling, that she wants to outplay him.

They need solid proof, she reminds herself, and that's when she knows she needs to tip the table to her advantage. Thankfully, she's learnt a thing or two from her father.

She doesn't answer his question directly, and hopes the smile that spreads on her face looks innocent enough. "I never knew you took an interest in architecture. It's almost as if I don't know you at all."

"Goddamn it, Naya—", Aidan's furious voice sounds in her ear again, and she needs to start calculating. It should take them two minutes to get into the cathedral, and another six to move past the threshold and climb the stairs to the Gallery of Whispers.

All in all, she's got about five minutes to make him confess.

"Maybe you don't," Patrick answers, but there's something off about his tone.

Naya murmurs in silent agreement, and sits down. "Why don't you tell me a little bit about yourself then?" To emphasis her interest, she pats the seat next to her. "Just you and me. What do you say?"

He smiles, and Naya's not so sure which Patrick she's talking to — the spy or Lucas's best friend.

"I say you are playing a dangerous game, Naya."

Naya leans back, thinking that she has four minutes left now. "How is it that you have managed to stay undetected for so long? I have known Nathan for a day maybe and he doesn't strike me as someone who wouldn't notice."

Her directness catches him off guard, and he stumbles over his steps in his haste to do as she suggested and sit down. Naya just remains smiling, and crosses her legs, showing she is not a threat.

"Nate has had his attention elsewhere for a while. All I did was take advantage of that."

She nods in understanding. "I suppose that's clever." She stops for a second — three minutes left, maybe, she thinks. "What did Joshua offer you in return, Patrick?"

She doesn't know if that will make him confess, but he seems happy not having to pretend anymore, and maybe that's what he was looking for — acceptance.

"You're not mad?" he asks instead.

It doesn't take a genius to figure out what he is inquiring about, but she does her best to look as clueless as he expects her to be as she tilts her head sideways and asks, "About what?"

"Me siding with Joshua against you, against Lucas—"

"I'm not," she lies and puts her hand on his knee. It releases all the tension from his body, and she squeezes his knee with a soothing gesture. "I think Nathan is a bit upset, though, but I'm sure we can find a solution to that too."

When he speaks next, his words come in disarray, like he knows he doesn't have much time but still wants to make sense; still wants to have Naya on his side and show her his reasonings. "I'm not the first one to betray The Order, you know? There have been deserters from the Mavro Order too. There is one I know who went entirely rouge and—"

When he stops, Naya knows that just like her, he can also hear the footsteps, hurried and furious. But Patrick's eyes lock on hers. "There's so much you don't know," he lowers his tone. "You can't trust them, I—"

"It seems like I can't trust anyone anymore."

Patrick smiles, and it seems wicked, but nonetheless genuine. "It has come to my attention that you already have an autonomous ally, someone you can trust..."

He trails off, but Naya knows he's talking about George. For once, she's unhappy to see Aidan at the threshold of the gallery. He looks dishevelled, and he takes in the scene before him, giving them a few more seconds of blissful silence.

"If they do not kill me, I will gladly switch to your side."

Naya wants to say how little his word is worth. How she would not choose him as her ally even if it would make her face certain death. But she can't, because Aidan calls his name and it forces her to pull her hand away just in time for Aidan to lift the spy from his seat. Patrick is still looking into Naya's eyes, hypnotised by something that she's not sure she wants to know.

CHAPTER TWENTY-FIVE

As subtly as they can, both men force Patrick to cooperate and take him to a safe house not far from St. Paul's. The street isn't busy, as such, but she hopes they seem inconspicuous as they go. Naya goes after them, anxiously watching whatever they do, especially as they thrust him into one of the rooms in the house, that looks more like a warehouse than anything, and chain him to a chair.

Naya has to tell herself that this man isn't the Patrick she knows.

In a matter of seconds, he has shed the mask he so effortlessly put on for her and her friends. She watches closely as Aidan moves nearer to him, stepping silently like the hunter that he is, and she catches her breath as he kneels before him.

His posture is tense, and although this strikes Naya as odd, she should have made the connection that Patrick holds some sort of significance to him. So she averts her gaze to look at Nathan, who seems much more collected than his partner, but it's only when he feels her staring and turns to look back at her that she understands that he is just as agitated.

Nathan tilts his head at the door and opens his mouth to speak but is stopped by Naya's unwavering eyes and folded arms. She shakes her head to disobey his order before he even manages to spell it out, but she assumes he won't give up.

Except he does, and stands next to Aidan instead. It's a show of feat — to show her who is part of their world and who isn't, and mostly to show her where she belongs.

For once, she decides not to say anything.

Nathan seems to be content with his small victory, and circles the chained man, tugging on his bindings, to tighten them.

It is unnecessary but, once again, a demonstration of control.

Aidan speaks first, releasing the spell of silence in the room, managing to both reassure and worry Naya at the same time. "I am hoping for an honourable chat with you," he tells Patrick. "Me being such an honourable man and all, right Nate?"

His companion chuckles, and Naya visibly winces when he takes advantage of the chains behind the spy's back to bend his hands in a manner that is sure to break them. "Most of the time," Nathan replies, casually.

Naya wonders how far they are willing to take this and stares at Patrick. He shows no pain, but a grunt escapes his mouth when Aidan's tattooed hand closes around his neck.

Thinking that there must be a better way than this, she gasps unable to stop herself, drawing both Anax Order member's attention to her.

She takes a deep breath and stares at Aidan. His hand loosens around his victim's neck, but the damage is done, and she sees the red mark on Patrick's skin. Aidan doesn't look too bothered, but his eyes soften at her remorseful expression.

"We won't hurt him," Nathan promises, snapping her out of her thoughts.

"Too much." Aidan throws the words at the spy, unwilling to let Naya decide his fate.

If Naya was in that chair, she would be scared to her very core, but Patrick is calm, composed and almost serene like. She feels pity towards him — how used to this life he must be to not be remotely worried.

Then his lips curls into a smile, and he throws his head back in laughter, although it has little to do with humour and everything to do with contempt.

"And you wonder why they're keeping you in the dark," he mocks her, enjoying how her eyes trace

Aidan and Nathan's faces in search of answers. Instead of letting him continue, Nathan draws out a blade and presses it against the man's neck, efficiency shutting him up.

"Let him talk," Naya demands, challenging Nathan to do something more.

"Naya—", Aidan starts, but her glare shuts him up.

"I said, let him talk."

Patrick takes the chance he gets. "Isn't it funny, Naya, how monsters wear the same faces as humans?"

She doesn't hear anything after that; not Aidan's curses, or Nathan's threats. The only thing that is somewhat coherent is her own heart, accelerating at hearing a saying she used to hear constantly while growing up, and her throat tightens at the thought that Patrick knows the person behind it.

Unable to take it any longer, she leaves the room, needing to clear her mind.

There's a simple explanation, really, Naya keeps telling herself. Patrick must know her father somehow, but it doesn't feel like a satisfactory answer. She tries, on a hunch, to call her father, but he doesn't pick up his cellphone, so she tries his home and the shop, only to get the same result.

Uneasiness settles over her, so she turns to the only one she knows might know how to help.

She finds Nathan outside, standing guard at the building's entrance. The street is deserted, and save for the sound of a moving train not too far from where they are, it's extremely quiet. It's nighttime already, and the thick layer of fog wraps around them, almost too dense to see through. It is fitting really, and a perfect parallel to her own mind at the moment.

The man next to her doesn't spare her a second glance. She thinks that, with how silent the night is, even she would be able to hear if something were to happen.

"Aidan's inside," he breaks after a while, but other than his words, gives her no acknowledgment.

"I'm not looking for Aidan," she folds her arms, looking up at him. Up close, he looks even younger than she first thought, perhaps a couple of years older than her, and he reminds her of someone, but she can't really place who. "I was looking for you."

This piques his interest, and his gaze finally leaves its post, fixing his grey eyes on her. "Really," it should have come off as a question, but he doesn't sound too surprised.

Naya takes it as an indication to carry on. "How well do you know Patrick?"

"I don't see why it's any of your business," he replies.

"Considering I helped catch him, and considering he's manipulated me and my friends—"

"He didn't manipulate you. He had to get close to you, and he did."

"I would say that I deserve to know how well you know him."

Nathan is as stoic as ever as he looks in her direction. It looks like he's calculating the endless amount of information he knows and could probably provide her with, but then he's silent again and looks ahead, like she's not even there anymore.

Rude, but she can work with it. It's easier to think of what's at stake when he's not looking at her.

"Monsters wear the same faces as humans," she repeats Patrick's words and focuses her vision on the car parked not far from them. "My dad used to say that quite often, and as far as I know, no one else uses it on a daily basis."

She hears Nathan shifting next to her, but doesn't dare to look. "What's your point?" he asks.

"I need your help," she cuts straight to it, not even bothering with Patrick anymore. "I think Joshua's done something to my dad, or maybe he has him, or… I don't know, but the point is that I need to go and find him. I need to know he's alright."

Nathan considers it, and when he turns to look at her properly, she almost loses her resolve. It's hard asking for help, especially when she knows there's really nothing she can do without either of them, but it's even harder when he looks at her like she's mad to even be talking to him.

"Surely your father can take care of himself." He sounds so certain that she doesn't know what to make of it.

"I know he can, but Joshua's got an army, and my dad has no one but me," she says, refusing to meet his eyes because she knows she might cry, and that's the last thing she wants to do right now. "Please," she lets out the word slowly. "You have to help me."

Nathan finally agrees after deliberating with Aidan. She still doesn't understand their dynamic, but when Nathan tells Aidan he will accompany Naya to look for her father, Aidan relents quite quickly.

As previously, they fall into action easily, and it's astonishing just how well. Nathan has her covering all possible scenarios, and despite not believing a word she says, he still works hard to ensure her father's safety.

"Tell me a bit about him," Nathan says after her tenth failed attempt at calling him. "What's his routine, habits, characteristics, just about anything."

She has no idea what this has to do with anything, and almost thinks twice about the whole thing, but the words flow right of her mouth without even trying. She tells him of the small shop in Chiswick that used to belong to her mother, and about how he raised her to be independent and strong, and even about the way that every single sentence out of his mouth is calculated, deliberate and well thought of.

"It always seems like he knows something he's not telling," she concludes. "Kind of like you."

When Nathan looks at her, his features give away his reaction. His mouth twists just slightly and then his forehead creases. While she knows that he is dying to say something, he does not.

"Have you tried phoning the shop?"

Naya nods, still thinking back to how her description of her father is supposed to help. They are both silent. Nathan looks deep in thought, and Naya's mind is running wild just to keep track, so she just waits.

"What makes you think Joshua has him?"

In all honesty, Naya doesn't know. It's a hunch. Why else would Patrick say something so vividly about Dom without having some sort of agenda?

"I think it's to get me to come to him," Naya says after a while. "The last time my dad said that was when we were visiting my mum's grave at Highgate, so maybe that's a clue."

"Highgate is Mavro territory," Nathan says. "You know this is a trap, right?"

Naya had thought about it, but she was hoping she was exaggerating. "But it is a chance we are willing to take, right?"

Nathan says nothing for a while, until his cellphone pings, signalling a new incoming message. "It's Addie," he explains, even if Naya wasn't looking for answers. "I asked her to go and check your dad's flat and store…" He mumbles at the end as he looks at whatever Addison sent him, and then turns the device around so Naya can see it.

She would have rather stayed ignorant, than have seen the destruction in his shop and flat. She hopes it doesn't mean what she thinks it means, but by the grim look on Nathan's face, he too fears the worst.

He stands up abruptly and packs up his belongings. "We're going to Highgate," he says and Naya immediately collects her coat and cellphone. "But we do what I say, when I say it, and if I say we leave, you come with me, no matter what. Understood?"

Naya nods, and he leads them out without so much as a goodbye to Aidan.

Highgate Cemetery looks like the last time she saw it, except now, at half past midnight, it appears much more ethereal and eerie, both at the same time.

Nathan opens the gates, which is the first indication that they are not alone, since it's usually locked at this hour, but they continue on.

For a while, it's just the sound of their footsteps along the stone pathway. They're not hurried, yet their hearts are beating, partially in sync, as if they are walking into a trap. Naya knows it's the truth, but she fears more for her father than anyone else, and she trusts Nathan will do whatever he can to help and keep them safe.

There are shuffling sounds around them and, in a matter of seconds, they're surrounded by men carrying swords with Joshua in front of them — a clear indication of who is in command.

Nathan instinctively moves in front of Naya, so that his body is shielding her from Joshua. It's futile, since they are surrounded, but she still appreciates the attempt.

Joshua notices the gesture, but his stare quickly turns to the gun Nathan draws slowly.

"There is no need for violence here," Joshua says. "I'm just here to talk."

Nathan scoffs. "Fine. Ask them to leave, then."

There's a moment of silence, in which Joshua looks thoughtful, but eventually he orders his men away by the flick of his hand. Naya is surprised, since she didn't think Joshua would agree, but it is a good natured gesture, so she feels brave enough to ask about her father.

"Your father isn't here, Miss Tellus. I have no idea where he is, if that is what you're asking." Joshua shrugs, and as genuine as he looks, Naya doesn't truly believe him. "If I had to wager, I'd say he ran away as soon as you found out your true heritage, in fear you would learn the truth about him and his Anax Order ways."

"Stop selling her lies—" Nathan starts, but Naya stops him.

At this point, she thinks, why would Joshua lie? "My dad?" she asks.

"Oh, they didn't tell you?" It doesn't take a genius to pick up on the hinted joy or the fake wonder Joshua's voice holds. Out of the corner of her eye, she sees Nathan tense up, which only appeases the older man.

"Haven't you ever wondered about the lack of family? Why your mother died, and what your father hid from you? Surely, you have connected the pieces yourself. Kaia was the heiress to the Goddess Gaia, as are you, and Dominic was entrusted by the Anax Order for her benefit. Except... things have gone sour lately, and motives and agendas keep on changing, so to speak."

Naya had, in fact, thought about it for quite some time, but the realisation her father is part of the Anax Order, or used to be, is doubtful. What is really bothering her is how Nathan is tongue-tied, and it doesn't seem to be out of shock. The information about her father doesn't seem to be news to him.

He cannot even look at Naya.

"A long time ago, Naya," Joshua is happy to explain, "your ancestor was left for dead by the one who swore to protect her bloodline to the very end. So, she was forced to ally herself with the Anax Order, that took the same oath of loyalty to her and her kin. Except some of them couldn't resist the temptation to use her powers to create a new reality, so they separated themselves from those stubborn fools that claimed they were far more superior because they weren't after her blood."

He pauses, probably just for dramatic effect, and looks over at Nathan. "Would you rather tell her the rest, or should I?" Joshua doesn't get a response, other than Nathan's silence and audible grinding of teeth. "Didn't think you would," he says.

The man stares at Nathan, his silence proof of Nathan's defiance. Behind the storm of Joshua's eyes, Naya sense very dangerous tones. It is getting too personal between them, and the history lesson is cast aside quickly. "It's quite clever that they would send you of all people here," Joshua all but laughs at the man in front of him. "Or maybe I should say, ruthless?"

Nathan grits his teeth, and it's clear Joshua knows his weaknesses all too well. "Stay behind me, Naya," he mutters at her, hardly looking her way. To Joshua, he finally answers, "I will not hesitate to kill you, and even your summoner won't be able to help you then."

"I had no doubt that following the Anax rules was beneath you. You, who has long since forgotten those who gave you a home and shelter when you had none," Joshua speaks as if every single thing about the Anax member offends him greatly. "I wonder how long it will take for them to realise you've been itching to work against them this whole time."

Naya doesn't understand any of this, so she asks, "What are you on about?"

Joshua turns to look at his purpose of being there. He stares at Naya like she is a prize to be taken, and less than a human being. "I suppose they have not surrendered their true nature just yet."

The man's words make no sense. "Nathan?" She chooses to try her guardian.

"Of course they have not," Joshua cuts off whatever Nathan starts to say. "No, that would be far less suitable. You see, my dearest Naya, I had been true about my intentions all along, while I reckon you think I have done some things wrong by your book… They have done much worse."

"None of us have lied," Nathan says casually, his tone remaining the same, while his fingers grip his gun so hard they turn white. "We haven't hurt her friends, or used them as leverage and we haven't threatened her life."

"You may not have done all that, but you did not tell her why it was your duty to guard her."

"That's because I don't agree with it," Nathan seems to be talking to Naya more than to Joshua. He turns to look at her, and then back at the Mavro member. "This isn't show-and-tell, Adams. There's nothing you can do to change her choice."

Joshua's smile is merciful. He is looking at Nathan completely differently now, and it worries Naya just how well he replaces emotions, as if they were at his disposal to change by choice. His mouth curls upwards in pity, and she wonders what he has on Nathan to make him feel sorry for him.

"You have your reasons to disagree with your duty. That, however, does not change the motives of your partners, or those of your scared council either," Joshua says, then turns to Naya. "You see, you should have accepted my help when I first offered it to you."

Nathan cuts him off. "I swear to God, Adams—"

But Joshua isn't having it. When he stares at Naya once again, she is sure that for a moment she sees pity there, and that angers her. "God isn't here to stop either of us. The gods are not here to make us change our lives and they're not here to play the hero. We choose our own path and it is high time we choose to reshape reality, and since our goals are the same — you require her blood as well as I, why don't we work together as one?"

The revelation that her so-called protectors plan on using her blood as well is enough to throw her off-balance. The words take a long time to sink in, and by the firm posture of Nathan beside her and by how dumbfounded he is by Joshua's nerve, it is safe to assume there's truth behind it.

Joshua's game is far from over, though. He smiles wickedly at the both of them, thinking it would benefit him, and his next words to Nathan question her entire understanding. "You should be grateful to me, Nathan. If it was not for me, you would never have been reunited with your sister."

CHAPTER TWENTY-SIX

The betrayal is there. She can't deny it; she can't change the fact that Nathan's eyes are glued on Joshua, unable to look at her, proving to her beyond anything else, that Joshua is speaking the truth.

She tries catching Nathan's eye, to feel the pull of unspoken words, but then narrows her eyes at Joshua. He seems delighted to tell her the truth, and tear apart what trust she has, to show her they are unworthy of her confidence.

No one speaks. There's no need for that. Suddenly what's left unsaid between them is irrelevant, and all that remains is the betrayal. She tries not to choke over her feelings, not to feel the shortness of breath or her unsteady heart, and most of all she tries to clear the fogginess in her mind. She can feel the anxiety striking, and she knows there is no escape. She's trapped between two enemies, and she's not sure which one is worse.

"Remember what I said, Nathan," Joshua drawls, enjoying every second of it. "We're just going to talk."

Naya doesn't react, and neither does Nathan. The information is sinking in as slowly as one can expect, and she feels detached, like she's observing the scene and not really in it.

Joshua doesn't stop there, though. He seems adamant on twisting the knife. "Alas, you have already made your alliance clear, Naya. I did warn you, though, and now it's too late."

"Naya," Nathan speaks, even if he's still not looking at her.

"By all means," Joshua gestures at the direction they came from. "Take her away. Do not forget, Naya, that I gave you a chance, and now... now you need to face the consequences."

The call to flee should be refreshing, to ease her anxiety and slow everything else down, but instead her heartbeat accelerates to the maximum, leaving her no room to think or function properly. She knows she should snap out of it, order her legs to move and get the hell out of there, but it seems impossible.

Then she feels hands, a touch that is supposed to feel reassuring but instead feels hot, in complete contrast to her frozen body. She knows it's Nathan, and she can't make out the words he's saying, but she is not irrational enough to push him away.

In some sane part of her mind, she knows that he won't kill her right away, and if he can get her out, she can escape them and seek refuge somewhere else. They move quickly, Nathan pushing her forward, and she is half thankful for the fact that he is not talking to her.

By the time they reach the street, the silence is too harsh, Nathan makes sure there is no one following them. Naya comes to terms with the fact that Joshua's spy was there just to lure her here, to prove her wrong, by showing her that she has trusted the wrong people.

There's not much she can say. He did warn her, after all.

"Naya, listen to me," Nathan says; she hadn't even realised that she had begun walking away.

"No," she replies, running now instinctively.

"You need to let me explain," Nathan insists, but instead of trying to physically stop her, he just walks by her side. "This is wrong," he says when she does not answer. "You're supposed to trust us with your life, and we're supposed to protect you. Just please listen. You have to trust me—"

"I did trust you!" she exclaims, her strained voice piercing the night. "You used this trust to crush me."

"Joshua—"

"Be honest with me, then," she cuts him off again, turning around to face him. "Was he wrong? About any of it?"

Nathan huffs, sounding annoyed. "This is what he does! Joshua takes the truth and manipulates it to suit his purpose. Do not let him get into your head!"

"Was he lying? About The Order's true intent with me? About you being my brother?"

She has plenty more to confront him with, but this is enough. Nathan doesn't reply, he can't contradict anything, Naya knows it. She knows that Joshua, for all intents and purposes, is a master in deception, but even he wouldn't lie wholeheartedly.

"No," Nathan says eventually. "He wasn't, but The Order's agenda is different than ours, I swear—"

Naya can't listen to him anymore. "Don't dare lie to me," she says, and she's surprised with how lucid her voice sounds. "Patrick was right, I can't trust you either. Leave me alone, Nathan."

What shocks her more than his pained expression is how he does what she asks. He doesn't follow her when she walks away, and more than that, she hears the car door slamming angrily before she turns the corner and uses her cellphone to order a cab.

She automatically puts in the Royal London Hospital address and thankfully, despite the late hour, the cab arrives quickly, and Naya breathes deeply.

She's not even looking at the road, not really. The only thing on her mind is what the hell she has gotten herself into, and is terrified of what tomorrow will bring. The consequences of which Joshua spoke cannot bode well, and now she doesn't have anyone by her side.

The cab driver stops the car by the hospital's main entrance and, as Naya gets out, she sees the one person she had not expected to encounter anytime soon.

Aidan stands by the front door, clearly waiting for her, but Naya doesn't have the energy to face him.

"Naya—" His voice is strained, and she knows what he wants to say, but she doesn't want to hear his apologies, she doesn't need his reasons or his excuses.

She doesn't look at him, can't is more likely, but she knows she will have to soon enough. She misses the way his lips curl at the sight of her or how he hides her insecurities with a joke or two. She misses the banter between them and how he used to be a beacon of safeness for her, and she knows she is hurting because of her attachment to him.

Try as she might, she won't lie to herself that she even misses him calling her Little Bear.

But it's all been a lie, she reminds herself, and so she moves past him, not even able to talk properly, and walks into the hospital, hoping he will get the message and leave her be.

He does, and doesn't follow her in.

The nurses refuse to let her visit Lucas, and considering that it is past one in the morning, neither Lara nor Logan are there. In the end, she stops trying to convince them to show her where Lucas is.

It was been a waste of time going there, but thankfully Aidan isn't outside anymore and she can call another cab driver to take her home, hoping to get some rest.

Nothing about the dream feels different, and while Naya doesn't remember it in detail, she knows it was about her mother. It wasn't frighting like her usual nightmares, but she's still left with the feeling of complete exhaustion and despair that comes after.

Her breathing is labored, and it takes forever before she can properly exhale and inhale. Her throat is dry, and her mind is foggy with dread. She takes a moment to collect herself until she knows her limbs can function and gets out of bed. It doesn't take long for her to waddle into the kitchen, barefoot, silently rummaging through the cabinets in search of her favourite mug and camomile tea.

While the water boils, she gathers her thoughts and wonders when the last time was that she spared her mother a single second which involved emotion and not memories. It must have been when the whole thing started, when she was so fixed on solving yet another puzzle she never realised that she was walking into a trap.

She can't even be mad at anyone, she's just so tired.

The mug nearly slips from her hand as she goes back to her room, praying that Logan is still sleeping. For once, whatever deity is out there, listens to her and she escapes to her room.

Naya puts the mug on the window pane, the one that doubles as her bedside table in her too small bedroom, and focuses on the street below. There are perhaps, two cars in the street driving by and a few people here and there, and by the time the clock turns to four in the morning she has finished her tea and had enough of watching people.

Despite never having a mother to hold her when she was scared or had a nightmare, she can relate to the feeling of yearning that comes over her as she allows herself to drift in thought. But she can't understand what she feels now. The deep longing and craving to know her mother just for one small second — just to have her arms around her, holding her securely as the world revolves and moves past them. It makes her want to cry, to choke out the feeling and put it as far away as possible.

However, she has to remind herself that she can't mourn over a choice that wasn't her own. The quietness of the night makes everything worse for her, like a thick blanket that swallows her — nothing good ever comes out of the darkness, and she forces herself to go back to sleep.

Morning comes with the slamming of the front door, and Naya is sure Logan doesn't even know she's there to keep the noise to the bare minimum. She knows she should text him, see how everything is, but at this point she's more afraid to involve anyone.

The incoming cellphone call makes her jump, but she relaxes a bit when she sees that it is just Julie.

"Hey, Jules," she clears her throat so it doesn't sound like she was sleeping.

"Julie can't come to the phone," the feminine voice that answers her doesn't come close to sounding like Julie, and Naya's heartbeat picks up again. "I'm afraid Mr. Adams had stated there will be consequences, and here they are."

The voice rings a bell, and Naya is filled with the need for revenge. "Theresa," she says, "I swear, if you touch her—"

Theresa just laughs, but it's a mocking one that sounds more like a choke than anything else. "You and what army, Naya? You're all alone."

Naya doesn't answer, because she knows she doesn't have leverage.

"You have twenty-four hours to come to us, or the girl dies." Theresa hangs up, and Naya is left, unmoving, with the cellphone still by her ear.

Her mind is racing in every direction, from the words Joshua spoke, to the threat Theresa clearly confirmed and to how she is, in fact, on her own, and what she can do. She doesn't even know how and where to find them, and when she tries Julie's phone again, it is disconnected.

Suddenly Patrick's words ring like an echo in her mind — an *autonomous ally*, he had said. She jumps out her bed to put some decent clothes on, knowing each and every second counts.

On her way out, she dials the number George gave her, telling her it's for emergencies only. When he gives her an address as soon as he picks up, she guesses he already knows what has happened.

The address is in Notting Hill. She can't risk the time it'll take on the underground, so she takes another cab, hoping the streets won't be too busy. She asks the cab driver to go as fast as he can, since it's an emergency.

Mickayla's at the door waiting by the time Naya gets out of the cab, and while Naya isn't thrilled to see another Order member there, she has a feeling that Mickayla is more aligned with George than the rest.

Naya would have been happy to observe the architecture of the place, but Mickayla is leading her through the corridors and into a well-spaced living room and so she is left with taking in the brown wallpaper and wooden floors. The room is much more personal than George's office back at The Order's headquarters, with a spacious sofa and two armchairs in front of his great oak table. George gets up from his own chair at the other side of the table, and looks at her.

"How are you, Naya?" he asks, seeming genuine enough.

"You said your interests aren't the same as The Order's," Naya cuts straight to the point. "You said you wanted to be my ally, despite The Order."

"Correct," George says. "The matter is still the same, Naya."

"Help me, then. Joshua has taken Julie, and I have less than a day to find her, I have no idea where she is, and—"

However, George doesn't let her finish the sentence. "I can't intervene, unfortunately."

She hadn't expected that. While she hadn't expected to fully immerse him into helping her, she didn't think she would get a 'no', especially in light of what he had claimed. "What?" she asks, and it comes out as a shaky breath.

George sighs, at least looking miserable about it. "If it doesn't put you in direct danger, I'm forbidden from helping."

"But I don't know where to go or what to do or—"

"I can't intervene," George says again. "But you still have allies that can."

She knows who he means, of course, but it's pointless. "You mean Aidan," she clears the unspoken message.

"I know you must consider him the lesser of two evils," George says. "But perhaps he's the only one who can help."

The only thing that worries Naya is — at what cost.

CHAPTER TWENTY-SEVEN

Aidan answers on the first ring, which makes Naya wonder if he was waiting for her call.

"I need your help," she manages to say.

He doesn't hesitate. "Where are you?"

The street name comes out as three garbled syllables, but she isn't surprised that he's able to hear it clearly. When she thinks she hears the sound of his motorcycle starting, she sits back down on the sidewalk, too exhausted to hold herself together.

"I'm on my way," he shoots out. "Be there in ten minutes."

Her mind is blank, but she forces herself to think of where is he, or why he would jump to help her after she made it clear she didn't want him in her life, but most of all how to resolve the situation.

She doesn't know if he arrives in ten minutes or more, but eventually she sees him, through her tears. He is like a silhouette of the person she knew before, in more ways than one. On the surface, he's the same. Even his hair is styled like it usually is, but his steps waver as he approaches her carefully.

It reminds her of how hunters come close to a wounded animal, in fear it will attack. The thought of attacking would have probably been the first thing on her agenda if it hadn't been for Julie.

Aidan closes the distance between them, helping her to her feet, until she is able to balance herself. "Where is she?"

Somehow, Naya manages to let out a bitter laugh due to the obvious fact that he knows exactly what has happened. But she refrains from commenting — too tired to speak. The only thing running through her mind is how she is to blame, how they had all warned her something would happen, but she hadn't listened.

"Hey," he brings her back from her thoughts. "Look at me, Naya."

"Why did you come?"

The mask of indifference vanishes, and she sees true and raw emotion in his eyes. It's so strong it manages to take her by surprise. She's not even sure he'll reply, because all he does is hold her in place, their bodies inches apart, and it baffles her how tempted she is to lean in and hug him.

"You needed me," he says after a while. "What else was I to do?"

She wonders if she looks as jaded as she feels, but when his warm hand moves to take hers, like he has done many times before, she flinches. He doesn't bother hiding his hurt, probably thinking he deserves it.

"You should know by now," Aidan states. "Order or not, I'll do anything for you."

Naya chooses not to respond, because she doesn't like how how truthful it sounds, and she doesn't know what to believe. She does know, however, that she needs to use whatever resources she has to find and help Julie — no matter the cost.

"I don't know where she is," she stumbles over her words, crying just a bit. "I don't know where to start looking, or how, or—"

Aidan stops her babbling, and she's thankful for that at the very least. She feels so confused, so out of it and so helpless. "Nate and Addie are already working on it. They have sent their agents all over London to try and see what we can learn."

Naya doesn't ask about the implications of such help; she will have to deal with it later.

When Aidan's cellphone beeps, he finally looks away from her to check the incoming text. "Joshua has been sighted in Mayfair," he says. "We'll go there now, and Nate and Addie will rendezvous with us once they arrive."

Naya knows that without traffic Mayfair is not more than fifteen minutes away, and she is hopeful that at the very least, she can help Julie.

Aidan doesn't say anything else as he leads her to his bike parked not far from them, and they set off.

The road feels too deserted, but perhaps that's Naya's own testament to how she's not paying attention. She has never been where they are, so nothing strikes her as familiar, but Aidan is confident as always as he moves through the street, before pausing in front of a building. It's an old red brick building with arched windows at the top. The blue sign ordering to keep clear is Naya's only indication, and it's not much.

"This way," Aidan leads her to a doorway. Without much effort, he opens the sealed door and enters before Naya.

As she follows him, the door closes with a loud noise and, for a moment, they're in complete darkness, until Aidan turns on a flashlight and hands another one to Naya. He doesn't say much at first, and just leads her through a corridor, advancing slowly down a stairway.

"This used to be a tube station," he explains as they make their way down. Naya mumbles in return, not caring much for a history lesson. Aidan, however, probably thinks she could use one and continues anyway.

In the darkness, with only their flashlights to guide them, he tells her how the rich people of Mayfair rarely used the station, and it became one of many ghost stations in London, but not before Winston Churchill converted it to a bunker during the Second World War.

"A lot of good men and women in The Order fought in that war," his voice echos when they reach the platform, and its eerily quiet — save for his musing. "Most of them died serving amongst the common folk who had no idea about Gods and Goddesses and those that survived were cast out of The Order."

"Why?" Naya asks, not entirely sure what he means exactly. She keeps a short distance from him, unable to shake off the mixture of emotions within her.

Aidan fixes the light on the far end of the platform, trying to detect any threats. Finding none, he jumps off onto the railway, holding his hand out for Naya to make the same jump. She takes the help offered and once they're on somewhat solid ground he speaks again.

"They thought it was a noble cause, I suppose." He gently pushes her behind him and holds up the flashlight again. "Those who forget their place in The Order aren't allowed back," he says. His tone isn't judgmental, so to speak, it is more like a rehearsed thought that has just occurred to him.

She doesn't reply. The ways of The Order are unfamiliar and it sounds like a bad place to live in, and she wonders how it is possible for him and so many others to belong to such an organisation. Naya figures though that they probably don't have much choice in the matter.

"We should be there in about half an hour," he cuts into her thoughts. "We could get there sooner, but I wanted to avoid getting hit by a train, since they still use part of this railway for the Piccadilly line."

Naya nods. She thinks about asking him how he knows everything in such detail, but supposes he would just shake off the question in any case. Instead they continue walking in silence, with only the sound of squeaking rats and their footsteps as a soundtrack.

He lets her enjoy the silence as much as he can; but even he has his limitations.

"Killing comes with a price," he says slowly, hoping his true intentions will sink in along with his tone. "You can't kill someone and get away with it."

She is not sure it even surprises her that he saw her need for revenge, before the idea had even formed in her mind. Perhaps she's an open book to him, or maybe he is just making a logical assumption.

Naya isn't sure she would be able to even kill to begin with, but she humours his train of thought. "What are they gonna do? Judge me? I'm not even part of the same world."

He frowns and shakes his head. "No one in The Order cares about death, especially of the Mavro Order. That's not what I'm talking about though," he stops, probably to think about how to explain himself. "I'm talking about the mental price of taking a life from another person, even if it is in self defence."

Naya is about to respond, but just thinking about the act of taking anyone's life makes her stomach turn. Just thinking about how easy it might have been for Aidan to have grown up in a place where it is pitch black or blinding white, a world where law and order are different and defending oneself was a way of life, makes her want to offer him her sympathy. Her thoughts become entangled and, as she tries making sense of everything, she almost misses his next sentence.

"It is a price I'm not willing to let you pay."

It makes her angry, not because he cares for her, but because he has the audacity to worry about her, despite wanting to use her blood for some ancient Goddess she's not even sure exists.

"It would mean more if I actually believed you," the words shoot out of her mouth.

"Don't forget that you called me."

The accusation is precise, and it stings to know her only choice of help was trying to kill her not too long ago. She shakes off his hand, almost jerking away from his touch and takes a step back.

"Maybe I shouldn't have."

It obviously hurt him to hear it, because his expression sharpens and though she has become used to how well he can control his feelings, now he is not even trying.

"Don't kid yourself," he says in a voice laden with emotion. "You wouldn't stand a chance without me."

She scoffs, but it's hollow and humourless. "I'm far better off without you." She hadn't meant to say it, but it seems as if Aidan is giving her an outlet, so she might as well take it. "At least then no one will want to use me for my blood."

It's a low blow, and it's not fair. She sees the same scared boy she saw a few nights ago in the street, too afraid of her judgment

When he stops abruptly to face her, she stops in her tracks. There are mere centimetres between them, and her hands itch to close that distance for just that semblance of sanity it brings to her to be close to him. She settles for fisting his shirt, holding the fabric and twisting it in anger.

Aidan pulls her hands away from him, holding them between the two of them, and she can see how she's shaking. She must be crying, too, because her vision is blurring. The solid touch of their hands provides comfort to him as well, as he tightens his grip.

"You don't deserve this," he says after a couple of seconds, his voice shaking in a way she has never heard before. "You don't deserve any of this, and I'm sorry — there's nothing I could ever say or do to make this go away, but I am truly sorry."

Naya doesn't reply. There is no need. Instead, she leans forward, putting her forehead against their joined hands and breathes slowly.

"We'll find her," Aidan says, and it doesn't sound like anything but a promise.

She nods, and lets him go. In no time, they carry on walking, although there's lot more tension in the air now, and when the tunnel starts to close in on them, Naya wonders if they're lost.

"Something doesn't feel right," Aidan says, and it's Naya's thoughts exactly. "Nate and the rest should have met up with us by now."

"You think they were caught?"

Aidan only murmurs, with no particular response, but she sees the way his body is slightly flexed, as if he is getting ready for anything. There's no reception down there, so she can only hope reinforcement is on the way.

Suddenly, there is movement ahead of them, and it's enough to know they're being ambushed. The way behind them is still clear, and it's only because Joshua knows that they have come all this way for Julie, and will not leave without her.

Aidan is in front of her in a second; his posture high enough so he blocks most of her view. However, she couldn't miss Joshua's expression even if she tried. His voice speaks volumes enough, and it's more than pleased — he sounds ecstatic.

"I'm afraid for once, Mr. Hall, you're outnumbered."

Naya looks around and, true to his word, Joshua's men and women have them almost surrounded. What's astonishing, though, is that they are not carrying any visible weapons and, as much of a good fighter as Aidan may be, even he doesn't stand a chance against them all.

"I say we settle this like men, *Señor* Adams," Aidan counters back, and even using Spanish, his tone is of anger and sheer contempt. The way he says it, sounds more like an insult than respect for a title.

"You mean, like barbarians? Yes, I suppose that's what they taught you back in Mexico, but that's not how we do this here."

Naya can see the amount of willpower it takes for Aidan to restrain himself from launching at Joshua straight on. She knows, even if they have only talked about it briefly, how much Mexico means to him, and how proud he is of his heritage. Joshua is playing mind games, and it seems even Aidan understands this, judging by his clenched fists and evident tension.

After a while, he responds. "You would drag an innocent person by their hairs to a shrine for sacrifice, yet I come from a land of barbarians?"

Joshua smiles. Naya realises that she has grown afraid of that smile. It can never mean well.

"Of course not," he replies without a hint of shame. "It's best to pretend to care for them before you stab them in the back. Alas, it's a lesson best learnt, even moments before you die."

"It was never our intention," Aidan says, even if Joshua has already settled the subject, ordering his followers to separate Aidan and Naya. Aidan goes without a fight, knowing there's not much he can do. Naya's heart sinks even more, when Aidan looks her in the eye and says, "We were going to get you out, after the business with Patrick and New Years, before—"

"Quiet," Joshua demands, and Aidan, for once, does as he's asked. "You should be pleased, Mr. Hall. You will get to witness a whole new world order before you too will die."

Side by side, Joshua's guards lead them onwards, and even though she feels Aidan eyes on her, it does little to encourage her.

"Just stall," he whispers. "I promise, just... *Respira*, okay?"

Naya remembers the word being repeated in her ears

time and time again during her latest panic attack. She vaguely knows what he means, but she takes a breath as he has asked, choosing to trust him — for the moment.

CHAPTER TWENTY-EIGHT

Joshua leads his men through a series of corridors, which all look and smell the same as the ones Naya and Aidan have just gone through. It's like a labyrinth, and with every step Naya knows they're walking to their doom.

She's losing track of the number of steps they have taken, the corners they make and the time they have been walking. Her legs ache and so does her back from the man holding her, but she doesn't try to fight it.

Joshua pauses before an enormous brick door, and when she hears Aidan's sharp intake of breath, she knows that they have reached their destination.

The door opens into a large hall, probably as large as the one she had passed through at the Anax Order's headquarters, but it's a lot darker and clearly underground, so it feels stranger, more malevolent.

"I did try my best," Joshua talks, and this is directed solely at Naya. When his man pushes her past the threshold, she sees four black stairs, with the unconscious figure of Julie bound to a post at the top. Naya struggles against the man holding her, and she can only watch as Joshua ascends the stairs himself, holding his hand towards her from the platform.

"I did," he says again as the man forces Naya up the stairs. She almost stumbles and falls, but he catches her. Joshua is either oblivious or simply doesn't care, as he continues his speech. "I thought perhaps natural disasters might be the trigger for you. Maybe ironically you'll be the only one to care about the planet's welfare. I figured, maybe if you saw we had a common interest, you would cooperate…"

"We don't have anything in common," Naya retorts, and it only irks him.

"That is because you're a child, despite everything. You get offered the chance of a lifetime, to be a part of something great, and you toss it away, too scared to burn."

When Naya does not reply, it makes his mouth twitch in anger. When he moves behind her, the man lets her go. She doesn't move though; too focused on the form of Julie's unmoving body to do anything. She is still breathing, which is the only thing making Naya relax just a bit.

Then she feels something shackling her arms, but it's not the feeling of metal.

"These are a special kind of tree branches," Joshua explains and forces her to kneel. "They were grown in Ancient Greece for the purpose of killing without leaving marks. As you struggle, they will sink their thorns into your skin, and will release a poison that, even with the proper antidote, will work faster than the antidote can. So, I would advise against you moving too much."

When Naya feels the tips of the thorns she freezes.

"Eventually, even I had to come to the conclusion that you would not have come freely. I suppose I don't have the pretty face your Mexican friend has, but I do have a better master plan."

Joshua talks like they have all the time in the world, and Naya dare not move enough to look at Aidan for help. She knows he's there, probably somewhere behind them and bound just like her, but it doesn't ease her mind. All she sees is Julie; her blonde hair in a mess and her arms turning blue.

"You can let her go, now that you have me," Naya tries.

"I'm afraid I need both of you, Naya," he tuts her. "You are so easy to manipulate, aren't you?" He continues, and the branches are tightening their hold on her even when she's not moving. "You see, you should never have trusted them, but you should not have trusted me either," he says menacingly. "What a pity that all of your mother's work is going to fall apart."

He touches her key pendant, and when he releases it she swears its weight is much heavier and its touch burns on her skin. "You almost succeeded in tearing them apart from the inside," he smiles, and it's a wicked one.

"What the hell are you talking about?" Her words feel heavy, and it's hard for her to speak. Every syllable is difficult to push out of her mouth, but she will not give him the satisfaction of showing how much she's in pain.

For a moment he seems surprised, and then the mask returns. "Do not get sassy with me, girl. Do not pretend that it was not your mother's plan from the start. She had tried to do the same to your father as you have done to Mr Hall. And it is a shame," he pauses to lean closer, to whisper in her ear. "He was willing to betray his family for you."

Naya forces herself to think of how to get out; of anything except his words causing distress, together with the implications of it all. Joshua is desperate to get some sort of reaction from her.

"You're a believer," he says, looking at her Star of David necklace. "Tell me, where is your God now?"

Joshua's words are madness, and despite the throbbing pain all over her body and her immense sense of helplessness, she refuses to succumb to him. He's beyond furious, and Naya is slightly worried what that might lead to.

She looks at Julie instead, hoping to draw strength from her.

"It seems like it is easier to have a deity to pray to — to worship and to blame," Joshua says slowly, so confident in his thinking, "but there is nothing to pray for other than damnation and hell. I have seen the Elysian Fields, and there is nothing there! No gods, no spirits, nothing! There is nothing to look forward to."

Naya's words comes out as raspy breaths. "What is your answer, then?"

The man's smile is wicked and full of pity at the same time. He kneels next to Naya, looking at her and blocking Julie from view. "I will make it better. I will bring back the gods and destroy them. And then the world will know that there is no purpose in being here. There is no use for religion and there is no redemption. There is only the present and it needs to be fixed."

"Fixed?" Naya wonders out loud.

Joshua doesn't answer at first; he just stares ahead, just beyond her shoulder, and some part of Naya is positive he's busy picturing this reality as he envisions it. Then he smiles again, this time more out of empathy than anything else.

"First, we need you to wake up and take our side." His words make no sense, but she doesn't have time to ponder on them. He gets up and walks to Julie. Naya's words fall away, as her best friend is being tugged by her arms, and she starts to wake up.

"Julie—" Naya mumbles, as Joshua holds her up so that Naya can examine her. She doesn't look physically harmed, although Naya can see the bruises the restraints have left. However, she looks somewhere between alive and dead.

"What have you done to her?" Naya demands.

"She would never have been here if it wasn't for your stubbornness," he muses. "You can help her, Naya," he says. "She is dying, but you can help her — you can bring her back to you."

Naya doesn't hesitate with her response. "Tell me how."

"You have powers within you, powers you have yet to understand, but they hold the most basic role of the Universe. Everything has a value, but some things cannot be gained without first losing something in exchange."

Naya doesn't understand, but it doesn't matter. All that matters is Julie, and Joshua sees it on her face because he releases Julie, who falls back to the ground like a puppet, and then he approaches Naya.

"A life for a life," he says. "Would you sacrifice your own to save your friend's?"

Naya holds his stare for the longest time, but still seeing the golden dagger he is wielding out of the corner of her eye. She is willing to do her part to help Julie — of that there is no doubt.

The weapon comes close to her heart, almost beating in sync with Joshua's hurried breathing. He is confused, and as she turns to look at his hand she notices the way it's tightening around the object, like he was trying hard to push it forward and get it over with, but can not.

Then she understands that something is holding him back. Some hidden force, probably the same one which at that same moment, forces the weapon away from his hand, making them jump at the sound of the metal touching the ground.

For the first time in the short while she has known him, Joshua looks dumbstruck. He stares behind her back, looking for something that he know should be there, but in fact isn't and the hall remains eerily silent.

And then, the chaos begins.

Naya has no idea what's happening, except she hears a scream and her body shivers excessively. The branches fall apart and her body shakes as she collapses forward onto her arms. All she feels is pain, like thousands of needles piercing her skin and all her senses are on overload. Then there's a blinding flash and she sees Joshua being thrown aside along with Julie, and she knows something is terribly wrong.

She's at least free, and she hurries to Julie's side to see the dagger, Joshua had held not so long ago, pushed into her chest, and she is gasping.

Julie is awake, and looks at her with such despair Naya can barely contain. "No, no, no..." Naya mutters, and holds her best friend, wishing she can help, somehow. She would do what Joshua asked. She would give her life to save Julie's, but she doesn't know how. She can't look away from her wound or her face to see where he is.

The commotion behind them must be their reinforcements, and she hears the voices of battle but can't get herself to look anywhere, but at Julie. "Please, no... Stay with me, Jules, please, please... I can't..."

It's selfish to think she can't live without her, that she can't do any of this without her, but she's begging in any language she knows, with every sense she has, with her every being, not to let Julie die.

The cause for dying is there, and she knows none of this would have happened if it wasn't for her. She sees Julie's eyes struggling to keep awake, so she knows. She knows there's nothing she can do the moment Julie's eyes blink blindly at her, and she wishes she could fix it. She wishes she could fix her.

She wants to glare angrily at Joshua, demand answers or retribution for Julie — but she can't tear her eyes away from her best friend. Her best friend, whose total body weight is being supported by Naya, but she is clueless as to how to help her.

Even in her last moments alive, Julie manages to guide her. As she slowly seeks Naya's hand, interlinking their fingers, she manages to better the bitterness and to slow down time.

She doesn't say anything, and she shouldn't either. Her smile says it all, and while Naya knows she's probably dying in agony, there's nothing there but contentment. She's not mad, or disappointed or even sad. She's just... peaceful, and Naya hopes that her close proximity makes it somewhat better.

She allows herself to cry only when she hears the last breath Julie takes.

No one gives her enough time to mourn, and she is being torn away from Julie's body. She recognises Aidan's words in her face, begging her to work with him so that they can escape, and she sees Nathan hoisting Julie on himself, but she can't move without help, and her tears are blocking everything.

Everything after that is a blur.

When they take her away from there, back to Aidan's flat, she's pretty sure she's screaming, but everything is silent, her mind refusing to acknowledge the reality, too caught up in denying what has happened to wrap itself around it.

She lets Aidan lead her to his bed, and she's tucked in under the covers immediately, mindless of the state of her dress and the dirt. As he turns to leave, she stretches out and holds him by his forearm. He doesn't say anything, there's no use for words. She tugs his arm and pulls him down to lie down with her. His hand circles around her waist and his head rests on hers.

She's supposed to feel comforted by his touch, supposed to feel safe and calm and collected.

Instead she feels nothing.

CHAPTER TWENTY-NINE

Grief is not something she handles easily. In the week that passes, she loses all contact with the outside world, trying to stay as much as she can in her bedroom, not really knowing how to act anymore.

Time doesn't stop just because she's hurting, and the day of the funeral comes too quickly. She barely has the energy to leave her bed, but she knows she needs to be there to support Julie's family as much as she can.

At some point, the front door opens and she hears Aidan greet Lucas, who has now thankfully recovered. They don't fight, and she hears the conversation in the living room, which is not surprising considering how thin the walls are, but it's a good distraction from her own pain.

"How is he?" she hears Aidan ask, and she wonders how Aidan knew about Logan's love for Julie. Aidan sounds pretty concerned.

Naya knows Logan is almost as heartbroken as she is,

and can pictures him sitting at the edge of his bed, too wrapped up in his own agony to worry about anything else.

Getting ready for the funeral is methodical for both of them.

"What do you think?" Lucas's snide question is the only indication that he is feeling sad too. Naya knows he is trying to hold himself together for the sake of Logan and herself, and she really hopes Aidan doesn't rise to the bait.

"Losing someone is never easy," Aidan says instead. "It's even harder when there's nothing you can do to ease the pain, and it's a lot harder when you're hurting yourself."

"I'll be fine," Lucas replies.

Naya only hears Aidan mumble in return. The two of them don't utter a word for a long time and, as comfortable as the silence is, someone is bound to break it. This time it is Lucas. "The funeral is at East Finchley Cemetery."

Naya doesn't know how Aidan is reacting to this, other than his somber tone saying, "I'll take her, you worry about your brother."

"You'll make sure she's safe, right?"

It's a simple question, really, but it holds so many different layers. Naya knows Lucas is worried about her, but even she can't shake off the need to worry about what could happen should someone decide that the twins are next.

"Her life comes before mine, I promise."

She can only imagine Lucas nodding, but he doesn't say anything else other than, "See you there," and for a moment she forces herself to focus on finishing to get ready.

The reflection she catches in the mirror slightly alarms her. The woman looking back at her in the mirror looks nothing like her. Naya's stare is fixated on her face, half familiar and half brand new, worn out physically and mentally, with dark circles under her eyes and skin similar to the whiteness of the walls around her rather than her natural tanned one. Walls that used to feel like a warm embrace, now hold her captive, making her breathless and wanting to abandon her black dress and put on her pyjamas, particularly the one Julie bought her for her birthday two years ago.

She can't bring herself to think of her best friend in the past tense. She can't calm her breaking heart and steady its beatings. Even breathing seems hard now, a practice saved for the brave ones, to those who withstand the storm, but not her, anyone but her.

Her brain registers that Aidan is knocking on her door, and when she fails to reply — because really, how can she move a muscle without hurting — he lets himself in and takes in her appearance.

She doesn't ask why he is wearing black clothes that match her own, or how he knows when she is just about to leave, and most of all, she doesn't ask why he moves to stand by her in front of the mirror. He's silent as he turns her to face him, but she tries to look away.

"Don't do that," his whisper is demanding, but with a slight plea to it.

"Julie's dead," the words slip out of her mouth too easily, and she dares to look at him, to finally speak what she knows is right. It is odd, even when she sat down to tell the twins she never used the words, deeming them too final.

"Can I hold you?" he asks instead. The sentiment is everything, and she nods.

Aidan's arms are around her in an instant, the touch reassuring to both of them, and she lets him hug her tightly until all she can feel is his body against hers. By now, it is instinctive for her to wrap her arms around Aidan; perhaps it is natural for her to break down within his embrace.

"I'm sorry," she hears him say between her sobs. It's near inaudible, and she almost misses it, but she doesn't, and she doesn't stop to ask.

Time passes and she has no idea how long they are standing like this. Aidan doesn't try to provide any other comfort other than his body pressed against hers, no words of reassurance or false promises, and for once she's grateful.

Aidan and Julie had been somewhat friends, and it's selfish to look to him as a partner to mourn with and not as an outsider providing solace, but she can't help it.

In the haze of her emotions, Naya thinks how funny grief is. How in between her sorrow and hurt it has created a whole new level of intimacy between them. How his arms now seem like the safest place in the world, and how content they are holding each other.

He makes her look at him again, his hands holding her face so gently it's like his touch is barely there, with his thumbs barely brushing over her face, wiping away her tears. She understands the pain will never go away, and she wonders if it's only the beginning of something worse.

Aidan looks as distressed as she is, and deep in his eyes is an additional level of guilt she knows he feels to his very core. She wants to tell him she's not looking for anyone to blame other than herself, and he must see her mouth opening to give words to her thoughts, because he invades her space further, resting his forehead against hers.

It's calming, and even though she can remember the countless times that they have touched before, this feels different, even if she isn't bothered enough to find out why.

She thinks he means to say something, but as her arms tighten around him, all he does is draw back just enough to look at her again, and press his lips to her forehead for a few seconds.

At this moment in time it is all the comfort he can offer.

Not quite sure what to do with herself, Naya takes in the graveyard before her. Everyone is silent, and she takes refuge in between the umbrellas around her. Aidan doesn't leave her side, and she feels him pushing her slightly aside as he opens up his own umbrella to shield them from the rain.

Biting her lip, she finally dares to look at the photo near the burial site. Julie, in all her glory, is smiling happily, and Naya remembers exactly when the photo was taken. Her hand trembles when she realises she was the one that held the camera that day and had told a joke to make her smile like that.

The weight of her memories comes crashing down, flooding her mind and body. The guilt is too much, almost making her turn on her heel to escape. However, Aidan's hold on her is firm, and he's not letting her go anywhere.

She's left with only one option and that is to watch the scene in front of her, detached from reality, moving ever so slightly to really focus on the casket. There is a minister speaking a few words and praying, followed by a moment of silence to honour the dead. Only then do her senses slowly resurface and she can hear the soft sobbing sound coming from Julie's mother, and feel the touch of Aidan's hand in hers, intertwining their fingers, keeping her balanced.

The wind is blowing and it is in cold contrast to the hot trail of tears running down her cheeks.

She barely pays attention to the service, too busy staring at the wooden box her best friend is lying in, completely and utterly at peace, not amongst the living any more.

"Maybe going home might be a good idea," Aidan whispers in her ear when it's over, and everyone is turning to leave. "Little B—"

At the ceremony, Naya had been mortified to talk to Julie's mum, but now she knows she must. The woman had been like a mother to her all through university, when both Julie and herself had been studying together, and she has been caring ever since.

As Josephine Bennet stands in front of her, her words get stuck in her throat, only to drop down into her stomach, making her feel sick again. The woman doesn't say anything, just puts her arms around Naya's shoulders and pulls her closer for a hug. There's nothing to stop Naya's tears to fall freely, and she takes as much comfort for Josephine as the latter takes form Naya.

"I'm so sorry," Naya chokes on her words, but what's destroying her most, is that she'll never know what she's truly apologising for.

"You did what you could," Josephine says in return, and it makes Naya cry even harder, because there had to be something more she could have done. "I know you took care of my Julia," she continues, and Naya wishes she would stop talking all at once, because she can't handle the weight of her guilt together with the sickening feeling of deep regret and hate.

Each word is like another knife to an already bleeding wound, and eventually Josephine pulls back from the hug, still holding Naya at arms length, with enough force to prevent her from running away.

"Thank you for coming," Josephine says, as she pushes the hair away from Naya's face and leaves her hand there, cupping her face the way only a mother knows.

The touch is both soothing and aching, and sorrow is evident on her face. She doesn't say anything else, and offers Naya a smile as a token of gratitude and farewell.

Later, Aidan tells her that Mickayla had used her connections at the police to make it appear as if Julie had come to London to meet with Naya, and they were both ambushed by criminals who tried to mug them before it all went wrong. It doesn't help with the guilt, of course, but at least she knows Julie's family are safe from knowing the truth.

Naya stays at the cemetery even after everyone has long gone, and Aidan tells her that Addison made sure the twins arrived safely back home. She knows that she has been avoiding them, because she thinks they blame her. She blames herself enough as it is already.

It doesn't make sense to her that she is at a cemetery. She's stuck in a haze, in a cloud of denial and bitterness hovering above her, preventing her from facing reality. The only coherent thought in her mind throughout the funeral was how unfair to Julie this all is.

"I could have saved her," she says, summing up what she's thinking.

Aidan, beside her, doesn't say anything at first. His companionship offers little comfort at the moment and she has too many questions about the dark world that took Julie away from her. That same world that she was supposed to fit in somehow and accept without any doubt.

"No," he says finally. "No one can reverse death, Naya."

She scoffs. "Joshua said—"

"Joshua is wrong," he interrupts her rudely. "Even if your powers were at their maximum level, you are not able to reverse death. That power belongs only to Gaia, and probably not even to her."

Naya turns to look at him, red rings around her eyes with the tears she had shed, trailing down her face. With a freezing hand, Aidan cups her cheek, waiting for the tears that are sure to fall.

Except they don't. There's a flash of anger in her eyes that make her take a step back from his touch, almost like it has burned her. She shakes her head and clenches her hands, trying to contain her feelings.

"What good are these powers then?" she demands. "If all they bring is death then by all means, take them away. This is what you were after from the start, wasn't it?"

"Naya—"

She holds her hand up, to shut him up, somewhat thankful he didn't have the nerve to use her nickname. "No, don't 'Naya' me! My best friend is dead, everyone I know is in danger and I'm some sort of... of abnormality!" He's probably about to reply, but she won't have it. "You don't see it, do you? I killed Julie with my own damned powers! If it wasn't for me, she would still be alive!"

"There was nothing you could have done," Aidan says. He's so vehement about it that it makes Naya wonder if it's only for her benefit, or if he needs to say it out loud in order to believe it.

The latter makes her sick to her stomach.

Then something catches Aidan's attention, and she turns to see what.

Dom is standing not too far from them, and immediately she knows that, judging by his black suit, he was there for the funeral as well.

"I'll wait for you outside," Aidan says, and she watches as he moves through the graveyard and into the street.

Dom doesn't say anything at first, and suddenly the man doesn't look familiar; any and all memories of him holding her when she came back hurt from school, patiently explaining her about one thing or the other, or even teaching her how to cook has faded away from memory.

He stands two steps away from her, not attempting to advance towards her, and the remnant of the person she knew as her father moves further and further away.

"You are a part of them," she mumbles. She has plenty to say, from accusations to insults and everything that would make her feel better, but as the seconds move on, she finds she can't really face him. Most of all, she wants Dom to be the comforting father he used to be for her, and she wants nothing more than to just forget about everything she has found out.

"I was," he admits, his voice measured enough. "But not any more. Not since you were born."

"When were you planning on telling me?"

"Never, if you hadn't taken your mother's necklace."

The honesty and accusation in his words are a bit too real for her. She had expected him to apologise, or at the very least give her a solid excuse for why he had kept her in the dark, but this is different. She doesn't know how to react to different.

"You are not a monster, Naya," he says, and the words sound rehearsed, like he has spent a decade telling himself the same thing. "You are the final piece in a puzzle you don't quite understand, and you can't see or know the whole picture."

"Then help me understand, won't you?"

Dom's features harden. "This isn't the time or the place for that kind of discussion."

Naya huffs; she feels like a little girl being told off from meddling in the adult's conversation. It makes her even angrier at Dom than she is at Aidan and the others, for not being completely honest with her, but she knows one piece of information that will throw him off guard.

"Do me a favour, when you find it in you to tell me the truth, don't bother hiding the fact that I have a brother, okay?"

She waits to test his reaction, and when his face morphs into something more shameful than the poker face he was maintaining, she realises it was never his intention to share that with her, either. It is a game to him, seeing what he can get away with and what she would find out on her own. In a way to return the childish gesture, she sets it as a task for her to figure it all out, without his help.

"Thanks for coming to my best friend's funeral," she says and moves away from him, walking down the same path Aidan had.

CHAPTER THIRTY

Once again, the days pass by, and even a month after the funeral, everything still feels hazy. Naya hasn't done much, nor has she had the motivation. Logan is pretty much the same wreck as she is, but after a while, he needs to get back to work, so she's left alone with her thoughts most of the day.

Josephine calls her almost daily, asking if there's anything she needs, and so does Lara, unsurprisingly. She knows both women want what's best for her, but still can't gather up the nerve to do much with her life.

Aidan has been a constant presence in her flat, and while she knows that they need to talk over everything, she's mourning and can't bring herself to take away one of her only forms of comfort.

It's on a Tuesday morning when she hears a knock on her front door. Slowly, she moves towards it, looking out of the peephole and takes a deep breath, when she sees Dom is outside.

Despite everything, she can't send him away, so she opens the door and gestures him inside.

"I suppose I owe you some explanations," he cuts straight to the point.

Naya feels there's no need to go round in circles either. "You acted like I was crazy," she shoots.

"Naya, let me explain—"

Unfortunately, she's not looking to listen. "No, you said all those awful things as if I was a conspirator! And all along, all this time — I was right! Something was off, and I…"

She trails off, knowing there's no way she can finish the sentence without triggering her guilt again.

"I'm sorry," Dom says, and Naya thinks it might be the first time she has ever heard him apologise in such a sincere manner. "I didn't tell you because I was scared, but I guess it was inevitable."

The words clearly hold more meaning for Dom than for Naya, though she can't quite fathom how she knows. She watches him wearily, wondering what else he's hiding from her, silently awaiting his explanation.

"You've been asking questions ever since you could talk," he pauses and sighs, rubbing his eyes. "Always the why, the how and who or what... It was endless, you were relentless. So when you decided to become a journalist, it made sense."

She almost opens her mouth to speak but he waves her off, undeniably feeling her determination.

"I should have known you would find out the truth, but your mother made me swear not to tell you anything until you were old enough... and I guess you never were, not for me, not for the truth. I wanted to keep you in the dark for as long as I could. I wanted you to have the perfect life I was never able to have."

The raw emotion in Dom's words dispels her anger. She has never seen him like this, so honest and in tune with his feelings. He sits down on the sofa and she joins him, patiently waiting again.

Dom takes a deep breath before he talks. "Kaia... she knew, you know? Knew The Orders would catch up, so she proposed using Nathan as your protection in The Order. She thought, maybe, if we had an inside man, we could divert the Council's attention elsewhere. But it didn't work, Kaia died and Nathan resented me too much to fully trust me, so here we are, I guess."

She ponders on how just talking about her mother makes Dom different to the stern father she knows. How Kaia, even in death, manages to have such a huge impact on his life, and she smiles softly, noticing the slight changes in Dom's demeanour.

During her adolescence, Naya barely mentioned her mum, let alone asked questions about her. She just accepted her death as inevitable, and soon enough the person Kaia was and what she had stood for was pushed to the background, and she became a stranger rather than a mother.

"What was she like?" she forces out the question.

Dom grins, probably reminiscing about his lost love. "She was a lioness, that one. Resourceful, intelligent, always getting her way… But she trusted no one and it took me forever to actually get her to talk to me."

Naya has a feeling there's something else he isn't telling her, or he has twisted the truth somewhat to suit his memory of Kaia, but she decides not to pry.

"She was stubborn, like you, and rarely listened to anyone else…" He trails off, a look of sheer hurt appearing, before disappearing in a flash. He wipes his hands on his trousers, letting them linger there in clenched fists.

Pushing aside one's emotions, or bottling everything up, according to Logan, are the traits Naya likes to brag about mastering, so she is able to tell when someone doesn't care to speak about something in particular. Dom's hands and feigned expression of normality are enough of a hint, and she easily changes the subject.

"Who were you, in The Order?"

Dom looks surprised. "Nathan's role once belonged to me. It goes from parent to child, and I was the Spymaster when Kaia met me. It was my job to know everything about her, and we were tasked to do the same as your friends in The Order, except we thought we knew better."

Dom doesn't elaborate, so Naya doesn't ask, for now.

"I am not asking you to trust me again," Dom says after a while. "But know that whatever I did, how badly you think I acted, I did it for you. My life has been dedicated to The Order, then to Kaia, and now you."

Naya can only nod. Even after knowing what she has learnt, there's nothing to hold her back from forgiving him. She has lost too much in the past month, so she moves to hug Dom. She knows she can't go through the pain of losing her father.

A few days later, Aidan asks to meet her to have a proper talk, so with a heavy heart and a paranoid mind, she arranges a time to go to his place. Truthfully, she should have known that he would be waiting by the entrance to the building, but she still jumps when she hears his footsteps behind her.

Aidan tried, in his defence, to move slowly, but she still panics.

Wordlessly, he puts his helmet on her and ignites the bike, and they drive off. Naya doesn't pay much attention to her surroundings, and even the concierge doesn't say anything as they walk past him.

Aidan is silent all the way, until they reach his flat.

There, in the safety of his own living room, he speaks. "Joshua was right, you know."

Naya moves past him to sit on the sofa. "Which part?"

"Me willing to betray my family. Nate had tried to tell me years ago, that what we were doing was wrong, how we shouldn't take advantage of someone for a ritual... how the greater good isn't good but just a lesser evil, and that we should find another way. I wasn't convinced until I met you, though."

Naya considers it all. "Then why did you lie?"

"I never lied to you," Aidan responds quickly.

This is true, of course, but it isn't working. "But you haven't told me the whole truth yet either."

Aidan chuckles. "Would you have believed me, if I told you at our first meeting?"

"I suppose not."

Aidan just shrugs. "Nate and Addie were against me telling you, but after a while, I didn't care... You deserved the truth, and you deserve better than this life. I would give it all to you, all of my secrets are yours to keep, from now on."

Naya wants to say the feeling is mutual, but she's not sure it is — just yet. They are getting there, though. If she can find it in her to forgive her father, she will be able to forgive them too. She thinks for the first time in a month, that it's what Julie would have wanted. It is what she would have advised.

Aidan kneels on the carpet in front of her, taking one hand in both of his. "The Order put me on trial for what happened, and if my father hadn't intervened, I would be in jail right now, or worse." He lets out a sigh, and she hopes it's not a goodbye. "I don't know what will happen next, but I couldn't stomach the thought of you not knowing, should I disappear…"

Despite his tough exterior, Aidan looks scared now, and she doesn't know what to say, so she can only act. She pulls him towards her, and wraps her arms around him, giving as much comfort as she was getting. She hopes it helps, somehow.

Eventually, they fall asleep, and Naya is pulled into dreamland quite easily.

The dream starts the same. She is in an unrecognisable street in London. Everything is quiet until it turns black, and she finds herself in between buildings. She's alone for a while, but then the shadow before her takes the shape of a human male body — tall, firm and intimidating in every fibre of its being. The shadow creature raises his smokey hand and gestures Naya forward.

Walking ahead, her eyes fixate on his face, composed out of the same smoky shadow, with is hawk-like features. Nothing about him seems natural, as if he was an embodiment of artificial and inhuman. Naya has the distinct feeling that he went to great lengths to appear human.

His eyes are a bottomless pit; staring into them feels like losing one's sanity. Yet he forces her to hold his stare for a long time, until he is content. The creature sneers at Naya, his foreign lips shaping up in a mocking grin.

There's something oddly familiar about his presence, though hardly comforting. She feels as though she's supposed to turn on her heels and run away, but something draws her to him, and she knows her curiosity is too strong.

"Is that why you do not flee, Little Lamb?"

His lips don't move, his harsh voice speaking inside her head. The question shoots right into her soul, and it's almost enough to paralyse her in fear.

"Who are you?"

The creature ignores her question. "I have little expectations from you, Gaia's daughter. In fact, I have only one: you cannot die."

"You're in luck — I have no intention of dying," Naya mutters against her better judgement. Whoever this creature is, it's clearly not wise to upset him. His rage over her statement scares her to her very core, and he moves to stand closer to her.

He is scrutinizing her, and under his scrutiny she fidgets. Nonetheless, Naya is determined to hold her head high, answering his dare. She knows there's really nothing to fear in a dream, and she knows the creature wants to see her scared, to see her try and escape.

"Funny, there was a time where all humanity feared me, even if they had never heard of me," he speaks in her head again, but there's some puzzlement and admiration in his tone. "But not you, Little Lamb. You challenge, and you are different from the rest of your bloodline." His hand holds her chin, smoke and shadows caressing her cheeks.

Naya takes a step backwards, hating how cowardly it is, but his presence is too much to take. "Don't touch me," she manages to hiss out.

"You are as much mine as you are Gaia's," he says flatly. "I can do as I please, and no mortal will dictate to me otherwise, not even you. Had it not been for me, you would have died with your enemies."

His words makes her think how the dagger shot from Joshua's hand, and while she had blacked out everything else, she remembers the smoke that followed them and the shadows that grew wherever they went.

"Why save me?"

"You cannot die yet, Sweet Lamb. I cannot allow it."

Naya grits her teeth. "Why?"

The creature holds his hand up again, to slowly touching her face again but this time she's prepared and faces him bravely. "You have a destiny to fulfil, and I cannot forsake you until you do so."

His promise holds no good in it. While his intentions

and personal gain from her life are unknown, she is sure there's something more to all of it.

"I'm not sure I want your help," she says.

He smirks. "You will need all the help you can get, silly human, and I am here to present you with the best help I have. He will come for you, Lamb, fear not. And you shall not need any human to defend you any longer."

Giving her no more explanations, the creature puts his index finger to her forehead, and before she can defy his gesture, he speaks again, "Sleep now in your ignorance. Help is coming, I guarantee it. Just stay alive."

Naya jolts awake, and feels Aidan doing the same next to her. Her anxiety intensifies in light of her dream, even though it didn't feel like a dream at all. Aidan moves to put his hand on her cheek. It reminds her of the creature in her dream, and she pushes his touch away, needing a moment to differentiate the dream from reality.

Aidan gives her the space she needs, and when she calms down after a while, she can only scoff.

"I hate this," she says, looking everywhere but at Aidan. He has seen the worst of her anxiety by now, and while there's no reason to hide anymore, it's uncontrollable. She can't avoid him forever, even if he keeps his distance.

It bothers her a little.

She wouldn't say it out loud though, and just sighs. Aidan doesn't push her to talk, and it takes her quite a long time to mumble out the words. It's the catalyst of everything that has happened, and she's not even talking about her dream anymore.

"Sometimes it's too much, and my thoughts run at a hundred miles an hour, only to end up choking me from the inside…" The tears are sliding down her cheeks now, flowing in an unstoppable stream. "It hurts so much that I don't even know what's going on. So much so, sometimes I feel like I might die."

He's silent, for much longer than she likes, but she understands — most people are, once she exposes herself like that. It's worse when she's really hoping for the right words to soothe her though, when she's hoping for the right words to cleanse her.

"What helps, usually?"

Naya finally looks him in the eyes, and she's not sure what she finds there. It might be understanding, or compassion or concern. It's difficult explaining and answering his questions when her mind is messed up as it is at the moment.

He asks if he can hold her again, and her body automatically moves toward him. She sets the tone, and lies down on her side, facing him and he does the same. His arms are wrapped around her as tight as possible, and he leans his forehead against hers.

"Is this what you hate most about yourself?"

She wants to say how inappropriate his question is,

but she knows he's referring to what she said earlier, and she silently agrees. "I wish it wasn't like this; I wish I would stop feeling like such a coward all of the time… I used to take anti-anxiety pills. They made me feel, I don't know, artificial, but I was seventeen years old, so what did I know, right?"

He murmurs, but she's not sure if it is in agreement or if he is just filling the silence. She's exhausted, which makes sense, and sighs once again. "I feel like my body is fighting itself, and I'm just so tired…"

She is at the point of rambling, and forces herself to shut up.

Then, he asks, "You deal with this daily?"

She nods. "Sometimes even getting out of bed feels too much."

His response comes way too quickly for someone who thinks about things. "There's nothing cowardly about dealing with anxiety and moving on despite it."

Naya tells him of her dream as they wait for sleep to come, and while Aidan doesn't offer much in return, she feels content for the first time in a month. She thinks, that maybe Julie would understand, as she snuggles closer to Aidan, that he is her comfort now.

According to Aidan and Nathan, the worst is behind them. Joshua is in jail, Theresa has vanished and the Mavro Order members are caught up in a war amongst themselves in light of everything that has happened, so they are distracted enough.

The Anax Order is still debating on how to proceed from here on out, and Naya doesn't understand much of it, but there are more pressing matters that are not related to her, apparently.

It gives Naya partial peace of mind to walk unaccompanied, and on an unusually sunny afternoon, a few days before her birthday, she takes a walk to Primrose Hill, enjoying the sun on her skin.

In one of the hidden spots of the park, she sees him, and everything comes to a standstill.

Naya has to focus all her attention to look at the lanky figure. The boy, probably no older than eighteen, looking almost inhuman, so implausible that it takes her a few moments to understand what she is looking at. His hair is so black and his skin is so pale in contrast and she is sure she can see right through him. This leaves her in shock.

He gives her time to take him in and she wonders if he is doing the same. His sharp face lights up in a grin spreading on his thin lips, and she ignores the air of malice and the threat he might be.

He gives her no reason to be afraid.

Yet.

She's silent, not willing to take the first step for introductions. His expressions change too rapidly, and she understands that he has no idea what to make of her either. A few moments pass, and he settles on giving her a pleasant smile, and something clicks in their dynamics.

Slowly he opens his mouth to speak, making sure to do it as loudly and coherently as possible, to ensure she will have no doubt of what he is saying.

"Hello, my other half," he drawls, and she's sure he hears her heartbeats quicken. There is something about his words that make sense and yet doesn't make sense at the same time.

He doesn't let her think more about it, and says, "My bloodline has been waiting a lifetime to meet you again."